A.L. BIRD lives in London, where she divides her time between writing, working as a lawyer, and running around after her young family. She loves writing dark, twisty thrillers. Bestselling *The Good Mother* was her first major psychological thriller for HQ Digital, and *Don't Say a Word* was her chilling standalone next book. She has an MA in Creative Writing from Birkbeck, University of London, and is also an alumna of the Faber Academy 'Writing a Novel' course. Amy is a member of the Crime Writers' Association. For updates on her writing follow her on Twitter, @ALBirdWriter.

D1427242

Also by A.L. Bird

The Good Mother
Don't Say a Word

The Classroom

A.L. BIRD

ONE PLACE. MANY STORIES

This novel is entirely a work of fiction. The names, characters and incidents portrayed in it are the work of the author's imagination. Any resemblance to actual persons, living or dead, events or localities is entirely coincidental.

HQ
An imprint of HarperCollins*Publishers* Ltd
1 London Bridge Street
London SE1 9GF

This paperback edition 2018

1

First published in Great Britain by
HQ, an imprint of HarperCollins*Publishers* Ltd 2018

ISBN: 9781848457676

For more information visit: **www.harpercollins.co.uk/green**

To my parents, in recognition.
To my two little miracles, in joy.

Part One

Prologue

She puts the letter to one side. Today isn't about that. Not in this moment. Today is about Harriet. Her, and Harriet, making a fresh start, together. Away from all this nonsense. If the letter shows anything, it's that they need to make that fresh start even further away. There'll be people looking for them. And Harriet is so pretty – people will notice them. England is too small. She needs to go abroad. They need to get tickets to France or, ideally, somewhere outside Europe that doesn't need a visa. Somewhere not hugely swamped with international newspapers. She gets out her phone, begins Googling destinations. That's stupid, though. She should just take Harriet to the airport, see what flights they can get. And go.

Resolved, she gets to her feet. Thank God for Harriet being well looked after this morning, while the fresh crisis was breaking. She can imagine her now, playing happily on the grass. Soon, Harriet will be playing happily in another country, doting eyes on her. They'll be happy together. Of course they will.

At first glance, she doesn't notice, when she gets outside.

The absence.

She looks around another time.

It's then she realises: Harriet isn't there.

Just the woman who was supposed to be looking after her, sitting all alone.

Chapter 1

KIRSTEN, 4 SEPTEMBER 2018

'I just wasn't sure about the headteacher, at the new joiners evening, you know?' Kirsten says to her husband, as she gazes at little Harriet. She bites her lip, as she resists the urge to hug her daughter another time before getting her into the car. Harriet looks so smart and grown-up in her new uniform, but Kirsten doesn't want to deliver her to the destination: first day of reception.

Ian lays a hand on Kirsten's shoulder.

'The headteacher was just fine, darling. You know that. You got on like a house on fire.' There's a wryness to his delivery, probably born of being a headmaster himself. He knows the conversations that go on.

'And what about the other kids? They say that the most important thing is the cohort your child's in. What if they're mean?'

Ian shrugs. 'There's bound to be one mean kid there. Maybe it will be Harriet.'

Kirsten shoots him a poison dart with her eyes.

'Joking,' he tells her. 'Harriet's no bully. But they're five, Kirsten. No one's going to be selling drugs, or making them down alcohol.'

Kirsten looks at him more carefully this time. It's an oddly chosen example, considering.

She sees Ian notice her look. 'Whatever,' he says. 'What I mean is, she'll be fine, you need to get her in the car, or we'll both be late, OK? You've been taking her to nursery for three years. School's no different, really. She should be so lucky, going somewhere like that. We can catch up this evening.'

Kirsten nods. But she doesn't agree. He doesn't get it. Or maybe he does: he gets what's on the surface. The anxiety that she's actually expressed. But there's the deeper anxiety, the one she never shares. The one she never knows whether dads truly face too, or if it's just the mums, the worried mums. The need that can suddenly seize you to know exactly where your child is at all times. The sudden rush of panic that they could be with anyone, with any number of terrible things befalling them. And that even if they were meant to be in safe hands – with relatives, at school – it would always ultimately be your fault for making the choice that day, that hour, to outsource their care. To not be looking after them yourself.

The guilt, Kirsten knew, would always linger. And it worked the other way too: if she was indulgent enough to take a day off work, that particular day would be the one when their route to the Fun Activity was favoured by terrorists, or a gas explosion, or a sinkhole.

'Can I go to school now, Mummy?' Harriet asks.

Kirsten tries to shut her anxiety down. She'd made such a thing of school being Grown-Up and Very Important that Harriet can't be blamed for wanting to get there sooner. But it's still too soon. Only a moment ago, Harriet was a newborn. Kirsten still remembers looking at those amazing owl-like eyes, wide and unblinking, as Harriet sat in the back of the car on the journey home with Ian – their little miracle. He'd been a bit cold, nervy with the weight of responsibility, but she'd been transfixed. If she'd known, really known, how enchanting a newborn could be, it would have got her through the discomfort of all those rounds of IVF – the injections, the hormone reactions, the tests – with much less heartache. Or maybe more, knowing what she was missing.

'Of course, darling – it's so exciting. I'm so proud of you!'

Kirsten watches as Harriet clambers into the back of the car. She tries to capture the moment in her mind. It's just as significant as the ride home with the newborn, those life milestones every mother faces. Kirsten knows she'll only get to savour them once – there are no more children after Harriet. So she must enjoy them now.

But she also really must get to work. Kirsten sees the time as she turns on the car ignition: 8.25. Shit. Not only were they meant to be at the school five minutes ago, her first appointment is fast approaching, as well. And as emotionally rewarding as it is to gaze dotingly at Harriet, it isn't financially rewarding. Those financial rewards have kept the roof over her daughter's head. OK, so Ian may be laudably busy managing the struggling comprehensive school he heads up out of special measures, before the Ofsted inspection – but he doesn't get a bonus for the hours he works. The more Kirsten works, the more she gets paid, and the less they have to watch the overdraft every month.

Harriet begins complaining that she's left one of her new special pencils in the house and says that they'll have to go back and get it. The gloss of the first school day becomes tarnished. The usual negotiations (or bribes) kick in. By the time Kirsten drops Harriet at school, she is thinking very positively about the benefits of being able to deposit your child elsewhere for someone else to deal with.

As soon as she has that thought, she wants to run back after Harriet and apologise. Never wish away something so precious. Never try to abdicate responsibility for one so dear. The school staff seem good on health and safety, but what if they aren't?

She considers calling Ian, asking him what he thinks. Should she go back in and make sure Harriet is properly settled? But no. She knows what he would say. It's fine. The school is a good one, excellent parent feedback, and the teachers are fully checked for criminal records. She's safe, Kirsten tells herself. She's safe.

Chapter 2

MIRIAM, 4 SEPTEMBER 2018

Miriam stands at the front of the still-empty classroom, mentally hugging herself. Finally, she is here – about to embark on teaching at St Anthony's. All summer, the thought of it had been her best thing – the one that gave her hope and excitement each morning. The one that made her happy to exist as she curled up in her bed at night. She'd think about all those little faces, staring up at her, yearning for knowledge.

She knew how the first morning would go. Pick out one particular face, that natural teacher's pet – all blonde, dimpled, cute floppy hair. Then look to the one next to them. *That's* the one you want. The one you should go for. Maybe their hair is red or brown. Maybe they don't smile. Maybe they have glasses, or their lack of a smile suggests they've learnt the hard way that everything doesn't go hunky-dory just because you're a kid. Maybe they wouldn't be the archetypal cute kid on the bleeding heart 'Missing Child'-type posters, or the pictures that stare out from papers hauntingly when sad news hits. But it's that little one, the less than obvious one, that you want. That child will change your life. It's worth taking the rap for that kid, if something goes wrong.

She'd seen her formative teachers choose the less obvious kids, and she knew for herself that it made an otherwise average teacher become truly memorable.

And it was that thinking that got her the job. Not her own personal goal for where all this is going, of course. But the emphasis on child-focused attention. Thinking beyond the normal line of duty. Looking beyond the obvious to achieve results. She replays the interview in her head. So nervous. All her dreams depended on it.

'Ms Robertson, where do you see yourself in five years' time?'

She'd wiped her sweaty palms on her dress. She'd bought it specially but hated it already. Why did she go for acrylic peach? She'd read in some magazine one time that you look confident in pink. This was not the right pink and she did not feel confident. What she felt was hot and grimy, and the dress wasn't helping. She could literally see her palm marks on the fabric.

'In five years, I'll be … I don't know, maybe married, with my own child, maybe two children?'

The headmistress had stared back at her, stifling a yawn. How many other twenty-somethings had she tried to imagine being five years older that day? It was a world away. Miriam had to up her game. She tried again.

'So. Five years. I'd hope to be well on the way to making an early Deputy Head at a school like this one and be helping out in the co-curricular activities – running a breakfast club, that kind of thing? I see you don't have one, but I'd be more than willing to start one. But I guess I don't need to wait five years – I can start it sooner, if parents want it. It's so important to have these extra conveniences, isn't it? Happy parents, happy children, that's what I always think.'

And she'd smiled brightly, hoping it was enough, that she wasn't just gushing madly. And it was enough. The headmistress's yawn had gone. She was leaning forward. Rapt. Thank God. Miriam took a sip of water. The next twenty minutes were a formality. The job was hers. The other twenty-somethings could go home; the school had found 'The One'. Maybe she wasn't the best choice, objectively speaking – if the school had all the facts at its disposal. She certainly didn't have the best childcare credentials (her sister had still never forgiven her). And if she'd told them where she really wanted to be in five years – well, they might, in their misguided way, have called the police. But she was the choice they made.

Summer holidays done, here Miriam stands. Finally. Behind her desk, waiting for her assigned class to potter in for registration. Waiting for that one little face that will make or break her heart. Not wearing peach today. Baby blue silk (OK, viscose) shirt with a pussycat bow, and a blue tweed skirt. It looks professional, approachable, maybe a bit sassy. She hopes.

They start to arrive. Dribs and drabs at first. Little poppets in their burgundy uniforms. How lucky their mummies and daddies are; how much she wants one of them for her own. The boys in little ties and caps, the girls in pretty pleated skirts. They are meant to have just turned five, but some of them are tiny. One girl, she's far too small for the chair. She brings her knees up to her chest, and sits there, curled, thumb in her mouth, *Peppa Pig* lunch box clutched to her. But then you have the boys – big enough for a rugby team, some of them. Could overpower the little girls in an instant, get them into a scrum tackle. Maybe they are already in kiddy rugby teams; they're in North London after all. It's never too early for stretching your children.

'Good morning, class,' Miriam says, in her best Miss Honey voice. Try not to let it shake. Try to smile the words. Remember the lesson plan. Remember you're in control, this time. Kids trust adults who assume authority. And that's what she wants. Their trust. That's central to her plans. To get close.

'Welcome back to school, everyone. My name is Ms Robertson, and I'm delighted to be working with you all. Let's go through the register. Stand up when your name is called, please – it helps me learn who you are.'

11

Miriam had their photos already, of course. She'd studied them over the summer. But it looked like some of them were about two years old when they registered; nothing beats seeing them in the flesh. So she calls the roll. And they're away. Names fly by, some the latest crazes (we have several Olivias), some more traditional (welcome, Peter). They're nearly at the end when she stands up. The girl. And Miriam knows, instantly, that this is the one. She squeaks her name: Harriet White. Doesn't even meet Miriam's gaze at first, just fiddles with her messy plaits. But then she looks up and Miriam sees those beautiful hazel eyes.

And there she is. Miriam's vocation. Miriam catches a breath. Because it's a big moment, isn't it? When your life's purpose is suddenly right there in front of you. Tantalisingly close already. But so much work required to get there. Little by little, she'll secure it. She'll secure her. She must.

Chapter 3

BECKY, JULY 2012

Becky rubs her eyes and puts her maths textbook down. She needs a break from calculus. Besides, they're done with exams for this term, so why bother really? She throws herself onto her bed and looks into the full-length mirror at the end of it. She pulls her glasses down on the end of her nose, and pouts into the mirror. 'Pretty Geek.' That's how people know her. She could live with either of the labels separately. But together – well, it's sort of like she's not good enough to be one or the other. She's only an acceptable geek because she's pretty, and only acceptable for her prettiness because her IQ is higher than average. Try to devote herself to being either one of them? Wouldn't work. She'd be even more of a social outcast.

Her middle sister never seems to have that problem. Quite the opposite. Becky hears, sometimes, about the boyfriends and parties at university, somehow juggled with first-class marks and doting tutors. She wishes she could be more like her.

And yet … Becky doesn't mind her own image as much as she should. Leaning over to her desk again, she pulls out the leaflet for drama summer school. Her parents were amazed when she signed up for it. She knows, she's not stupid – she overheard all those conflicting conversations downstairs. They went like this, basically:

Mum: Oh, our little darling is finally getting some social skills.

Dad: But drama makes people stupid. What if she fails her exams?

Both: We only want her to be happy (as long as she gets good grades and doesn't have S. E. X., of which God might not approve. And as long as she doesn't catch Acting, distracting her from a good career as a doctor or a teacher or something Solid – which she and her sisters must do).

Then there's some disagreement – it escalates into a row and Becky tunes out.

OK, Becky was summarising the part she listened to, but that was the gist. And she kind of understood, because yes, she was surprised with herself too. If it weren't for Caitlin, she wouldn't have agreed. And Caitlin wouldn't have pressured her if they hadn't both caught Andrew Carmichael staring over at them in Maths. (Becky was busy concentrating on finding what n equalled, so Caitlin had to nudge her.) Becky assumed he was looking at Caitlin, because Caitlin is gorgeous, in a way that is the opposite of everything about Becky (blonde to Becky's mousy brown, long-limbed to Becky's wiry petiteness, twenty-twenty blue vision, compared to Becky's black-framed myopia). Becky isn't totally sure how they managed to become friends. But they seem to be, and it doesn't do to prod the proof under the microscope, or it might burst.

Besides, apparently the timing worked out well for her parents because Becky's other sister, the boring one, was coming to stay with The New Baby. The baby had been new for the past, what, year? And it hadn't learnt to sleep, or was it swallow, or had forgotten while it got its teeth, or something, so Becky's sister needed Help and everyone had to make way for the invasion. Becky just hoped she didn't come back to find her room full of nappies.

So anyway, at school, Caitlin had been convinced Andy (divine Andy) was staring at Becky, and vice versa. Unlikely. But later, by the notice boards, it seemed like Caitlin might be right. Becky was looking for the algebra club meeting, when she heard a voice behind her. A male voice.

'Are you signing up to the drama summer school?'

She'd looked round to see Andy just there, almost kissing distance away. Could smell the minty intrigue of the gum he was chewing. Pulling her gaze away from him momentarily, she followed it to where he was looking. A sign-up sheet for drama summer school, with a few flyers in a little plastic folder pinned next to it.

There were two spaces left on the sign-up sheet. Under Andy's name.

Becky had smiled shyly. 'Oh, it's not really my kind of thing,' she said, and made to turn away.

'What she means is,' came a loud, springy, female voice behind her, 'she'd love to go, and so would I!'

Caitlin. She grabbed a pen from her ponytail and filled in her own name first, then Becky's.

'I went last year,' Caitlin said. 'It was amazing.'

That was six weeks ago. Now, the course was only four weeks away. A two-week summer school, with gorgeous Andy. And Caitlin.

'Get some contact lenses,' Caitlin had advised her.

But the optician had said there were none suitable for her eye type. Pretty Geeky Freak. Or at least, none that she could comfortably use to look at computers with. So Mum said no. The drama course was expensive enough, and she wouldn't have Becky ruining her eyes over it.

Still, she could take her glasses off if she ever got close enough to Andy to warrant it. Or he could take them off for her. Caitlin said Becky was still in with a chance – said that's what she was giggling about with Andy in the cafeteria. Seeing them together

15

had sparked something in Becky's chest. But Caitlin was a good friend, wasn't she? So it must be true. You had to trust your friends.

Chapter 4

KIRSTEN, 4 SEPTEMBER 2018

'Jess, you're a legend!'

Kirsten takes a sip of the green tea that her PA has put on her desk. She secretly wishes it was coffee, but she's trying to be more Zen. Come on, brain, arise calm, clear, out of befuddled mummy mode, please.

'How's Harriet?' Jess asks Kirsten.

'Oh, she's great – thank you,' Kirsten says. She knows there's a blush spreading over her cheeks. She can't help it – even now, when she talks about her, it happens. It's like you're in love, permanently, isn't it? When you have a kid? And now they know that Harriet will, sadly, be their only child, their little empress, so she gets all that love. After the baby that didn't … work out. Every day, Kirsten tells her: 'You're the best thing that ever happened to us.' Ian, he always raises an eyebrow when she says that. But despite everything, it's true. See the silver lining; that's the motto.

'It must be tough leaving her all day,' Jess continues. 'I know when I have kids …'

She trails off. Kirsten raises an eyebrow. Maybe her PA has

remembered Kirsten is her boss, so this is forbidden territory: do not discuss any plans for fertilisation with the one who pays your wages. First female rule of the workplace. Or maybe she remembers that this is the same passive-aggressive 'why do you work rather than stay at home?' bullshit that mums put up with on a regular basis, and decides to shut her mouth for the good of the sisterhood.

This is Kirsten's bugbear. First day at nursery, the keyworker had said to her in front of a teary Harriet: 'Oh, you must feel so guilty, leaving her here like this.' Well, thank you, Ms Judgemental. Thank you so much. Kirsten had gone back to her car and cried, more than Harriet ever did. Until they invent a self-paying mortgage, Harriet is going to have to be dropped off in places that emotionally blackmail Kirsten. Good, safe places that will broaden Harriet's mind.

They did a study, didn't they, that said girls who go to nursery, and then to school, while their mothers go to work, actually do a whole lot better than those whose parents stay at home? Yes, it got a whole bunch of ridicule in the press. But maybe Kirsten could bring copies to hand out at the school gates (or get the au pair to do it – looks like they're going to have to get one: she can't start offering 7.30 a.m. appointments if she has to do the school run).

'So, are we fully booked today, Jess?' Kirsten asks.

'Right up to the brim,' Jess reports. 'And the first patient is waiting outside now!'

'Good. Give me a couple of minutes, and send him in.'

Kirsten needs that two minutes. Because as much as she loves Harriet – and she does, she loves her, she loves her – it takes more than one sip of green tea to go from desperately cajoling: 'Harriet sweetie, get back in the car, come on now, you know you want to! You don't need the second purple pencil. One is enough! No, honestly, no one's going to judge you. We're going to be late – please, come on!' to her best calm bedside-manner-infused: 'Now, what seems to be the matter today?'

But she's got to. Because it's a business, this private practice GP surgery. She can't just rock up like at a NHS practice each morning, with the attitude that people should be so lucky that they've got an appointment, and she'll do what she can but hey! she's no brain surgeon. Yes, NHS GPs are the front line of medicine. Some surgeries are brilliant. And many GPs are fantastic. But some are struggling. Over-run with patients and paperwork, having to lay down ridiculous rules to reach even more ridiculous targets (Six minutes late? You'll need to rebook your appointment!) and then giving advice in a rush – it's tough. Sometimes she'd felt like she was just a gatekeeper for prescriptions, rather than providing meaningful advice. Which was why she left. Set up on her own. Maybe a bit earlier than some people – she could have waited a good decade – but if you have a dream, why delay?

And now, people are paying for a service with more than their tax. They are investing in their health, investing in Kirsten personally, as a service. So she needs to put her mummy service to one side. Not be the nice, slightly harried, always doting but ever failing mummy. She has to be polished, professional Dr White. She puts on her glasses. Slips on her jacket. Lines up the blood pressure monitor neatly on her desk. The desk she herself built from an IKEA flat pack at 1 a.m. the day before the surgery opened. And, of course, makes sure Harriet's picture is tilted to where the patients can't see it.

There are pictures of her and Ian too, in the montage Ian had put together for one of their anniversaries. Kirsten and Ian together back when she was a student – how young she looks, particularly next to Ian, who always crashes through the important birthdays long before she does. Then Kirsten and Ian in their climbing gear. She doesn't angle that frame away. A young, fresh, physically bold couple. A good advertisement for a healthy outdoor lifestyle, if nothing else. What she doesn't have is a picture of her niece, the one she can't see anymore. It makes her too sad.

Then the first patient of the day comes in.

And Kirsten is glad she had that calming hot drink. Because it's a special gut-wrencher, a tear-jerker: the sweetest couple, with fertility problems. Can she help them? And can she prescribe the wife some mild anti-depressants? Because now it's really starting to affect her sleep. And her ability to function in the world without crying.

Kirsten risks a look at her lovely Harriet's picture. Beautiful Harriet. Safe and happy at school, now. What a big girl – hard to believe she's turned five. Someday, the bubble will burst; the picture will shatter, won't it? The dream of Harriet is too good to be true. She experiences a sudden urge to run out from the surgery, away from this couple with their traumatic failure to conceive, and to go to school and gather up her own gorgeous child.

She doesn't, of course. Because although Harriet might be the most important thing in the world, this is Work Kirsten. So she stays put, sits, listens, empathises and prescribes, while a little part of her brain rejoices in Harriet, her girl.

Chapter 5

MIRIAM, 4 SEPTEMBER 2018

As they approach mid-morning break, the children are happily drawing pictures of their holidays. Miriam didn't ask them to draw their families – she felt it would be too upsetting for some of them. Can be a bit unorthodox, the set-up. Sure, everyone's cool with kids having two daddies these days, but if your first venture into the classroom is to find out you're completely different, and someone giggles at you, it's going to mar the school journey, right? Put the children first, not preachy societal values. If she'd learnt nothing else, she'd learnt that.

Besides, it would be upsetting for her too. She knows the family she wants. Her, plus-one. The plus-one being a child. Not just any child, of course. She'd done two short stints at other schools, but there hadn't been the connection that she feels here. But that experience had, in part, got her this job. Nothing is wasted.

So they do holidays. The EasyJet generation – they've all had a summer getaway. Even if it was a staycation, it had to be a cool one. Who knew that five-year-olds went glamping? Or maybe it was just a campsite, and the slightly cash-strapped Brexit worriers have sought to teach their children the socially acceptable face of a muddy tent break.

There are the usual shout outs of 'We went to Disneyland!' and 'Mummy says the only way to fly is business class!' or 'The French Riviera is perfect at this time of year!' (Would the parents be embarrassed or proud if they could hear the precociousness of their children?) Miriam makes sure the quieter ones get a say, too. She walks between the desks, asking about the pictures.

Harriet is covering her drawing, making a little circle round it with her hands and her plaits as she draws. Miriam bends down. She sees the girl up close now. Her hair is not just light brown, it is so many colours: copper, oak, dark blonde, all woven together in those silly messy plaits. But cute little bobbles at the end of each one. Unicorns, they look like. Someone cares about her, then. Someone other than Miriam.

'May I see your picture, Harriet?' Miriam asks her gently. Start soft; build the rapport gently. That's the way to win them over.

She shakes her head vigorously, sending plaits flying out, the unicorns given wings.

'But surely you want to show me where you went on holiday?'

She shrugs.

'Well, I'd like to see,' Miriam tells her. 'Even if you don't want to show me.'

Miriam leans slightly closer, and tries to prise one of Harriet's little hands away from the paper.

Reluctantly, Harriet lets her, and lifts the other hand away too.

Miriam looks at the picture.

At first glance, it's a playroom. There are lots of toys, and a low-level table. Miriam's about to ask what her favourite toy is, but then she sees that there's a little cross on the door, like the ones you see on ambulances.

Miriam's heart lurches. Oh no! Is this lovely little girl ill? Has she spent the summer at a hospital? Her mind flits back to that

22

summer, years ago. When they didn't go to hospital when they should have done. After Miriam did what she did. The little girl she misses every day.

'Where is this?' Miriam asks her.

'Mummy's work,' she says.

Miriam mentally readjusts.

'Mummy is a doctor?' Miriam says, like she didn't know. Of course, the picture makes sense now. All the parents filled in their jobs on joining forms. And Miriam had read them all carefully. But you have to play the game, don't you? Just like if you Google someone in the evening, looking for pictures of their kids, imagining being their child's mummy, the next day you have to make with the questions to eke out answers you already know.

'Mummy is very busy and I have to play with the toys,' Harriet says. Poor little thing, thinks Miriam – *if only I could give her a big hug, show her some love.* Miriam had a teacher who'd done that with her, and she'd never forgotten it.

'But surely you went away on holiday, too?' Miriam asks. 'What about Daddy?'

Harriet shakes her head. 'Mummy can't have a break because she works so hard. But Daddy was away, because he does school work all summer even though everyone else spends time with their family, Mummy says. Daddy says Mummy and Daddy would go away together if they could, but not me.'

Alarm bells start ringing. 'They wanted to go away at the same time, without you? Would you be home alone?' Miriam wouldn't have thought at this school, with this child, her first thoughts would be about alerting social services.

Harriet shakes her head and gives her a grin. 'I'm only five, silly. I can't stay at home alone, and Mummy wouldn't let me stay with Granny.' Thank God. Miriam's heart rate slows a little. 'Daddy took me with him for a week, and I watched the big children play.'

Miriam's heart rate increases again. It sounds like things are not being done right. This is why Miriam needs her own child – to show how things should be done.

'Was that fun?' Miriam asks. 'Did Daddy make time to play with you too?'

But Miriam doesn't hear the answer because the child on the other side of her announces he needs to do a poo. NOW.

The teaching assistant ushers him out of the room, and Miriam turns back to Harriet but the bell goes, and it's time for break. The moment's gone. Harriet, like the rest of the children, jumps up from her seat and rushes out of the room. Before Miriam follows them, she looks again at the picture Harriet has drawn. Fancy spending the summer at your parents' work and no holiday! It's not like they lack the cash. Unimpressive. For everything Miriam's parents didn't do for her, they at least gave her a holiday. Norway, Holland, France – abroad, but not far flung. Until they flung her out. But then, that was her fault. Or so they said.

Still, this isn't about her. It really isn't. It's about Harriet. And the other children, of course. About making sure they're all as happy as they can possibly be.

True, the happiest place would be at home with her. But you can't have too much, too soon.

So for now, if they aren't happy, then she'll need to change things. One step at a time.

Chapter 6

KIRSTEN, SEPTEMBER 2018

How is it always 5 p.m.? However much Kirsten asks Jess not to book in 4.30 appointments, it's somehow always five when Kirsten's running out of the surgery, slinging her bag in the back of the Lexus and revving like mad to pick up Harriet on time. First nursery, now school. Thank God for after-school clubs, and that she could choose to set up her practice only a ten-minute drive away from Harriet's school. But really – how the hell were working mums supposed to do it? Could she pay Jess to collect Harriet? Probably, but also probably not. She needs her to help run the business, not her personal life, however much the two coincide.

Besides, Kirsten knows she always melts when she sees Harriet again. It's a joy to pick her up from school, isn't it?

And there we go. The switch from busy doctor-mummy to mummy-mummy. Of course she can make time for this. Yes, Ian should do more – it would be good to alternate. He keeps telling her it's just a phase, while he gets his school over the Ofsted approbation. And yes, she admires his dedication to the failing school, his social conscience, his commitment to the kids from less advantaged homes. His quest for unimpeachable integrity. And she understands the particular source of his middle-class guilt. But you'd think he'd help more at home too, considering. You'd think that day-to-day, Kirsten would have more leverage.

But no. It's like he can't bear to spend the time with his daughter, sometimes. Kirsten's seen him look at Harriet like he hates her. Oh, sure, he thinks he hides it well. But Kirsten sees him. A wife knows her husband. Leaving the room at strange moments, when Kirsten's telling Harriet how much she loves her. That time he got disproportionately angry when Kirsten let Harriet play around with her make-up – she's five for God's sake, she's not being sexualised, she's playing at being Mummy. There'll be a time for rules about that (of course there will, Kirsten isn't stupid), but that time is not now. And the other day, when Harriet was messing round with his phone, Kirsten honestly thought he might hit Harriet. Well, OK, not quite that bad – because she'd never let him do that – but he stared at that phone with such rage, Kirsten was almost frightened.

Other times, though, he looks at Harriet like she's the love of his life. Which maybe she is. The love of both their lives. Kirsten remembers when she and Ian were that precious to each other. Or were they? Can you ever truly love your spouse as much as you love your child?

Ah, parking space! Ian says if Kirsten got a smaller car she wouldn't spend so much of her life worrying about where to put it. Her verdict is that he can play the ruffled headmaster turning up at his school in his Golf – it wouldn't do to look too posh. It's different for parents collecting their kids. Kirsten needs to show up at the school gate looking like it was worth being late. Like she earns as much as people think she does. Otherwise, they ask themselves what the point is. And she starts asking herself that too. Which is stupid, futile, dumb and a waste of dreams – because Harriet needs a role model. And Kirsten needs to provide one.

OK; mummy mode. Fine. Ready to jump out of the car. Go!

A woman calls out as Kirsten moves away from her car. 'Hey, Kirsten!'

Kirsten panics. Is she a patient? Are they going to get into discussions of UTIs out here in the street? But no, she has a child attached to her, so she's a mum. In fact, two children – one swaddled to her breast, one jumping along at the end of her arm.

'Hey …' Kirsten says. She's sure the alpha mummy has a name but she doesn't know it. They've probably been introduced, but too late now.

'You bring anything for the nearly new sale tomorrow?' the woman asks Kirsten.

Ah, she's a PTA mum. No wonder she knows Kirsten's name. The guilt shifts slightly.

Kirsten wrinkles her brow. 'Sorry, maybe next time,' she says. 'Work and everything, you know?' Kirsten feels like she's at the start of a bad American movie. Of course, the woman knows about work. She probably works too, as well as bringing up the kids.

The woman rolls her eyes. 'Tell me about it. Geoff hasn't left the office this week. Don't worry, I know it's hard to juggle.'

She effortlessly unswathes the baby from its sling, and in one seamless move, places it in her parked Maserati. Jesus. Other people's lives.

Kirsten taps the entry code into the school gates, buzzes herself in, and goes to find Harriet. Deep breaths, onwards, into the school.

There she is. Kirsten's beautiful little darling. Didn't every mother's heart just soar when she saw her child? It's chess today, by the looks of it. She'll be a little champion in no time.

'Harriet! Darling, time to go home!'

Harriet turns around but keeps on playing. Kirsten remembers when Harriet used to run up to her with open arms. Is that

27

innocence gone already? Perhaps Ian was right about the make-up. Perhaps Kirsten is letting her grow up too fast.

Kirsten walks up to the game. Harriet's playing with a staff member. Kirsten sees, now, that all the other children are being packed up to go, their parents having arrived a long time back.

The staff member stands up. Nice clothes, nice hair – not 'look at me' fashionista but professional, stylish. A good role model for girls in her care. 'Hi, I'm Miriam Robertson. You must be …'

Kirsten puts out her hand. 'Kirsten. Kirsten White. Harriet's mother.'

The teacher looks at Kirsten's hand for a moment, then takes it. A soft handshake, almost like she doesn't want their hands to touch. Kirsten can't have offended her already, can she?

'I just started here today,' says the teacher. 'Harriet's in my class.'

'Oh, that's great,' Kirsten says, withdrawing her hand. Here she is, making those famous connections with her child's school. 'How did she get on?'

Harriet, tiring of her chess game, gets up and starts trying to swing herself between Kirsten's legs like some kind of monkey. A novel show of affection, but she'll take it.

There's a pause from Ms Robertson.

'Everything OK?' Kirsten asks.

The teacher smiles. 'Of course it is. I'm sure Harriet will be a pleasure to teach.'

Kirsten tries to extract Harriet from between her legs. Sure, Harriet's having fun, and there's a pleasing embarrassment in having a child so free with your body, but Kirsten suspects it will lead to a wardrobe malfunction soon – note to self, wear trousers in future.

'She's showing real promise in her drawings,' says the teacher. 'We haven't done much maths or English yet, so let's see. The main thing is that she's happy.'

Kirsten nods. So true. That's what should matter to all of them

– being happy. But we just find so many ways to put it off, right? *If I can just make this bit of extra money ... if I can just lose this extra five pounds ... if I can just have a child ... then I'll be happy.* But we never stick to our promises.

Harriet is looking up at Kirsten. Kirsten knows this is meant to be Harriet's happy time.

'What were you drawing, sweetie?' she asks, stooping down.

'Holidays,' she tells her.

Kirsten flicks a look at the teacher. 'Oh God, don't tell me – was it her time at Daddy's work or mine?' She tries to grin away the guilt.

The teacher looks at her steadily.

'Yours,' she says simply. Kirsten can smell the disapproval.

Well, screw that.

'Ah, yes, holidays at Mummy's office – you had a lovely time, didn't you, sweetie? All the toys and the books? Charming the patients?'

Harriet nods, semi-happily, and takes Kirsten's hand.

'Me and Mummy do everything together, go everywhere together,' she recites in a sing-songy chant. The line Kirsten fed her for the patients (doctors struggling with childcare isn't a confidence booster). Harriet totally owned it.

Good girl. Kirsten mentally promises them both Tuscany, some happy year in the future. Ian wanted to go this year, just the two of them. Suggested leaving Harriet with Kirsten's parents, but it didn't feel safe. Hyper-vigilant of her, maybe. But she can hardly believe in Harriet sometimes, or how fortunate they are. Harriet could be wiped away in a heartbeat and Kirsten knows she needs to be there to see her every single day. Sadly, Ian doesn't quite understand.

Kirsten straightens up and talks to the teacher.

'Well, I dare say I'll see you tomorrow,' Kirsten tells her. 'Same time, same place.'

'Harriet does after-school club every day, then?' the teacher asks.

Is that *another* judgement? Kirsten is so sick of this – don't offer a service if you then berate people for using it.

'Not every day,' Kirsten says. 'But I work, her daddy works. It's a lifesaver to have this club. To be honest, I could do with a breakfast one too – real wrap-around childcare.'

The teacher nods thoughtfully. Oh, like they'll ever take the suggestion into account – the staff probably find it a wrench enough already getting out of bed at 7 a.m. Or they imagine some idyll of the whole family breakfasting together, chattering calmly about their day ahead. Not *Peppa Pig* blaring away as one parent desperately advocates another spoonful of Weetabix while the other sets a world record for showering after the alarm failed to go off. Kirsten wishes they'd make teachers have children before they take up teaching, so they know what it's really all about.

'I understand,' the teacher says. Like hell she does.

But then, looking at her, Kirsten thinks she might understand. Genuinely, somehow. She feels her guard slipping slightly. She gives a little 'pity me' shrug. She lets the teacher pat her on the shoulder. And her eyes well with tears. But she blinks them away.

'Come on, you!' Kirsten says to Harriet, hoisting her up into a hug. 'Time to get you home to Daddy!' He probably won't be back yet, but it's a good line to get Harriet moving.

'Have a lovely evening!' says Miriam, waving after them.

As they leave the room, Harriet turns back to wave again, so Kirsten does too. Miriam is hugging herself and gazing after them. Their eyes lock. Kirsten shivers a little; she doesn't know why. Perhaps it's the intensity of Miriam's gaze. But still, Kirsten nods to her, and she nods back, lifts a hand a little in a wave. Kirsten's about to shout 'Goodbye', but Harriet pulls her out of the room.

'Don't be so rude!' Kirsten admonishes her.

And Harriet pouts, doesn't answer, and refuses to budge a further inch. So Kirsten has to drag her from the building and forcibly put her into the car. On the way home, rather than prattling to Kirsten about her day, Harriet stares out of the window.

Why did Kirsten have to take it into her head to do some 'parenting'? Maybe Harriet just wanted some alone time with Mummy, hence the dragging away from the teacher, and Kirsten spoilt it.

Another evening started all wrong.

And it doesn't get much better. By the time Ian is finally home, dinner is burnt – the period it took to placate Harriet exceeded the optimum cooking length for chops – and half-eaten. Kirsten is trying to salvage the evening. A glass of red wine down, she is curled up on the sofa, head resting against Harriet's as they read a book.

Ian blusters in, breaking the hard-won calm.

'Evening, all!' he says, taking off his coat, and throwing it on a sofa.

Kirsten resists the urge to mutter 'Finally'. Instead, she nods to the wine on the table.

'Want some?' she asks, half-heartedly.

Ian shakes his head. 'Nah, I'll leave it to you.'

Kirsten finds implicit criticism that the bottle of wine will soon deplete. But he's probably right.

Ian plants a kiss on each of their foreheads. Harriet gives him a big hug, which he accepts but only fleetingly returns.

'I'll go and rescue the supper, shall I?' Ian says.

'We've eaten,' Kirsten tells him.

'Anything left for me?' he asks.

She shakes her head. 'Didn't think you'd be back in time. There'll be something else, though. Check the fridge.'

She turns back to the book. She tries to re-create the mood, but it's gone. Harriet is distracted. Soon, Ian mooches back in with some pitta bread and hummus.

'How was Harriet's first day?' he asks. 'How was it, sweetie?'

'We had to draw our holidays,' she says.

Kirsten shares a look with Ian, seeing his understanding.

The conversation moves on.

31

'And how was your day, sweetheart?' Ian asks Kirsten, rubbing her shoulders. 'Any tricky patients?'

'It's not the patients that are tricky, it's trying to run a business while trying to raise a child basically single-handedly. That's tricky!'

'Hush, Kirsten, not in front of—'

Shit, he's right, of course. She should have bitten her tongue – every time she snaps like this, she gets one step closer to being her parents, everything turning into an argument. 'Sorry. Sorry, both of you. Bit stressed.' Kirsten kisses both of them on the forehead, then sits back on the sofa.

'But, Ian, do you know, all my competitors offer early morning and late evening appointments?' she continues. 'All of them, without exception. I'm never going to make it, working in school hours only.'

'So go back to the public sector,' he says, joshing her. It's a running joke, that she's gone private, while he remains wedded to the state sector. She rolls her eyes. He grins. 'Or, more realistically, take on a partner,' Ian tells her.

He says it like it's so easy.

'I can't afford to take on a partner until there's a business case, and there won't be a business case until I make more money!'

'So we'll get an au pair, like you said,' Ian counters.

'It's not about an au pair, Ian. It's about you … being here.'

Sometimes, late at night, they sit on the sofa and listen to each other's concerns. Address them all rationally, over an equally split bottle of wine. This is not one of those occasions.

Harriet gets up and leaves the room.

'We're not really bickering, darling, come back!' Kirsten calls after her.

'Sweetie, it's OK—' Ian joins in.

Kirsten stands, ready to follow Harriet.

'It's not, though, is it?' Kirsten says. 'It's not OK.'

Ian climbs off the sofa and kneels in front of Kirsten.

'It is OK. You're just stressed. I'm sorry. I'll try to get home earlier. OK? Maybe I don't need to shadow all the teachers running up to the inspection, just the problem ones.'

'You sure you won't miss the time with the students?'

The comment hangs in the air. Their shared past, ever present.

'Kirsten, come on. Let's try to salvage this. I'll go and find Harriet. You put your feet up, do work emails, whatever. You deserve it, OK?'

She nods, but she feels her jaw pumping.

Ian stands and kisses her on the top of her head.

Together, they go up the stairs to Harriet's bedroom. She's sitting on her bed, talking to her teddy bear. Kirsten gestures not to disturb Harriet so they hover outside the room. Ridiculous, to eavesdrop, but it's the only way inside Harriet's head sometimes.

'You do not do that, no no no!' shouts Harriet, in a little kiddy shout. 'Bad bear!'

And then she hits the bear across the face.

Christ. Who has she learnt that from?

Kirsten makes to go into the room, but Ian holds out a hand to stop her.

'Let me,' he whispers. 'You did this afternoon. Go downstairs and put your feet up.'

Kirsten shrugs, lets him go in. But after the bear exchange, she's not about to leave Ian alone with Harriet. She wants to be sure of what goes on. So she moves out of the doorway, does some loud stepping on the spot to imitate going downstairs, then stays where she can hear.

'I'm sorry about the shouting, sweetheart,' she hears Ian say.

She can't see Harriet's reaction, but Ian continues.

'Sometimes grown-ups just get a bit angry with themselves, and they take it out on each other.' It's a platitude, but Kirsten's not sure she could do better.

'As long as they don't take it out on their children,' says Harriet, very seriously. 'Children are there to make people happy.'

Kirsten blinks back tears. She makes it sound so simple.

'That's right, sweetie,' Kirsten hears Ian say. 'Did someone teach you that?'

'My new teacher, she's great,' Harriet says.

There's rustling, maybe a hug. 'I'm so glad you like her, sweetheart.'

'And the playground is brilliant. Look, I got two more scabs.'

Harriet showed them to Kirsten earlier. Kirsten had kissed each one of them. She can't see how Ian reacts, but hears 'I love you, Daddy'.

'I love you too, sweetheart.' So. He's being good, caring Daddy now. Makes a change. But credit where it's due. Kirsten is about to sneak away downstairs, when Harriet speaks again.

'I love Mummy too but please will you tell her she doesn't need to shout? We can still hear if she uses her gentle voice.'

Kirsten closes her eyes and leans against the wall. Her child shouldn't have to say this.

'I can ask her, sweetie, but I don't know if she'll listen,' she hears Ian say. Great, so much for spousal support.

'You'll have to make her listen.'

Then Ian again: 'You're right, sweetheart. I'll have to make her listen. One way or another.'

Kirsten feels a little chill spread over her at the words, then shakes it off. He's just trying to reassure their daughter. She could walk into the room, say she is persuaded, that she will use her gentle voice from now on. Ask Ian to explain what he means. But no. Gentle voice here means retreat. Don't spoil this rare father-daughter bonding session. Retreat. Pad softly downstairs and leave them to it. Whatever 'it' is.

Chapter 7

MIRIAM, SEPTEMBER 2018

Miriam's stomach rumbles. She should eat. She looks from her lesson plans to her watch: 7.30 p.m. Kiddy bedtime. Imagine them now, all the parents, tucking in their kids. If only it could be her. Brushing those strands of beautiful hair away from the little ones' faces to make room for a kiss. Maybe another bedtime story, another lullaby. Then turn off the light, leave the room to be lit by the glow-in-the-dark stars on the ceiling.

OK, they can't all do that – look at stars. They can't all have had the same bedroom ceiling as Miriam did. Back when things were sweet, innocent, untrammelled. How she used to stare at those stars, be soothed by them, when things were bad. They were her little bits of magic, adorning the ceiling. She'll never see that room again.

Miriam puts down her pen and gets up from her desk (i.e. the one table her flat possesses – mean old landlord). She can't plan anymore. First, the lesson is the most over-planned one ever. (She had the full first week planned the day after she got the job.) Second, how can she enthuse children when her empty stomach is making her maudlin? The big picture is too distracting – after all, she became a teacher so that she could one day hope to have a child of her own. The right one. The one that she could win over, slowly but surely, so that the parents sort of … fade away. Individual planning of lessons seems too trivial compared with that, even though she knows that gently, gently, little by little, is the way to win that trust.

Plus, the fridge is calling to her. She walks over to the kitchenette and opens the door. The glow illuminates the room and she realises she's been working unlit. Terrible for the eyes and the mood. Happy thoughts, please – dream job, dream children, dream future. That's what it's all about.

She fishes out some noodles from the fridge, adds a bit of extra soy sauce. She contemplates the desk/table, wondering if it's worth the effort to clear stuff away just now so she can eat. Probably not – sofa's just as good for dining alone. She picks up the school-issued A4 picture sheet of the children she teaches, and takes that and the noodles to the sofa. Gingerly, she puts her feet up on the edge of the bucket that's meant to be catching the drips. (Seriously – when is her so-called landlord coming over? She needs to text him again later.)

How unalike so many of the photos are to the children they're trying to capture. Harriet, for example (of course). She looks so washed-out, so wall-eyed, and her hair dulled. In the picture, that is. In the flesh, she is so much more … nuanced. A living, breathing child, not just a mark on a bit of paper. Look at all the others. So beautiful to their parents – and not unbeautiful to Miriam, either. Or each other, as time moves on. Miriam wonders who Harriet's little friends will be. The ones she'll stay friends with in future, right through high school. The ones who'll mess her life up if she lets them.

She'll be asleep by now, probably – they all will. What will Mr and Mrs – sorry, Mr and Dr – White be doing? Hold on, maybe she doesn't want to know! But no, maybe more likely sitting downstairs with a big glass of red wine each? Reminding each other all the ways Harriet is wonderful? Such a cosy notion of parenthood. Is it like that, being in a marriage like theirs, with the little one asleep upstairs? Or is it just tapping away at smartphones, preparing for another working day? Where Miriam's work involves teaching Harriet, their work involves palming her off on teachers. Not that it would do for her to be home-schooled. Certainly not.

Miriam places the photo sheet carefully on the floor and exhales. *Come on. Enjoy this. It's what you've been working for. It's a success! First day in a new job, no disasters, all the kids are compliant, the other staff are fine. You have your special child to make a project of. All good.*

She looks up at the ceiling. No stars to gaze at here. Perhaps she could catch a shooting star out the window? Make a wish on it? Because unfortunately for Miriam, a good day isn't enough. The anxiety never goes away. What if the kids are unhappy? What if they aren't treated right? What if they end up … well, like her?

She needs to take her mind off this. So she does her other usual favourite/least favourite thing. She summons up Facebook on her phone and looks into other worlds. Or rather a specific world. A woman with her young daughter. A girl she's no longer allowed to look after. Apparently Miriam's judgement is 'off'. But look at that girl. Such a pretty little thing, eating an ice cream, hair all done up with ribbons. Miriam would so love to be the one posting those pictures. She remembers holding the little baby, how small and precious it was, how she wanted it to be with her for her own, always. It wasn't meant to end that way. So she'll just have to Facebook stalk. For now.

Chapter 8

KIRSTEN, SEPTEMBER 2018

It was bound to happen.

Kirsten just wishes it hadn't been so public. That it hadn't been in front of Harriet.

Ian wasn't without fault. He knows the pressure Kirsten's under. Knows that this plus a little bit too much red wine on a school night – yes, she's a doctor, she should know better – isn't going to make the school run any smoother. Just don't take the piss. Not unless you want a fight.

But yes, she knows the rest is down to her. She messed up, big time. Again. She sits down at her desk and puts her head in her hands. Someone cancelled – thank God – so she has ten minutes between appointments. She pops another ibuprofen and chases it down with some sparkling water. The hangover's been replaced by a stress headache.

'Maybe you shouldn't have had that extra glass of wine,' was Ian's suggestion this morning, while Kirsten was struggling with the idea of wrenching herself out of bed.

She had to retaliate, right?

'Maybe you should have been there to stop me, rather than doing whatever the hell you were doing.'

'Putting our daughter to bed,' he told her.

'What – you do one thing, and suddenly I'm the alcoholic; you're the caring responsible one?'

And then, of course, Ian tried to play the grown-up. Kirsten could see him counting to ten, his jaw pulsing, nostrils flaring.

'Look,' he said, finally. 'Let's both try to get home on time tonight. Cook dinner. Spend some time with Harriet. Maybe we could watch a film. Like the old days.'

Sounded nice, didn't it? Of course it did. Maybe that was the problem. Maybe it would mean allowing herself to relax. So instead, she flew off the handle.

'These aren't the old days, Ian. We have a child. I'm trying to set up a business. When would I have time to watch a film?'

So he muttered under his breath: 'You don't seem to be trying very hard.'

Come on, really? She built up that place from scratch – selected the premises, painted the walls, did all the marketing, chose the sodding cushions, for goodness' sake! And she's got to keep on climbing; she can't just bail. She's committed too much, borrowed too much from her parents – they need to be repaid in the pride of being able to send cards to their 'Dr' daughter.

So they got on to listing what the particular demands on their time were. Kirsten recalls they were shouting by then. That may or may not have been what woke Harriet. But either way, she was at their bedroom door just as Kirsten was yelling: 'Of course I wish there was someone else to look after Harriet – I do not have time and you don't have the love!'

And he nodded to the door. And there she was. Harriet. Holding a little pile of bread on one of her toy plates, perhaps meant for one of her parents. But she didn't offer it to them; she just stood very still for a few moments then bolted, crying.

Exactly what Kirsten had promised herself she wouldn't be like as a parent. Her mum and dad fought constantly but refused to divorce 'for the good of the children'. She wasn't sure how their snarky, bitter quarrels, interspersed with crockery being thrown at each other was good for anyone, particularly the children. The great lesson Kirsten learnt from them was how to retort in a fight, how never to let things drop. But Harriet deserves better. Even Ian deserves better, probably.

So of course, Kirsten flew out of bed, sort of assuming that Ian would follow. But he didn't. Which meant it was Kirsten, going to explain to Harriet, tears in her voice, that sometimes adults say things they don't mean when they're angry, and that they both love her very, very much. Then she read her some books, played with some dolls – the usual. By the time they all met again on the doorstop, Kirsten had needed to resign herself to leaving home unshowered, badly dressed and carrying her make-up bag.

Then, the worst bit: Ian looked her up and down. *He looked her up and down.* And he said, 'Are you going in like that?'

Bastard. Kirsten, too, was sorry she wasn't ten years younger and couldn't slide on some lip salve, throw on a T-shirt and be voted 'Doctor with bedside manner of the year'. Sorry that looking professional and suitable for the outside world took time.

What she should have done was ask him to look after Harriet for ten minutes while she went and made herself look a bit better.

What she actually did was hit him over the head with her make-up bag.

Forgot, again, about Harriet. Got caught in the cycle of anger. And forgot, too, that foundation bottles are made of glass. So they create quite an impact. Though he was really over-egging it when he stumbled and leant on the car for support. Kirsten, of all people, knows concussion when she sees it – and that wasn't it.

But Yvette from next door didn't necessarily know. Which is

40

presumably why she came rushing towards them, remote-locking her white Audi as she did so.

'Oh, Ian,' she cooed, face all covered in concern. 'I saw everything. Are you OK?' Her hand on his arm, helping him up. A glance at Kirsten, like she was the devil.

'We've got it covered,' Kirsten told her. 'It's been a busy morning. But in my medical opinion, he's fine.'

She saw Ian gently trying to manipulate his arm out of Yvette's grasp. 'Honestly, Yvette, it's OK. I'd better be driving off,' he said. 'My class won't wait.'

But Yvette wasn't having it.

'Oh, you can't possibly drive after that!' she exclaimed. 'Kirsten will have to drive you.'

'Kirsten is very busy,' Kirsten said drily. 'She has to drive her daughter to school and then go to work.' Christ, she was thinking. *Come on, Yvette, just give us some private family time, OK? Stop interfering.* Maybe she was good-natured, but a good-natured busybody is still a busybody.

Kirsten turned to Harriet. 'Come on, sweetie, let's get you to school, hey? Sorry about this.'

She tried to hug Harriet to her in order to make the point, but Harriet refused to budge. Hugging her teddy bear seemed to be enough for her. Frankly, Kirsten felt the same – give her a day on the pavement hugging a soft toy over this mess.

Yvette then came out at her fake best. 'Oh, of course, I quite understand. You are so busy. I don't know how you do it. Let me drop Ian off then.'

'But it's miles out of your way!' said Ian. 'You can't possibly do that. I'll get a cab if you're that worried.'

'I was actually heading over your way to see someone about upholstery – so it's right on track. Come on, hop in,' she said, gesturing to the Audi. 'And I can bring you home again too!'

Yvette has some kind of pretend job Kirsten has never understood. Interior design brokering services or something. It basically means everyone else does the work and Yvette is mentioned in lots of magazines, which she reads out to people over coffee.

'Yvette, you know that's unnecessary,' Kirsten told her, voice low. But Ian was already walking (unsteadily) to the car. 'Ian, tell her it's fine,' she pleaded with him. They'd squabbled, sure, but it was their marriage, right?

Yvette turned to Kirsten, allowing herself a little smile. 'I know lots of things, Kirsten. Let me be the judge of what's necessary.'

Her words chill Kirsten, even thinking back over them again now. *I know lots of things, Kirsten.* What did she mean by that? She'd moved in just after Harriet came along. Bought the house through a private sale, friend of a friend of their previous neighbour. Who, if Kirsten isn't mistaken, didn't know anything about what mattered.

'Ian!' Kirsten called to him. 'I'm sorry, OK? We'll talk this evening.' She tried to muster up some tenderness that she didn't feel. Never start the day in the middle of an argument, right? But he wouldn't even look at her. She could feel her eyes tearing up – life was not meant to be like this, her *marriage* was not meant to turn into this – so she had to turn her attention back to Harriet.

She tried to persuade her into the Lexus with as little fuss as possible.

'Let's see if I've got any mini-cheddars, hey?' Kirsten asked her, in her best sing-song voice.

Harriet looked momentarily interested. Kirsten rifled round in her handbag and found a rustling packet.

'Ooh, ooh, this sounds promising!' Kirsten said, hoping it wasn't sanitary wear. She pulled out her spoils. Oh. Crisps. Not even kiddy ones – those posh Kettle Chip things, an emergency snack. 'Oh sorry, sweetie, it's not mini-cheddars. You can't have these.'

But of course, Harriet reached out her hand. Kirsten gave her the crisps, and stooped down to wipe away her tears. Harriet wriggled her face away.

'You'll understand one day,' Kirsten told her.

But Kirsten hoped she wouldn't. She hoped Harriet would always be innocent. As innocent as she could be, anyway, considering.

They had the same problem getting into school. After a difficult car journey, Harriet was on strike. Once they arrived, Kirsten had to sit next to her in the back, reading her a story. Then sit on the pavement and coax her out with the bribe of chocolate for supper (hoping she'd have forgotten by then). Thankfully, Kirsten didn't think any of the parents heard. Although, when she turned back to face the school, she saw Harriet's new teacher standing there. She didn't know what the teacher saw, but it couldn't have been the worst. Kirsten waved to her, made a little grimace, but the teacher went back into the building. Harriet, suddenly willing again, ran after her and was gone before Kirsten even had time to kiss her on the head.

Suddenly Kirsten was alone, the surreal, chaotic whirlwind of the morning finally over. Until she looked at her watch and saw her first patient would be there in fifteen minutes.

And so it has been, non-stop, until this break that is nearly over.

At times Kirsten secretly wishes she could have nothing more to do with Ian and Harriet. That she could just not get the weekly shop in, which she does so that Ian and Harriet are always well supplied with their favourite foods. Not sort out paying the bills, so they continue to have a warm, light home. Not read the books at bedtime with Harriet, then listen to Ian de-stressing from his day. Not have to do the school run. Just walk away.

But of course, she never would. Because she loves Harriet too much to do anything like that to her. And Ian too. Of course she does. It's just that – how is this her life now? How is it that, however hard she tries, she can't get everything right? She doesn't mean 'anything' – if she just had to get one thing right a day, that would fine. But to get it all right? Too much to ask.

Time was, she would have called her best friend and fellow former med student turned psychiatrist, Clare. They'd meet for a glass of wine, or if that was too difficult, they'd just chat on the phone while drinking their own. But she couldn't do that anymore. It wasn't that they'd drifted or got new best friends. Their friendship had become … compromised.

Chapter 9

BECKY, 1 AUGUST 2012

Day one of the summer school. Everyone is congregated in the hall for a warm-up. It's not Becky's school; it's a posher, bigger one. This is called the Main Hall, as though there are other ones. At the stage end, sitting with their legs swinging off the edge, are the cool girls. Caitlin is there in cut-off denim shorts, of course. She's not the only one. Maybe there was a message – this is what we're wearing today. Except Becky wasn't on the thread.

She waves at Caitlin, expecting Caitlin to beckon her over. But no – she just gives a dismissive wave and carries on talking to Gwen Collins. Of course she does. They can flick their long blonde hair around together and share candy-cane lip gloss. Subtle? No. Effective? Probably.

Instead, Becky ties her cardigan round the waist of her (long) denim dungarees and waits for the session to start. No sign of Andy.

But then, a tap on the shoulder.

'Hey,' says a voice behind her.

It's him. Andy. A little thrill caresses her spine as she turns to face him.

'Hey,' she says back.

'So, you feeling all luvvie, then?' he asks her.

Is this flirting? she wonders. If so, then maybe she should half-flirt back. You know, just in case he isn't, but maybe he is.

'I could—' she starts.

But whatever her comeback was going to be, it's cut off by the authoritarian clapping of hands at the front of the room.

'Right, let's make a start, shall we?' It's a man, casually dressed in a black top and black jeans. He's in shape. His clothes fit well and he looks like a bona fide actor. Except then he introduces himself as a teacher.

'I'll be leading the course,' he says. 'First off, I want you to warm up your bodies and voices. Make space – reach out so your arm span is wide enough for you to just avoid touching fingertips with the person next to you.'

Andy and Becky reach out their arms. They manage to just *not* avoid touching fingertips, and Andy gives Becky a little smile as they both hold their pose. Becky looks down modestly at the floor. When she looks up, Caitlin is magically by her side, with Gwen. Looks like she wants to play the same game with Andy. Becky moves over. After all, the long legs and short shorts are bound to get Andy's attention eventually.

But Andy leans in close to Becky, certainly not regulation distance away.

'If they want us to be in pairs, we're a couple,' he whispers.

She smiles. Her lips may not be coated in candy gloss, but she hopes she makes up for it in genuine emotion.

'OK,' she whispers back.

Andy stays by her side through the warm-up exercises, until the leader announces they should sit down and take a break. Becky sits, hugging her knees to her chest. Andy, Caitlin and Gwen sit next to her. Becky notices some sweat darkening the underarms of Andy's maroon T-shirt (and also, to her satisfaction, those of Gwen's bubble-gum pink one).

'So, you'll all be wondering what performance we're working up to this week. Well, we're going classic musical.' He waits to allow muted cheers/boos to subside. 'I want a medley of Rodgers and Hammerstein – I've selected scenes from *South Pacific*, *Oklahoma*, a couple of others. There's enough there to give you an intro to song, dance and some serious acting as well. Tomorrow morning, I'll be doing auditions for those of you who want principal parts. The rest of you are very welcome to the chorus roles – but I'll still be divvying up some lines of the score for all of you. Sound fair?'

Some nods.

Becky doesn't nod or shake. She would rather just hide in a maths textbook. What was she doing signing up to this? The idea of singing in front of everyone – Andy, Gwen, Caitlin, and all the thirty or so others is mortifying.

'Eurgh,' she says, just as Gwen says loudly, 'Well, I'll be the girl who just can't say no, then.' Gwen then laughs loudly.

Becky looks at her blankly.

'It's a reference to *Oklahoma*,' Andy whispers to her. 'I hope.'

'Right, got you. Thanks,' Becky replies, grateful but embarrassed not to have known. What is she doing here?

'You auditioning then, Bex?' Caitlin asks.

'Um, that would be a no,' Becky replies.

'Oh go on, you must!' Caitlin says.

Andy looks at Becky. 'Go on. You've got a sweet voice, I bet you do. And you're pretty. They'll give you a part.'

Becky shakes her head. 'Really, no – I'm the back-of-the-chorus-line girl. No way am I singing in front and centre.'

'I will if you will,' Andy says.

Gwen starts making chicken noises. 'Scaredy-cat,' she says.

Becky figures this probably isn't the time to be pointing out mixed metaphors.

Just then, the teacher comes round. 'Hi again, Caitlin,' he says. 'Nice to see you back this year.'

Caitlin preens.

'You kids all auditioning then?' he asks.

'You bet!' say Caitlin and Gwen.

Andy says, 'I'm only auditioning if this lady next to me does too,' nodding in Becky's direction.

Becky could kick Andy. This is not her scene. She's only here because of … him.

The leader looks at them both, then round the room.

'Ah, come on, then – both of you should. We've got way more girls than guys here, and I need some male talent. Don't stand in the way of my dream – what's your name?'

'Becky,' says Becky.

'Right, Becky, you're up first tomorrow morning.'

'But—'

'No buts. And this young gentleman is going straight after you, so he can't break his word.'

And away walks the leader.

Becky looks to Caitlin for some sympathy. She must know how hideous this is for her. But Caitlin has got her arm linked through Gwen's and is whispering something in her ear. So much for best friends for ever.

Chapter 10

MIRIAM, SEPTEMBER 2018

Later that week, Harriet doesn't arrive in Kirsten's car.

Or her daddy's car.

She's in a white Audi.

No grown-ups get out – just Harriet. Bundled onto the side-walk.

Miriam moves away from the window.

It's no way to treat a child. Not how she would treat her own, if the day ever came that she was the one doing drop-off and pick-up.

Miriam's preparing for the day's lessons. One of the kids in the class has a new foster sister – from Syria. Maya. Doesn't talk much, by all accounts. Hardly surprising, if you think what the little thing must have been through, and now separated by so many miles from her parents. Anyway, they're building up to the little girl hopefully visiting the class, when she's ready. Miriam wants to give the girl a chance to meet what would be her peers, in a welcoming environment. Maybe help her flourish in her new country. Show the kids that she, Ms Robertson, can provide a place of sanctuary.

She has to make sure first that the kids will provide a proper welcome, make sure they understand the context – in a way that is kiddy-appropriate. Today, they're looking at journeys – over the sea, in crowded boats. Nothing scary. Nothing *real*. They're far too young to lose their own innocence as well. Just enough for them maybe to understand, a little bit, when the little girl arrives.

So now, Miriam is preparing the vessels. Crêpe paper sails, cardboard hulls. Everything has to start somewhere, right? Cut, cut, snip, snip, make them pretty. Bright and cheerful for happy thoughts.

Why was the white car dropping Harriet off? Why wasn't she with Kirsten?

Snip, snip, keep going. Miriam reminds herself she's not a social services detective. She just provides safe harbour for refugees.

Her phone buzzes with a message. *Can you give us a hand downstairs?* Mrs McGee, the deputy head. Fine. Sorry, boats. Maybe the kids will hoist your sails instead.

She heads downstairs.

What's happening?

There's a swarm of children gathered around one child. Miriam hears sounds of crying.

'What's going on?' she mouths to Mrs McGee.

But then the circle clears, and she sees who's at the centre. Harriet. And another little girl. Izzie.

Izzie is clutching her hand and leaning against Mrs McGee in tears. Harriet is trying to move out of the circle, but the other kids aren't letting her.

'What's going on?' Miriam asks again, this time loudly.

'She broke Izzie's finger!' one of the girls around Izzie shouts out. There's an accusing point towards the *she*. It's Harriet.

Miriam moves to the girls and bends to their level.

'Harriet, what's going on?' she asks.

'I've got this,' says Mrs McGee. 'Can you just focus on registering the other children? The TA will be back in a minute. She went to get a bandage.'

'Harriet, did you hurt this little girl?' Miriam asks.

'Seriously, Ms Robertson, I have this – go and see to the other children.'

Miriam doesn't have much of a choice, so she does what she's told. As she walks away, she hears Mrs McGee saying to Harriet: 'You're a very naughty little girl, and we'll have to tell your mummy and daddy about this.'

Miriam's eyes fill with tears. Look at the wider issue! It's so rarely the kid in the centre of it that's the problem. Who was around her? Who was egging her on? Was it a dare, a bet?

Come on – you know you want to! One little sip, you'll be fine. Everyone else is.

Miriam shakes her head. This isn't about her. It's about Harriet. The same day she arrives in a different car, she's apparently violently molesting her peers. Has Mrs McGee not read any of the case studies on how to spot unhappy children? Worse: at-risk children. Or problem parents?

A little clammy hand forces itself into Miriam's. Miriam looks down into the heavily bespectacled face of one of the kids in her class. Little Winnie the Pooh plaster on the glasses frames. Sweet, vulnerable, but not who she wants to be looking after.

'What can I do for you, Wendy?' she asks. Reluctantly, Miriam gives her the appearance of her full attention. She's still trying to listen out for the Izzie–Harriet scene but it's hard with all the noise going on.

'I'm a little teapot!' Wendy announces.

'Are you? That's nice,' Miriam tells her, craning her head to see over to Mrs McGee and her Victorian ideas of Naughtiness.

'No!' says the child so sternly that Miriam has to look at her. '*Sing* I'm a little teapot!'

Then all the others begin clamouring for it too.

So there we are. By popular request, Miriam is soon tipping up and pouring out (here's my handle, here's my spout). All the others are joining in too. She feels like Mary Poppins, and she sees Mrs McGee shoot her a look of gratitude.

Miriam catches sight of Harriet fiddling with her fingers and staring at the floor. Everyone's been so interested in Izzie's tears – have they been interested in hers?

But the bell goes for morning lessons, so that's not allowed to be Miriam's concern. The children in her class are suitably responsive to the boat theme. They are incredulous when she suggests how many people might fit in the boats. One gives a little whimper when she says that yes, mummies and children, or sometimes just children, will be in them. So Miriam backtracks. Makes it just about the boats again – bobbing over the waves, whee! Isn't it fun!

Some of the boats get eyes drawn on. Some get mascots. It's all very civilised. Poor invisible Maya. Her boat probably had neither eyes nor mascots. Just the unrelenting beat of the sea.

While they are in mid glue and stick mode, the door opens, and Izzie walks in. Her hand is flamboyantly taped up, and she is holding it aloft.

Boats forgotten, everyone crowds round Izzie.

'Are you OK? Does it hurt? Can we see?'

Miriam does her teacher bit, tells them to sit down and do their work. It has limited effect, so she goes over and joins in.

'What exactly happened, Izzie?' she asks her.

'I was doing beads with Karen, and Harriet came over and said could she play, but it was a private game, so I said no, and she still wanted to play, so I said no again, and then she tried to grab one of the beads from me really hard and hurt my finger deliberately on purpose. It's very serious.'

'Would it not have been nice to let Harriet play with you? I'm sure there must have been enough beads to go round?' Miriam asks Izzie.

Izzie stares at Miriam as if Miriam has missed the point. Miriam sees her lower lip pucker. Oh dear. She's about to start reliving her moments of glory with Mrs McGee all over again.

'Don't worry,' Miriam tells her. 'Those bandages will do a great job, I'm sure. You'll be playing beads again in no time!'

'Not with Harriet,' she says.

'Let's see – I'm sure you can be friends again,' Miriam says.

'We were never friends in the first place.'

Why did you let those girls talk you into it? They aren't even your real friends!

A memory of her mother flies in, unwelcome. This is not the moment.

Get into the moment. Boats.

Soon enough, the classroom gets its buzz back. Miriam mutters her excuses to the TA and slips out of the classroom.

She needs to know what has become of the other little girl in her care.

* * *

Miriam finds Harriet siting in the corridor outside the head's office. Another Victorian approach. Harriet's just waiting there, staring at her hands. Maybe that's the point. Maybe she's meant to be reflecting on what she's done.

'Hey, Harriet,' Miriam says gently. She wants Harriet to see her as a confidante, a friend. They can build things up from there.

Harriet looks up, but doesn't say anything.

'You doing OK?' Miriam asks her.

She shrugs.

Miriam sits down next to her. 'I know you didn't mean to hurt Izzie,' she tells her.

'Yes, I did,' Harriet says.

Right. OK.

'Why's that, then?' Miriam asks.

'Daddy said if someone doesn't give you what they want, you have to twist their arm until you get it. But it was her fingers that had the beads in, so I twisted them.'

'Why did you want the beads so badly?' Miriam asks. She doesn't want to get into the Daddy issues today. That sounds like a separate conversation.

Harriet shrugs again. 'They were pretty. I thought there were enough for all of us. And I couldn't bring my own toys today.'

'Why's that?' Miriam asks.

'Mummy and Daddy were not able to bring me to school today because sometimes they have to work very hard. Auntie Yvette drove me very safely in her car.'

Miriam wrinkles up her nose, trying to pick between the obviously parent-schooled phrases.

'Are Aunty Yvette and Mummy and Daddy kind to you?' Miriam questions.

'They don't let me have beads either,' she tells her.

Miriam nods. 'Sometimes grown-ups are mean,' she agrees. Harriet gives her a shadow of a grin. Good. They're getting somewhere.

Miriam stands up. 'Give me a moment,' she tells her. Miriam's about to knock on the head's door, but she stops. She bends down to Harriet again.

'Harriet, do Mummy or Daddy, or Auntie Yvette, ever do anything that makes you unhappy?' she asks.

Harriet shrugs, avoiding Miriam's gaze.

'Harriet?' Miriam asks again.

Very slowly, she looks up at Miriam.

'Yes,' she says.

It's all Miriam needs.

Chapter 11

Sometimes all it takes is for someone to ask you a question.

A question it should be easy to answer.

A question like: 'How do you think things are going?'

It all comes out.

Or it doesn't. That's the test.

Kirsten realises she's failing it when she hears herself saying to Harriet's headmistress '… and then her father just won't come home on time – or do *anything* around the house. And I want to keep the family together, for Harriet, because I didn't have that, but sometimes it's just so hard, you know?'

Harriet's headmistress looks at her sympathetically (at least, Kirsten hopes it is sympathy).

Kirsten clears her throat. 'What I mean is, we're all a bit busy, aren't we?'

The headmistress nods. 'But we have to prioritise our children, don't we?'

Yes, yes of course they do. Even though Kirsten will have lost, what, about a grand because of today's antics? That's just direct costs. And then more in reputational costs – people let down at the last minute, who will spread toxicity about the practice. No more custom, no chance of getting a partner. Maybe all because Ian was trying to make a concession to her, getting Yvette to drive Harriet in, unsettling Harriet.

But sure, whatever the antics, you always have to put your children first. No one seems to understand that if you put them second for a bit, it's because you're trying to earn enough to put their food on the table and shoes on their feet, and keep a roof attached to a gargantuan mortgage over their heads. No one apart from Kirsten.

'You mustn't let Harriet pick up on whatever ... difficulties there are at home,' the headmistress says.

'Ian and I love Harriet very much,' Kirsten says. 'We don't let anything get in the way of that.'

Listening to herself, even she is unconvinced. She hugs her thoughts of Harriet to her, holds them tight, kisses them. She feels tears forming, tries to blink them back. It's not just about Harriet; it's the thought of having had to run out of the surgery, again. Putting Harriet first always seems to create a conflict.

Perhaps she can send her back to class, rather than take her home? Maybe she doesn't need to cancel all the afternoon's appointments, can still rescue the afternoon? She flicks a glance at the clock.

'What lessons does she have this afternoon? Ones she'll be happy in?' she asks.

The head answers, 'I'm sure Ms Robertson has got some lovely plans for them.'

Yes, Ms Robertson. She seems nice.

'Great, well, perhaps I don't need to take her home, perhaps she can still go to those?' Kirsten says, trying to sound bright.

The headmistress frowns. 'I'm not sure, in the circumstances ...'

'It's a little playground tiff; let's not over-egg it.'

Kirsten regrets her words immediately. She can see the woman drawing herself up.

'Listen,' Kirsten says, before the head can speak. 'How about Harriet goes to Ms Robertson's lessons this afternoon, and then we see what measures we can put in place?'

While the head's busy ushering Harriet to her classes, Kirsten can call Jess, tell her they might still have a chance for the 1 p.m. appointments.

The headmistress sighs her assent. Kirsten follows her outside the room, where Harriet is waiting, and she tries for a kiss on her daughter's forehead. At first, Harriet doesn't respond, but then she flings her arms round Kirsten, and buries her head into her legs for a long hug. It breaks Kirsten's heart to tear her away. Maybe she could just take her to the surgery with her now?

But no. That's no way to run a business. Or to parent. Is it?

'I'll see you later, sweetie,' Kirsten tells her. The headmistress prises Harriet's hand away. As they go off together, Kirsten notices Harriet's socks don't match. They're both white, but one has a frill, one doesn't.

Kirsten waits in the headmistress's office. She doesn't call Jess immediately. Instead, she gives in to the tears. What is she doing? How has she misconfigured things so much that her little daughter, at what is meant to be such a beautiful age, is turning to violence? If Kirsten can't even manage to dress her properly in the morning, is it any wonder? Is Kirsten even present when she's with her? Does she need to phone Clare, get some sessions, some pills? No. No, don't phone Clare more than needed. Not these days. Keep the distance, keep her sweet. Kirsten will have to prescribe herself something, maybe. But what? Mothering instinct? Magical hugs?

Maybe it's just a phase. Maybe when Harriet's older, and Ian and Kirsten are hopefully still together, and have cash for everything Harriet wants, maybe Kirsten will still look back and cherish this stage. Because as people keep telling her, your kids are only this young once.

Kirsten blows out her cheeks, still regrouping.

And then, of course, Jess phones *her*.

'Oh, I didn't expect you to answer,' Jess says. 'I was going to leave a message. Everything OK?'

'Yep, fine,' Kirsten says, wiping away her tears with the back of her hand.

'Right,' Jess says. Jess is remembering, Kirsten is sure, how she ran out of the office in a flap, past the patients in the waiting room, shouting that she had to go to her daughter's school for an emergency. 'Anyway, that's good, because people are complaining up a storm here.' Jess lowers her voice. 'One patient is refusing to leave. Says she was guaranteed an appointment. They go on holiday tomorrow, and if she doesn't have her coil fitted today she says she'll sue us for the inconvenience.'

'Christ's sake, can't she just use a condom?' Kirsten mutters.

'Sorry, didn't quite catch that – what did you want me to tell her?' Jess asks.

'Nothing, nothing. I'll be back as soon as I can.'

'Good, because I've just seen a comment up on the website – someone complaining you're unreliable. I mean, we're unreliable – the practice.'

But of course she means me, Kirsten thinks. I'm unreliable.

The tears threaten to return.

'Don't worry, I'm coming back.'

Kirsten gathers up her things. She'll leave a little note for the headmistress, say she'll make an appointment – work emergency, very sorry.

The headmistress walks in just as Kirsten is rummaging round the desk for a Post-it.

'Mrs McGee, I'm going to have to run – everything's kicking off at work, and …'

She's met with a stony stare.

You don't get it! Kirsten wants to scream. I'm just trying to be good!

But instead, Kirsten half sits, half stands, at the chair by Mrs McGee's desk.

'Ms Robertson had some suggestions to make,' the head says. The tone is chilly, different somehow to when they last spoke. 'And I think they might help you out. How does a breakfast club sound to you? And some casual extra after-school lessons – to help Harriet with these behavioural issues?'

'Yes, yes, of course,' Kirsten says. She wants to shout that Harriet doesn't have behavioural issues. But the clock won't stop ticking.

'Ms Robertson also had one slightly more … controversial … suggestion. A child psychologist? She thinks psychologists can have a really powerful effect – work wonders.'

Christ, the irony … Kirsten knows full well what wonders they can work. It's why her sister still won't speak to her.

But no. This is going too far.

'Tell Ms Robertson I appreciate her concern, but I don't think we're at that stage yet. My daughter just wanted to play with another girl's toy. And she's only just five. She doesn't need a shrink.'

'Research suggests—'

But Kirsten cuts her off. 'No, Mrs McGee. I'm sorry. I have to get back to work.'

You can see the disappointment lines on Mrs McGee's face – little pinches round the corners of her mouth, a special line amongst the crow's feet round her eyes.

Kirsten draws herself up and remembers suddenly the power of being a working mum. She knows how to pull rank.

'I have emergency patients waiting for me. If there are any additional fees for these clubs, over and above what we already pay you, then of course we can pay. Now I really must go.'

And of course, at the mention of emergency patients, of fees, Kirsten sees Mrs McGee remember Kirsten's place in society outside these walls. That this matters too.

'Yes, of course,' the head says. 'I'll see you at parents' evening in a couple of weeks and we can catch up then.'

Maybe Kirsten actually flinches. She must do something,

because the head follows up by saying, 'There'll be an email reminder coming out soon.'

But Kirsten doesn't acknowledge she's forgotten about parents' evening. She just goes. And then, finally, she's on the way to the clinic. Stress levels rocketing. In the olden days, she'd have called Ian, calmed down that way. Now she relieves her stress by channelling it into anger towards him, practising the argument she knows they'll have later on. Not just about this.

Because this is all his fault. If it weren't for him, they wouldn't be where they now find themselves. They wouldn't have to rely on Kirsten trying to be in two places at once. Or on Ms Robertson's breakfast clubs. But thank God they will now have those. Because they can only be a change for the better.

Chapter 12

BECKY, 2 AUGUST 2012

Becky can't find Andy at breakfast. She can't find Caitlin either. So she heads to the audition room, thinking maybe Andy will be there too.

But no. It's just the course leader.

'Hey, you made it!' he says.

She shrugs, clutching the brand new *Music Theatre Compilation* book her mother bought her. It's medium voice because that seemed to Becky to translate into 'average'. Sopranos were special. Before she grew up and became a boring mum, her eldest sister had been soprano in the choir at school. Voice of an angel. So pretty. Et cetera.

'Where's the male talent – Andy, isn't it?'

'I don't know. I figured he might be here.'

'OK, well, let's give him a minute. Are you warmed up yet?'

She shakes her head.

The teacher gives her a look of mock disapproval. 'You must always warm up. Protect those vocal folds.'

He takes her through some exercises. They have to bend down low, swing their arms around as their heads nearly touch the

61

floor. Becky becomes conscious her bra is on show – not a cleavage enhancer, just one that makes her breasts look flat and squat. She tries to pull her top back into place, unsuccessfully. The teacher seems not to notice. He is just saying, in calm, steady tones: 'Now, wind yourself back up, vertebrae by vertebrae.'

She does as she is told.

'Relax your neck. Set it squarely on your shoulders, then rock it gently from side to side.'

She does as he says.

'Now stretch right up. Come on, hands up, stretch out your fingers!'

Again, Becky does what he says. This time, it's her belly that's exposed, her top riding up. Please let there be no flab hanging over my waistline, she thinks, as she stretches extra hard to make her tummy as taut as it will ever be. The teacher seems to be having the same problem – even his big baggy top isn't long enough for this exercise. It rides up, revealing the dark grey waistband of some Calvins under his black jeans. She catches a glimpse of tummy flesh too, covered in black hairs. They look soft, masculine. She realises she is staring and looks away.

That's when she sees Andy and Caitlin in the doorway. Andy is looking between them both, while Caitlin whispers, giggling, in his ear.

Becky drops her arms down, and pulls her top back over her midriff, crossing her arms over her waist. She sees the teacher follow her gaze, and he changes his posture too. Except he is relaxed, welcoming.

'Ah, Andy – you made it!'

'Yup,' Andy says, noncommittal. Where's the enthusiasm of the previous day?

'We were just warming up,' Becky says, feeling an explanation is needed.

'Are you warmed up?' the teacher asks Andy.

'Yeah, I'm good – thanks.'

'I could do with a warm-up,' Caitlin coos. 'I just feel really ... tight, you know?'

Becky stares at Caitlin. Is she flirting with the teacher?

There's a beat.

'Let's do some arpeggios and jazz hands, then!' says the teacher, brightly. 'Loosen everyone up. Ready?'

So off they go. No one comments on the fact that Andy and Becky's audition seems to have become Andy and Caitlin's personal training session. Becky stands at the back, watching Caitlin show off her hair, her legs, her voice. Andy sings pretty well, but he's not a drama queen – just quietly capable. It's one of the things she likes about him. Liked. She doesn't understand where she stands this morning.

The teacher gets them to sing back some song lines to him, as a group, then individually. Becky tries, but her voice is reedy and weak. She peters out on the high notes, and the low ones suddenly come out too strong.

But it doesn't mean Caitlin needs to giggle.

The teacher seems to think so too. He shoots Caitlin a dirty look.

'Everyone's just trying their best here – it's not competitive,' he says.

Caitlin smirks. 'Even though some people are better than others.' She sticks out her chest. Caitlin, Becky notices, *is* wearing a cleavage-enhancing bra. But the teacher doesn't look in that direction at all. His gaze remains firmly at eye level.

'Some people may be naturally gifted, but this summer school is for everyone. I'll let you know later what parts you've got, if any.'

Becky doesn't know why, but she suspects she might end up with a bigger part than Caitlin. She hopes she doesn't.

Andy makes to leave, and Becky quickens her pace to follow him.

'Hey,' she says.

But before he can reply, the teacher calls her back.

'Becky, can I have a moment?'

Reluctantly, Becky holds back. She sees Caitlin and Andy exchange a meaningful glance. Becky doesn't know the meaning, but Andy looks sad.

Becky stands in front of the teacher, arms folded round her music.

'Becky, are you OK with being on this course?' the teacher asks her. 'I don't want anyone to feel like they're being tortured.'

Becky shrugs.

'Come on, I mean it. I'll give you a part in the show because, well, everyone's paid up and it's meant to be fun. But I don't want it to stress you out.'

Becky debates whether to have the long conversation or the short one. She wants to follow Andy, find out where the connection went overnight. She'll go for the short one.

'I'm fine, honestly,' she says. 'See you later.'

'OK, if you're sure. Take care of yourself, OK?'

The teacher gives her the briefest of touches on the shoulder. She's surprised it makes her spine tingle. Suddenly, she wishes she'd gone for the longer conversation. But it's too late. Already, she's headed towards the door, Andy in her sights.

Chapter 13

KIRSTEN, SEPTEMBER 2018

Perhaps Ian thinks she's not watching him, as he gets out of the car. Look at him, he goes so slowly, like he can't bear getting a moment closer to helping his family. She puffs her cheeks out. Maybe that's unfair. The inspection is exhausting and stressful; she gets that. But Kirsten left him a voice message earlier, so he knows the deal. He didn't reply. Didn't even text to say he was coming home.

He's reaching the kerb when Yvette appears. Kirsten watches him hesitate, probably wonder how he can get away, but he's not quick enough. Yvette trots down the steps of her house. Is she interfering again? Sure, Kirsten's super grateful for the occasional help with school drop-offs but that doesn't buy Yvette the right to invade their family time.

'Mummy, can we read this one?'

Kirsten looks over her shoulder to see Harriet holding up a picture book, one of Kirsten's favourites.

'In a minute, sweetheart.'

She looks out of the window again, to Ian and Yvette. They look very serious. Yvette is leaning in close to Ian. Ian isn't leaning away. Kirsten would have loved to dissect the whole situation with Clare, like they used to, if she hadn't had to keep her distance.

'Please, Mummy, I want to read it now.'

Reluctantly, Kirsten tears her eyes away from the scene outside. Then she chides herself for her reluctance. No wonder her child has 'behavioural' issues, if Mummy would rather stare out the window at her interfering neighbour than read a book.

'Of course, sweetie,' Kirsten says, immediately over-bright. 'We'll read it on the sofa, shall we?'

She sits down on the sofa and gives Harriet one hundred per cent of her attention. Well, ninety-seven per cent anyway – the other three per cent of her brain is wondering when Ian will finally come through the door.

There's the usual fumbling as the key turns in the lock.

'Hi honey, I'm home,' Ian shouts.

Kirsten considers not replying, just continuing to focus (now eighty per cent) on the picture book. But Harriet's attention has shifted too.

'We're in here,' calls Kirsten.

Ian comes in, gives Kirsten a quick peck on the lips, kneels down in front of Harriet.

'Your mummy tells me you had a tricky day,' he says to Harriet.

'You got my voice message, then,' Kirsten says, the criticism for a lack of response only just beneath the surface.

Meanwhile, Harriet shrugs.

'You were a little bit naughty, though, I hear?' Ian perseveres.

'Maybe Yvette can solve it. How *is* the domestic goddess today?' Kirsten can't resist.

'Now now, Kirsten,' Ian says, flicking his eyes meaningfully to Harriet. 'Yvette's been kind to us.'

Whether it's her parents' tone, or Ian's question, Harriet's eyes go wide. Her lower lip quivers. Then she says, 'It's past my bedtime,' and picks herself up, trooping towards the staircase.

Kirsten looks at the clock over the mantelpiece: 7.15. Fair enough, it is late for her. Ian should have got home earlier.

'I'll come and tuck you in,' Ian calls after their daughter. But it sounds like a threat. Ian stands, as if to follow Harriet, presumably to go straight into his version of night-time routine, whatever that is.

'You need a bath first, Harriet darling!' Kirsten calls.

'I don't want a bath!' Harriet storms, from halfway up the stairs.

Kirsten rolls her eyes at Ian. A shared moment. Whatever is going on outside the house, for one instant they have a common cause – tame the child. She puts her head gently on his shoulder.

'Seriously, how can she not want a bath right now? Can you imagine how nice that would be? Bubbles, a long hot soak.' She groans.

'Yup, I'm with you,' Ian responds.

Upstairs, there's the sound of a slamming door.

'Oh, for goodness' sake!' Ian says.

'It's not her fault. She's overtired,' Kirsten sighs, choosing the same side to support as always. She takes her head off Ian's shoulder.

'*I'm* overtired,' he says.

'Sure you are,' says Kirsten, in a way that means she wants to say so much more. Then, she's off, running up the stairs after their daughter. 'Harriet, how about I run you a nice hot bubble bath, OK? Then I can jump in it after you?'

She hears Ian trailing up behind her.

No response from Harriet. When they get upstairs, Harriet is curled up on her bed, fully clothed. The curtains are open, and there's a grey, unlit gloom in the room. Her eyes are obstinately closed.

We aren't doing our bit, thinks Kirsten.

She sits on the edge of the bed. Ian moves to the window,

hands out to shut the curtains. They see Yvette on the street. She looks up, waves. Ian waves back. Kirsten bats his hand down.

'Don't encourage her!' she says. 'She's always watching us. It's weird.'

'Shh,' he says. 'You'll wake Harriet.'

Downstairs, they continue the conversation.

'Don't get het up about Yvette. Just accept her help – she can take Harriet to school, look after her occasionally. A safe pair of hands, just what we need.'

Kirsten exhales. 'Sure, you're right. It's just, I'm not sure she'll draw the line there, you know? Soon we'll find her weeding our flowerbeds or washing our cars.'

'She can be my guest!' Ian says, with such vigour that Kirsten laughs. 'Come on, have a glass of wine with me,' he says.

She should really work on her accounts, check Harriet's schoolbag for hidden homework or consent forms, and plan everyone's meals for tomorrow. And Ian should work on his Ofsted stuff. But just once, they deserve a bit of down time, don't they? Harriet is safe; it's twelve hours until the start of another working day. They can relax and be lazy – for once.

Chapter 14

MIRIAM, SEPTEMBER 2018

Miriam would be the last person to willingly label anyone. Labels hurt. They're destructive, demeaning, designed to force people to comply with one perfect ideal. Does anyone truly fit them? No. Neither does she. But some people feel they are qualified to administer them. Whatever the human price. The recovery from that label, stamped over your life, can take longer than any underlying issue.

The toast she's buttering for breakfast club is reduced to crumbs in her hands. Damn. She'll have to throw that piece away too.

Sometimes, though, there is a *compulsion* to label people. For their own benefit.

And here is how she would label Harriet:

1. An unhappy child.
2. Ought to be looked after by someone who truly loves her.

Here is how she would label Kirsten:

1. The worst type of mother.
2. Not someone who truly loves Harriet.

Miriam doesn't use those terms lightly. By *unhappy child* she doesn't mean that Harriet is on a downer because there aren't as many muddy puddle-jumping opportunities as *Peppa Pig* would have you believe. She means in the textbook sense. The unhappy child they teach you to look out for in teacher training college. Those telltale signs. Withdrawn. Violent behaviour. Turning up at school unkempt. Odd socks – one of those cases of children murdered by their fathers had the little girl turning up at school in odd socks and with bruises. A warning sign that went unheeded.

There they are, then. Classic signs of neglect. Or something worse.

And so to Kirsten. The worst sort of mother? Yes. Really. Unremittingly selfish. Putting her needs far beyond the needs of Harriet. Because what does a child need more than her mother? Why would anyone withhold that vital, vital bond? OK, OK, Miriam knows there are worse. She's read the cases. The sex offenders. The murderers. The unwarranted home-schoolers. And she gets that some families have to separate – the parents of little Maya, perhaps, left behind in Syria. But putting aside those non-normal limits – what is the worst thing you can do to your daughter? Teach her she doesn't matter. That her human relationships matter less than work. Making her a non-person. It's like making her dead, a zombie child.

But labels alone do nothing. Particularly ones Miriam creates in her head. She'd be the worst sort of teacher if she didn't do something with them. She doesn't just mean communicate them. Sure, she's told the headmistress her concerns. Written them in a report, ready for escalation if need be. That official approach only takes things so far, though. Doesn't do much for the child, if they end up in care.

What they need is someone else to look after them. Someone else to care for them.

Miriam takes out the heart-shaped cutter and presses it into the pile of toast. Perfect little hearts are broken out of the toast. Miriam bites into one; they are too tempting to wait until her charges arrive. She regrets it instantly, though – she's being just as bad as Kirsten, putting herself first.

Everything should be pristine, fresh, waiting for the first little child whose parents ascribe skewed values to money vs. physical presence. Get a job that enables you to actually see your child! she always wants to scream. Miriam would.

And then, they're off. The first child, for the first breakfast club St. Anthony's has ever held. Little Leo Holmes. Dropped off by a woman too young and delicate to be his real mother. Unless she has reversed the ageing process through focused yoga and cleansing chakras. Or CBT, or whatever mindfulness shit perfectly well people with merely an *interest* in *safeguarding their mental health* are allowed to choose. No compulsion for them. No labels.

Miriam holds out a hand to Leo Holmes.

'Morning, sweetheart. Do you want some breakfast?'

He looks up at her wide-eyed, clutching one of those 'kiddy-safe' tablet computers in his right hand, the other hand exploring his nose. Jesus, he's six. What kind of parenting is this? Miriam's surprised he's even out of nappies.

Leo looks round the empty school cafeteria.

'Am I the only one?' he asks.

'No,' Miriam reassures him. 'More of your friends will be here soon. Make the most of the food before they get here.'

So he tucks in. Miriam chatters to him, trying to warm up for the day, but he has an eye on his tablet the whole time.

More children come in. Some still rubbing their eyes, others bounding around in glee at extra time with their friends. Some dropped off by au pairs, others by not-the-worst mothers.

Then, finally, Harriet. Kirsten couldn't even get her here in time for the start of breakfast club.

Harriet's eyes are not swollen with tiredness. But Kirsten's are.

'Thank you so much,' Kirsten says, practically flinging Harriet at Miriam. 'You don't know how much of a lifesaver you are!'

Miriam does know. It's just that it's not Kirsten's life she cares about saving. It's Harriet's.

Miriam smiles at Kirsten – don't aggravate the wild animals – and takes Harriet's hand. Just like she did little Leo's earlier. But also nothing like. She feels the thrill of belonging with another human being. So Miriam leads Harriet over to the toast and jam, still holding her hand. Then she sits down in front of her, and gives Harriet her full attention while the little girl eats. Harriet needs to know, if she doesn't learn anything else today, that she matters. That Miriam sees her, gives her time, permission to exist, and for her existence to fill Miriam's world.

'What do you usually have for breakfast?' she asks Harriet. It's good to know if you're giving them something they're used to, or if it's a treat.

'Crisps,' Harriet chirps.

Miriam tries not to let her lips set into a thin teacherly line. Instead, she fetches her some Weetabix, a banana, brown toast and peanut butter. Get some nutrition into her, if her parents won't bother.

Once all the children have finished their breakfast, Miriam sits them down in a circle.

'Welcome to breakfast club,' she tells them. 'An exclusive club for all the coolest kids in the school.'

'I thought that was drama club,' one of the Year Six children – a leading little thesp, so Miriam's told – pipes up, giggling. Miriam feels herself blushing.

'Cooler even than that,' she manages to retort. The girl will be awful when she gets to secondary school. Even worse than Miriam's 'friends' were, at answering back, crossing the line of what's appropriate.

'We're going to run it as a sort of extra-friends club. I'd like you all to feel like you can say anything to me or your fellow breakfasters. OK?'

Mostly Miriam is met with blank faces. A couple of shy smiles. Harriet's face is impossible to read.

'I'd like to start today with a little confessional, and a big toast to Roald Dahl. He's the reason I'm teaching today.'

'What, you got the golden ticket?' Same girl. Miriam ignores her.

'Put your hands up if you have read *Matilda*,' Miriam says to the group.

It's about half and half. And of those, Miriam suspects that many are equating 'read' with having watched the musical. Harriet doesn't put up her hand.

'Well, for those of you who haven't read it,' Miriam continues, 'there's a teacher in it called Miss Honey, who does a really good turn to a talented little girl named Matilda. Her parents are truly awful to little Matilda. They don't care about her at all, and she hates them. Nothing like all your lovely parents at all, I'm sure!' Miriam adds, smiling around, looking to Harriet for signs of upset. Nothing obvious. Miriam continues. 'She provides somewhere safe and happy for little Matilda to go after school. Even though Miss Honey is very poor, she is rich in her heart through her love of the children. In the end – well, no, I won't spoil it for you in case you haven't read it.'

'They all live happily ever after,' pipes up one of the children in a sing-song voice. Maybe they shouldn't serve jam next time. Far too much sugar in it – the kids are getting rebellious and cocky.

'Yes, they do. But what I wanted to explain was, that's what opened my eyes to teaching as a vocation, a way of being who I wanted to be, and helping children who needed me. I've known some real-life teachers who've had a profound impact on me, just like Miss Honey. And I always keep a copy of *Matilda* next to my bed, to this day.'

Miriam scans the faces again. A few more responsive now.

73

They are more awake, which is something. And Harriet is gazing at her from those big hazel eyes.

'Now, children, it's time for your lessons. For the next couple of weeks we'll take it in turns for you to "show and tell" books that have inspired you, OK?'

From the older kids there are groans of 'More homework.'

'It's not homework,' Miriam says. 'It's sharing. There's no writing, no presentations – you can just mention a book you like. If it's a secret, you don't even need to say why. But if I haven't read it, I might just do so. OK?'

'Ms Robertson, can I bring in *Fireman Sam*?'

'Of course you can,' she says, only hoping it's not the sticker book version. 'Whatever book you want. Now, off you go. Have a good day, for those of you I don't teach. See some of you later.'

So as not to freak them out, Miriam doesn't stare at them as they leave. She turns her attention to the breakfast things and makes a vague pretence of helping clear some away.

She had to stop herself giving away too much of *Matilda*. For people who haven't read it, understood that joy between Miss Honey and Matilda, the ending might sound a little sinister. A bit like kidnapping. And why would any of them want to live with their teacher, rather than their parents? Even Miriam doesn't want that. Not if they're happy at home – it's always best for children to stay with their parents if they can. Social work 101.

* * *

At lunchtime, Miriam pops out of the staffroom, up the road to the shops.

'Hey!' she hears a voice after her. She turns. It's Ted, another of the teachers. Half-cute, half-nerdy. She's done the polite nodding and smiling at him in the staffroom, but they've not spoken properly. Perhaps he thinks this is his opportunity.

'Hey,' she calls back, not really slowing. She has some important shopping to do.

'Wait up,' he says.

Miriam tells herself not to look weird, so she waits, looking at her watch while she does so.

'You grabbing some lunch?' Ted asks her, catching up.

Miriam knows he wants her to say yes, to suggest that they go together, for it to lead on to a proper date.

''Fraid not,' she tells him. 'I have to run an errand.'

'Ah, woman of mystery.' He smiles. 'My favourite kind.'

She smiles back, despite herself, despite her rush. Aren't there rules against these kinds of workplace flirtations these days?

'Another time we'll have a not-so-mysterious lunch at The Wok Factory,' she says, nodding her head at the cheap-and-cheerful Chinese across the road. 'But now I must run, OK?'

He smiles again. 'OK. Would just be good to get to know the new staffroom face.'

She starts walking up the street, faster than him. 'Of course. Let me know when works for you. See you!'

And then she breaks into a run. Let him think she has a doctor's appointment or something. An emergency. But aren't all plans an emergency, when you want something really badly?

* * *

After the last lesson of the day, Miriam calls Harriet to stay back.

'I bought you something,' Miriam says. She unveils the lunchtime purchase, and hands it to Harriet. *Matilda.* A brand-new copy.

Harriet looks at the book, then at Miriam.

'I couldn't help noticing you hadn't read it,' Miriam tells her. 'When we were doing the show of hands at breakfast club.'

'Thank you, Ms Robertson,' Harriet says. Maybe she's not

75

completely badly brought up.

'I've put a message in the front,' Miriam tells her. It was meant to be a surprise, but she can't resist. Miriam turns her to the opening pages. 'I'm your Miss Honey, whenever you need me,' it says.

Bit of a risk. What if Kirsten and Ian see, and they freak out? Sometimes kindness can be misinterpreted, and she doesn't want to be sacked. But in another way, so what? Make them raise their game – realise they are parents first, individuals second. That's the way it should be, shouldn't it?

Chapter 15

KIRSTEN, OCTOBER 2018

Kirsten lives for the weekends. Everyone does. Right?

Perfect quality time with the family.

Except, somehow, it never seems to live up to the promise. Kirsten wonders if that's just her, or whether everyone feels like that. Tired, conflicted, stressed, like the rare beautiful happy moments are more staged than genuine?

She remembers the old days, when they were first together, her and Ian. The hours they could pass in a pub – quite incredible to think of now. And of course, there were the climbing expeditions, their shared hobby. But then Ian had a fall, didn't trust himself anymore, and the trips to the Peaks were off. The guide ropes and hooks packed away, growing dusty in the attic. Without that pursuit, she guessed they must have filled their time in other ways – slept, went to the gym, had unrushed ungrudging sex? Cooked, maybe? By which she means things other than chicken nuggets and meatballs. Yes, great elaborate meals, ingredients planned days in advance. Or they'd do something spontaneous, maybe, make up for the lost adrenaline of the climbs – a trip down the Thames in a speedboat, or the London Eye at night.

Now, spontaneity is a trip to the faraway playground rather than the close one. Halcyon times, those weekends, before everything else. And yet, she thinks, she still managed to be sad. The sense of being incomplete as a twosome manifested early. Maybe what she's thinking of is her pre-IVF self. The woman whose joy wasn't sapped at every failed attempt. Before she became the woman who wouldn't drink, ever, just in case they were pregnant. No wonder, maybe, that she has slipped so startlingly easily into the studied anxiety of motherhood.

Regardless, these days, weekends are a bit, well, different …

Right now, for instance, Kirsten is sitting on the sofa watching Ian and Yvette through the window. It looks like Yvette is in fact trying to wash their cars, or at least tell Ian he's missed a bit. Ridiculous. She should just go out there and tell her to mind her own business. But she remembers what Ian said. That she means well, and they should accept her help. Fine. She'll just rage inwardly then, rather than outwardly. And if she goes out and creates a scene, she won't be there for Harriet, if she's needed.

Harriet is curled up on her bed upstairs reading *Matilda*, of all things. It's far too old for her. Kirsten thinks she's probably only looking at the pictures. She can't be able to read much of it yet, surely. Kirsten asked if she'd like her to read it to aloud, or to read it page and page, but Harriet says she wants to read it alone. What happened to 'Me and mummy do everything together'? So here Kirsten is, staring out of the window, alone. This is pathetic of her. She should go outside, be civil.

So Kirsten ventures down the steps and approaches them. As she gets close, she catches the snippets of the conversation.

'… *really unfortunate* …' Yvette murmurs.

'… *so grateful* …' Ian mutters.

Yvette puts her hand on Ian's arm, lightly, so you almost wouldn't notice. But of course, Kirsten does.

'Well, this is quite the neighbourly catch-up, isn't it?' Kirsten says. It sounds catty, not breezy. Missed again.

'I was just talking to Ian about—' Yvette starts.

'Her taking Harriet into school the other day,' Ian cuts her off. 'How grateful we were.'

Kirsten nods. 'Of course,' she says. 'Really grateful.'

'Oh, any time. I know how hard it is to be a working parent.'

'Do you?' Kirsten asks, then regrets it. Time was, they swapped IVF stories, long after Yvette had given up hope. 'I mean, I know you do,' Kirsten says. 'We appreciate your empathy.'

Yvette lifts her chin, challenging. Kirsten sees Yvette knows the first comment was the one she really meant.

'Of course,' Yvette says, 'if I was lucky enough to have my own little girl, I'd give up everything for her. Work, yoga, the lot. Just to be with her. It's different for you though, isn't it?'

Kirsten's not rising to the bait. 'Every situation is different,' she tells Yvette. 'Besides, I want Harriet to have a role model.'

'Hmm,' says Yvette, thoughtfully. 'Anyway, I must be getting on. I've a weekend consultation this morning. Only a couple of streets away but such a bore having to work on a Saturday. Good talk, Ian. Thank you.' She puts a hand on his arm again, squeezes it, and looks deeply into his eyes. He does a sort of smirk. 'Kirsten.' And a curt nod is all Kirsten gets from Yvette.

When Yvette's gone, Ian puts away the chamois leathers.

'What was that about?' Kirsten asks him.

'Harriet,' he says.

'Giving her views on our parenting, was she?' she asks.

'Of course, but don't let it get to you. Like I said, Yvette is happy to take her in whenever we need her to.'

'Why are you always so determined to see the good in people?' she asks him.

He shrugs. 'I'm head of a failing school. My job and reputation are on the line. I need something to give me hope.'

'Ah yes, the failing school. The reason why your own child never sees you.'

Ian doesn't reply, just finishes up with the car. He's such a goody-two-shoes, avoiding conflict, when she's spoiling for a pointless fight. Not pointless – there's a lot of angry energy she wants to let out. About him, his fixation with that school, with his good name. But that doesn't mean she should direct the anger at him. They should talk in a civil way, like grown-ups. Or not talk at all.

While Ian finishes up, Kirsten goes back into the house and stands aimlessly in the kitchen. She meant to be good. She meant, for Harriet's sake, not to fight with Ian at weekends (or indeed, at all). If Harriet had a sibling, they could play together, ignore them. Kirsten's not stupid – she knows that's why she's in her bedroom, too tired of walking on eggshells to come down to see her parents. Kirsten decides she'll go up and check Harriet's OK, maybe offer to plait her hair, or do some drawing. Show her she means more than anything in the world to her.

But to Kirsten's surprise, before she can do that, Ian follows her to the kitchen.

He stands in the doorway, car-cleaning kit in hand. Kirsten can't understand why he doesn't just take the cars to a car wash like everyone else. False economies – it won't be the cost of some soapsuds that ruins them.

She tries to make her face look open, inviting.

'Listen, Kirsten,' Ian begins. 'Talking to Yvette just now, it made me think.'

'Go on,' she says, being the model wife.

'We should talk about it. The big one. Harriet.'

All thoughts of being a model wife fall away.

'Seriously?' she dares him.

'Kirsten, come on,' he says. 'Just think about it. It's not right, otherwise. You know that.'

'You do not get to lecture me about what's right!'

He glares at her. 'This isn't about us. It's about her. You can't play that historic card for the rest of our lives.'

'Oh, it's a "card" now, is it? The emotional torment, the uncertainty you put me through, the *generosity* I showed you?' She knows what he means. Of course she does. But it's a damn good card. And she's going to keep on playing it.

'Kirsten, you're milking it. Every marriage has its ups and downs, its indiscretions, we—'

She walks up close to him and puts her face right into his. Her voice low, she says: 'Every marriage, maybe. But every career, Ian? Come on.'

Ian tilts his head back and takes a deep breath. He starts to speak but she cuts him off.

'You knew my price, Ian. It hasn't changed. And it won't change. We keep things as they are. Except you need to pull your finger out. OK?'

'You can't tell anyone without dropping yourself in it too!' Ian protests.

'Want to test that?' she whispers at him. 'Because if so, game on!'

And she pushes past him into the hall.

'Kirsten, wait!'

Oh, he's all cajoling now. Of course he is.

'Kirsten, come on, let's not live like this.' He catches up with her, hand on her arm. Squeezing it like Yvette squeezed his. She shrugs him off. 'Kirsten,' he says. 'I love you. And Harriet. I love my little family. Can we please try to have a nice life, together? Put all this stuff behind us?'

She so wants to agree. She wants to lean her forehead in to his, and for both of them to rest their heads together gently like they used to. But somehow, she can't cross that divide.

'You're the one who brought this up!' she tells him.

He shakes his head. 'I know, I know. I just thought it was my moral duty, you know?'

'Your duty is to me. To us.'

He nods. 'I get that. I'm sorry. Let me make it up to you.'

And there it is. The card works every time, and yet he questions why Kirsten keeps playing it.

81

She gives him an encouraging nod. 'OK,' she says. 'You're on. I'm going to see if I can fish out Harriet from her room for a bit of mother-daughter time. Take her over to the shops, have lunch, or something. Then maybe tomorrow, we head to one of the museums? Do a family trip?'

He nods. 'Sure. Sounds good. Anything else?'

'Maybe I could get a bit of time looking over the surgery accounts, later? If you play with Harriet a bit when we're back this afternoon?'

'Of course,' he says.

So, they have a plan. But, of course, as with all plans, they don't always work out.

Chapter 16

BECKY, 7 AUGUST 2012

The morning of the first full rehearsal, Caitlin flops down on Becky's dormitory bed. Becky carries on sorting out her music. They've barely spoken the last few days, kept apart by sectional rehearsals – Caitlin and Andy in one group, Becky in another. In the evenings, Caitlin is among the group sneaking out to the pub. Becky doesn't feel she can. And she doesn't want to drink, so she doesn't see the point. Cider makes her turn red and stare at people. It's not a great look. Instead, she's stayed in the room, calling her big sister – the one who's still cool – and leaving voice messages. Once, they spoke for a few minutes, but student life is busy, apparently.

'So, here's the thing,' Caitlin announces. 'Andy still really fancies you.'

Becky stops, letting her music case fall to the floor. 'What?' she asks.

'That's why I've been spending so much time with him,' Caitlin says. 'Trying to big you up.'

'OK, so … what do you want me to do about it?' Becky asks. She's worried her face may be turning red, even without the cider.

'Dress up a bit. Show off your figure. You have an amazing figure. So curvy.'

Becky knows curvy means fat. But Caitlin's not giving up. She leaps onto the other side of the bed.

'I mean, look at those hips, girl! And what are you doing? Hiding them away in baggy jeans. Come on, let's see what you've got in that suitcase!'

And before Becky can stop her, Caitlin is rifling through Becky's bag, looking for 'more suitable' clothes.

'Aha!' Caitlin says, holding aloft the black body-con dress that Becky was saving for the after-show party. 'Wear this today!'

'Don't be ridiculous!' Becky says. 'We're rehearsing, not going out.'

Becky tries to snatch the dress back, but Caitlin is too quick.

'Rubbish! You should see what some of the girls in my group are wearing, trying to impress the boys.'

Becky looks over Caitlin's outfit. Skinny black jeans and a tight pink T-shirt. Hardly club wear but Caitlin doesn't need it to shine.

Caitlin looks down at her own outfit. 'Oh, I'm roughing it today. I have a bit part – but your character has a *name* and everything. Come on, dress like a star. I promise you, it will make all the difference with Andy.'

Becky eyes the dress, and the clock on the wall. They have ten minutes before rehearsals start. She reminds Caitlin of that.

'Well, we'll have to be quick, then!' Caitlin says. 'Come on, clothes off!' And she begins stripping Becky off. 'You get dressed. Now, where's your make-up?'

Twelve minutes later, they are running (as fast as Becky can in heels) to the rehearsal hall.

Everyone turns to look at them as they arrive. Everyone, of course, being dressed in casual clothes, flat shoes, and minimal make-up. Becky tugs at her hemline, feeling like she's on an uncomfortable walk of shame. Not that she's been on that walk. But she's heard about girls who have.

'Hi.' Caitlin beams at the room. 'Sorry we're late. Someone took a while getting ready.' And she jerks her head at Becky, putting her fully in the limelight.

Becky feels the whole room look her up and down, the teacher included. But also, she notices, Andy. Maybe Caitlin was right.

After the warm-up, before they get started, she finds Andy on one side of her, Caitlin on the other.

'I never see you in the pub,' Andy says. 'You should come with us later.'

'I don't drink,' Becky says.

Andy shrugs. 'So get a Diet Coke. That's cool.'

Becky shrugs back. 'OK, maybe I will then.'

'Great. See you then.'

And all of a sudden, Becky feels like she can do this. She can be the star of the show (well, a named chorus member anyway). She can sneak out in the evenings. And she can get the boy.

* * *

When they set off for the clandestine pub visit that evening, she's not the only one in a dress. The other girls look dangerous, exotic, dresses freshly squeezed into, make-up newly applied. Becky tries to smooth out the creases from her own dress, to brush off the white dust that somehow always seems to accumulate on the stage. She feels stale, trammelled.

'Maybe I should change?' she whispers to Caitlin, who is looking gorgeous in a red skater dress with a cut-out back.

'Don't you dare!' Caitlin whispers back. 'Come on, the boys will be there by now.'

They are hurrying out of the main door when a male voice calls them back.

'You girls aren't off to the pub, I hope?'

It's the drama teacher. Busted.

'Of course not, Sir.' Caitlin turns and gives him a look of wide-eyed innocence. 'We're just going for a walk.'

'Sure you are. Well, make sure your walk back is as sober as your one there. I'm meant to be looking after you all.'

'Of course, Sir, will do.' Caitlin does a great meek look. She should really be the star of the show.

'All right, off you go. Oh, and Becky?'

She turns back.

'Great work today.'

Becky smiles inside. She'd expected to hate every minute of rehearsals that day but, for once, she'd owned it. Thanks to Caitlin. Thanks to the dress. Thanks to the promise of the evening.

'Thank you, Sir,' she says. 'I enjoyed it.'

'Me too. Now off you go for your "walk".'

He holds the door open for them, and they scuttle off into the night.

* * *

The pub is overwhelmingly full. Becky was expecting maybe to have a table, and to sit chatting to Andy. But she can't even see him above all the heads, or call his name over the clamour at the bar. Her shoes are starting to pinch, and she wonders how long she has to stay before it's acceptable to leave. She turns to Caitlin, but Caitlin is no longer there – she has mysteriously vanished into the crowd.

She feels a tapping at her elbow. It's Gina, carrying a tray of shots. 'Here, help me out, won't you? I can't carry them all.'

'Oh, OK, sure.' Becky's not sure to be offended that the only time Gina has bothered to speak to her is when she needs help, or to feel pleased that maybe now, here in this pub, they are equals. She makes to take the tray from Gina.

'Hey, no, I don't mean that!' Gina squawks. 'Just take a couple and get them down you!'

86

'Oh, no, I'm fine, honestly – I don't really drink.'

'For God's sake. It's a pub. You need to drink, or they'll think you're underage and chuck us all out. Go on, do the shots.'

Becky looks around. Everyone, it seemed, was drinking. Another couple of girls from the cool crowd come over to them and grab shots, knocking them down their throats. They make it look so easy. Fine, then. If they can do it, so can she.

Becky grabs a couple of shots from the tray, and tips them down her throat. The burn is so fiery, maybe it really is the devil's liquor like her parents say. She wants to retch the drinks up. But she knows that's not allowed. So she just swallows them down and manages a fake smile afterwards.

'Great! Thanks,' she says.

'There we go! Right, come on, where are the boys?'

And off Gina goes, forcing her way through the crowd. Becky follows in her wake, watching as the occasional male hands are laid, in jest or lust, on Gina's backside. Becky gets herself ready to smack the hands away if she feels them. But she doesn't.

Finally, they reach the boys. And Andy. He gives her a smile, which is worth the pinching shoes and the revolting drink.

'Hey!' he says. Or at least, that's what she thinks he says. The music is louder over here. He leans in to her ear and says something else. She nods and smiles, not knowing what he said. Suddenly, he is ushering her out of the pub. She doesn't mind. It was too hot and too noisy. And there are some beer tables out here – perhaps they can sit down.

Andy takes out a cigarette and waves one at her. 'Here we go, as promised,' he says.

Oh, so that's what he must have asked her. Fine. She doesn't actually smoke, but what's one cigarette? She lets him push it into her mouth, and inhales as he lights it.

'So tell me, Becky,' he asks her, as they are both sitting astride the picnic bench, 'what does it take to let me kiss a star like you?'

Here it is, then. The moment. Now she has to find something decent to say.

'I think,' she manages, 'it would take your lips on mine.'

'Well, I agree that would be a good start.'

Andy stubs out his cigarette. She does the same. He moves towards her – not slowly, like in the movies – and suddenly there they are, his lips. And then there is his tongue. Finally, finally, she is kissing a boy. Really kissing one. And the boy is Andy.

It doesn't take long for them to be discovered. Soon, a whole gang of the others are out there, some wolf-whistling, some taking photos, some handing her shots – which she takes, because why not, she is young and happy. And her parents' beliefs are theirs, not hers. Andy is there, holding her hand, warming her lips.

At closing time, the group of them carouse back to the drama school building. Andy gives her a final kiss before she sways off towards her dorm. She tries to walk in a straight line, to sashay sexily up the stairs, but she is aware of linearity eluding her. Instead, she ricochets off the banister. When she gets to the top and turns the corner, she is sick on the carpet. She kneels, momentarily disgusted with herself, trying to dab it away with her coat. Then she hears footsteps behind her.

'Andy?'

But it isn't, it's the drama teacher.

Shit.

She gets to her feet and flees.

'Who's that?' she hears behind her. 'Becky, is that you?'

And then, when the teacher comes level with her vomit, she hears him groan. 'Oh for God's sake!'

She makes it to the dormitory, expecting giggly late-night chat, to be able to share her drunken escapade, and relive Andy's kisses. But the lights are off. All she can see are Caitlin's eyes, staring out at her in the dark.

Chapter 17

KIRSTEN, OCTOBER 2018

At 9 a.m. on Sunday the house phone rings. They're watching cartoons or messing around with various screens while Ian cools down after his usual Sunday morning run. He trundles out to answer the phone, still wiping the sweat from his face.

From his expression when he comes back, she knows the false peace of their weekend is shattered.

'It's Clare,' he says. Kirsten feels her heart leap with pleasure momentarily, as though the call means they can still be friends. But the soaring is transitory, as Ian continues. 'She's received a letter. I'm really worried. She sounded—'

Kirsten cuts him off.

'Whoa, whoa! Slow it down. A letter from who?'

But she can guess the answer.

'From *her*,' Ian says. 'To her home, not the psychiatric practice.'

Ian turns to Harriet.

'Sweetie, we've just got to go and sort something out, OK? I'll be right back.'

Kirsten allows Ian to put his hand on her back and steer her into the dining room.

'What's in the letter?' she asks.

'Oh, mad stuff, it sounded like – you're guilty, I know you misdiagnosed me on purpose; please confirm the correct diagnosis. She's scanning it through to you.'

Kirsten has her mail app open on her mobile, and is continually refreshing for new items. Ding! One appears.

'Here it is,' She opens it, and they crowd round the small screen.

Dear Dr Sergeant,
    You might remember me. I certainly remember you.
    You gave me a misdiagnosis. Said I couldn't be trusted.
    You must have known that wasn't true. You have ruined my life and more.
    I need you to revisit that diagnosis. I need you to give me a clean bill of health.
    Otherwise, think of the headlines. The Daily Mail *would love it. You know what I'm talking about.*
    You can reach me at the above address.
    Yours very very sincerely

And then the name. The name Kirsten dreads so much.

'It says she lives in Croydon,' Ian comments.

'That's too close!' Kirsten barks.

'We agreed that as long as—' Ian starts, but Kirsten cuts him off.

'I don't care what we agreed,' she says. 'It's too close.'

Ian puffs out his cheeks. 'So what do you want to do?'

But before they get to decide what to do, the phone rings again. Kirsten puts it on speaker.

It's Clare.

'Well?' she says.

'We've read it,' says Kirsten.

'And what are you going to do about it?' Clare asks. Her tone is chilly, abrupt. You wouldn't think that from medical school onwards they'd regularly dissected the world over wine, shots, and anything else the bar provided.

'We were just asking ourselves that when you phoned,' Ian tells her. 'Bit of a tricky one.'

Kirsten shoots him a look. His tone is too jovial, too unconsidered.

'What would you like us to do, Clare?' asks Kirsten, tone all placatory and schmaltzy.

'I'd like you to keep me out of it,' she says.

'Looks like she may have other ideas,' Ian says.

'Well, you'd better persuade her out of them,' Clare retorts. 'Seriously. I am not being pulled into this – I can't have my name dragged through the papers. I'm *this close* to getting a Professorship at the Royal College. I do not need this right now.'

'Of course, we'll do what we can, Clare, but—' Kirsten says.

'Just fix it, OK? We agreed you'd start talking to her around this point anyway. Work something out, something that makes sense for everyone. You owe me that. I don't expect to hear from her again, all right?'

And she hangs up.

Kirsten sees Ian look at him.

'We have to talk to her,' he says.

'We can't! I can't possibly – don't you understand? I just can't do it!'

And Kirsten begins sobbing. He puts his arms round her and she sobs even harder onto his shoulders.

'Maybe if we just talk to her, come to some arrangement …' he says.

'More money?' asks Kirsten. 'Yes, I suppose we could do that, but …'

'I didn't mean money,' he says.

Kirsten takes her head off his shoulder.

'No, Ian,' Kirsten says. 'That's not happening.'

'I just think …' he says.

'Whose side are you on?' she demands.

Ian smooths down her hair. 'Yours,' he says. 'And Harriet's. Which means …'

Kirsten shakes her head and backs away from him.

'No, do you know what? This is your mess. You sort it out. You go and see her. Tell her what is and what isn't happening. I don't want anything to do with it.'

'I thought you wanted me never to see her again?' he reminds her.

'Don't do your petty little point-scoring, Ian. Go and see her, sort it out.'

'Fine. I'll go see her. This afternoon, even.'

'Thank you,' she says.

Ian turns to leave the room.

'Where are you going? We're having a conversation.'

'To see Harriet.'

He carries on, presumably expecting Kirsten to follow him. But she can't. She needs a moment to push the rage and the fear and the panic back down inside her.

'You coming?' Ian asks her.

She wants to say something. Or, more accurately, she wants to shout and scream. But what good will it do?

'Sure,' she says instead.

She puts her hand on Ian's back, and they leave the room together.

Parenting: this strange bond that divides and unites them. Long after the marriage vows would have failed to bind on their own.

Chapter 18

MIRIAM, OCTOBER 2018

Miriam takes a small sip of her white wine and smooths her dress down over her thighs. The same one she wore for the school interview. She ought to chuck it. Always makes her nervous. Or maybe it always brings her luck. She's not sure which.

Ted's late. Why suggest a date and then not keep it? She's sick of people flaking out on her.

She looks at the bar menu for about the fifth time. Not that she's hungry. It's something to do.

'Hi!' There's a tap on her shoulder. She jumps.

'Ted!' she says, like it's a surprise.

They kiss each other's cheeks, look at each other for a second, then sit down. Here's where she should draw on her adult dating experience then ... oh, right, yeah – she doesn't have any.

'This place is nice,' she tells him.

'Yeah, it's OK,' he says, looking around him.

They're in Islington. It's more than OK. Ted's a bit keen – school stamping ground even though it's a Sunday. Or maybe that was his way of keeping it casual – 'I'm doing some marking this morning, fancy making my day worthwhile and grabbing a drink after?'

'What can I get you?' he asks Miriam, nodding at the bar menu.

'Oh, are you eating?' she asks.

'Are you?' he says.

One of them should make a decision.

'Let's share some triple-cooked chips,' she tells him. He goes off to order. She can't stare at the bar menu anymore, so she stares at her phone instead, flicking through the photos. Something to bring a smile to her face.

Ted returns and she shuts down the phone. Photos are private, right? Plus she can't teach the kids manners if she doesn't have any.

'They're on their way,' Ted says, taking a sip of some blonde ale or other.

'So how was the marking?' she asks him. 'Not too painful, I hope?'

He laughs. 'Thanks for your concern. A whole load of stories about the holidays – more envy-inducing than difficult. When do I get my villa in Tuscany?'

She laughs back. 'When you've earned it. So, maybe in another two hundred and fifty years?'

'Surely not,' he retorts. 'Surely our pay will have gone up by more than one per cent a year by then?'

'Hah!' she says, into her drink.

'So what brought you to this school?' he asks her.

She looks around herself, mock-surprised. 'What, is this the third-round interview?'

Ted looks bashful. 'OK, touché – bit of an obvious question. Let me try another one.'

Miriam smiles, taking a sip of wine. That's that one dodged, then.

'If you could teach any subject, to any age group, what would it be?' he asks her.

'Um, general ed to reception … like I do now … I love my work, Ted.'

'Oh come on, don't be such a goody-two-shoes!'

'Really!' she protests. 'That's why I'm teaching the group I do. Why, what's your fantasy group? A bunch of fifteen-year-old girls and sex ed?'

Ted blushes for her. And she does as well. She shouldn't have asked that question. Fine line, for both of them, and she crashed right over it.

'Sorry,' she says. 'Inappropriate.'

He shrugs. 'I've heard colleagues say worse things.'

'What, at St Anthony's?' she asks, wide-eyed. 'It's a private pre-prep, for Christ's sake!'

'No, other places,' he tells me. 'Where I had the displeasure of teaching that age group. And you know what? I thought girls would be the bitchy ones. Boys were just as bad.'

Miriam does a mock-pout. 'Oh, diddums, were they mean to you?'

He takes a sip of his pint. 'Nothing I couldn't handle.'

She mouths a silent 'Oh'. This date is not going the way she'd hoped. Or maybe he'd hoped. She's not sure what her expectations were.

'I was a real mean girl when I was at school,' she tells him. She doesn't know where that's come from. Must be the wine.

She still hasn't learnt, then.

'Really?' he says, looking at her thoughtfully. 'I can't imagine you as part of a group like that.'

'Yeah,' she says, giving a laugh. In her head she's thinking: even now, why will no one believe she belonged? 'A real pain for the teachers. There was a group of us, in lower sixth, always flouting the rules on make-up, skirt length, cleavage …' She sees Ted give a quick look. He can't help himself. Yep, those were the old days, she wants to say. More buttoned up now.

'Must have made life hell for the poor teachers,' he says, giving her a cheeky grin. 'I imagine you're pretty good school disco material.'

'Oh my God! That is such a lechy thing to say!' she tells him, mock-offended.

'What? I'm not saying I wanted to ogle a seventeen-year-old you, I'm saying—'

There's a silence, as they both realise that means he wants to ogle Miriam as she is now. He looks mortified. She begins to giggle.

'Maybe we should turn the topic away from school,' he says, blushing to the tips of his ears.

'Maybe,' she says. But the ice is broken. They lean a little nearer to each other, hands around their drinks on top of the table, knees a little closer to each other under it.

'So …' he says. 'What do you like to do when you're not at school?'

'Talk about school in pubs,' she jokes.

He smirks. 'You're not helping me much on the conversational side, you know that?'

'Sorry, I'll stop answering back,' she says. 'Um, outside school – just the usual, I guess. Bit of socialising, bit of shopping, bit of cooking. Nothing special.' She doesn't tell him she spends her evenings thinking about her pupils, drawing up lesson plans. It doesn't do to be the school swot.

'Cool,' he says, nodding into his drink.

If I told you everything, she feels like saying, you wouldn't be like that. You would take my hand across the table and I'd be wiping away your tears of pity.

Instead, she says, 'How about you? What do you do for kicks?'

'I'd like to say something cool, like martial arts, or opera, or something, but much the same as you – bit of this, bit of that. And I know it's sad but, lesson planning and marking takes up quite a chunk of time, right?'

'Right!' she says.

Obviously feeling more confident now, he continues. 'I mean I think if you have a job like ours which, let's face it, is a vocation—'

'Absolutely!' she says, taking another sip of her wine.

'Then that's your hobby as well, right? I can't just rock up at 9 a.m. each morning and see what my boss has in store for me.'

'Because it's what the children need, isn't it?' she says, agreeing. 'And we've got to anticipate it. Be ready. Know before even they or their parents have thought it out fully.'

'I was thinking more having the answers ready to their questions, having the energy to engage them but, yeah, that too.'

They nod. Maybe the safest topic is the most dangerous one. The most apparently boring one.

Miriam's phone starts vibrating in her bag. She should check it, but she doesn't feel like it. She's making a connection here.

'Have you spotted that once-in-a-lifetime pupil yet?' asks Ted.

She takes a sip of her drink. The phone starts to vibrate again.

'Oh, you know …' she says. 'They're all special.'

'Come on, someone keen like you – you're bound to have favourites, ones who make teaching really worthwhile.'

She keeps looking at him. Maybe now is the time to reach under the table and get her phone.

'I don't mean in any inappropriate way,' Ted says. 'Just, you know, the ones who make you not hit snooze on the alarm clock in the morning. Because you're looking forward to seeing them.'

Yes, he has it right. It's just like that. If she needed an alarm clock, that is. She always finds herself lying awake at dawn.

So she tells him.

'There is one girl, at the moment,' she says. 'Harriet.'

It's such a pleasure to say her name. The way it conjures up her face, and those pigtails full of her gorgeous hair.

'I don't know her,' Ted says. 'What is it about her that fires you up?'

She shrugs. 'There's just that something, isn't there? She draws my gaze. Sometimes feel like she's the only kid in the room.'

Ted is nodding like he gets it, so she carries on.

'I'm a bit worried about her, though, to be honest. I don't think she's being very well looked after. Always dropped off early, picked up late, not really smiling, bit violent towards the others.' She feels tears in her eyes and blinks them away.

Not before Ted notices though. 'Hey, don't worry,' he says, reaching out to touch her hand briefly. 'I have heard about her, now you mention it. That incident the other week?'

She nods. She wipes away a tear that's escaped.

Ted's hand appears again.

'It's good to care – but, look, you can't let it get to you. I'm sure she's fine. Her parents know what they're doing. Probably hot-shot City types, trying to make a buck or two for that place in Tuscany!'

Now is the time to divert herself by checking her phone. She lifts up her bag and starts rummaging round in it.

'You looking for a tissue?' asks Ted.

'No, my phone,' she says. 'It's been vibrating for ages. It might be important.'

Finally she finds it.

Seven missed calls and two text messages. One from voicemail.

She checks the other message. Finally, her landlord's got in touch.

'Listen, Ted, I have to go I'm afraid. Landlord problems.'

She starts to stand up out of her chair.

'Miriam, are you OK? If this is about getting upset in front of me then please, don't worry about it. Stay, have another drink.'

She shakes her head. 'It's not that,' she says. 'I really do have to go. See you at school tomorrow.'

And she goes. Because he's her landlord, right – he has the power to kick her back into the gutter if he needs to. And there are some things she'd really like him to fix.

Chapter 19

BECKY, 10 AUGUST 2012

Becky may not have been to the pub again after That Night, but she's not missing the after-show party. Just one more scene, and they're done. She waits in the wings. Across the other side of the stage, the drama teacher gives her a reassuring wave. She waves back. She's in his good books again. The day after the vomiting incident, she went to see him, apologetic. She'd had to – he'd threatened to impose a curfew on all of them due to the 'disgusting mess', unless someone confessed.

She'd gone from extreme popularity to object of resentment in just twelve hours. With everyone, including Caitlin, it seemed, but not Andy (although he'd had to endure some gags about 'vomit breath'). The teacher had been nice about it. Said it seemed out of character. Then he gave her a couple of paracetamols for her head, told her to be true to herself, and sent her on her way.

Now, though, it's all forgotten. There's such a buzz – everyone is on an adrenaline high, wanting to do their best not just for the parents in the audience, but for each other. Andy comes up behind Becky and takes her hand, kissing her lightly on the neck.

'Break a leg,' he murmurs. 'You're my shining star, babe.'

Becky feels an additional thrill of anticipation. She can't wait for the rest of the summer. Who knows where things might lead before term starts again? She might even be able to have *that* conversation with her sisters. Be a real grown-up in their eyes.

And then it's her cue. She takes a deep breath and walks into the spotlight.

* * *

'You were brilliant darling!'

'That was amazing!'

'I'm so proud of you!'

At the impromptu stage door (i.e. the entrance to the hall), the air is thick with parental congratulations. For all that the students have come of age that week, they still want the grown-ups' adulation.

Becky is no exception – she is almost jumping up and down with excitement as her parents pat her on the back.

'We never knew you could sing like that. Imagine – our little bookworm taking centre stage!'

Becky can feel herself glowing, and sees the glow reflected in others. Even Caitlin, who'd been oddly moody again since the pub the other night, meets her eye and grins.

The drama teacher comes over to meet her parents. 'I'm really pleased with how Becky's done. You've worked so hard,' he tells her, his hand briefly on her shoulder. Becky's parents look on proudly as Becky blushes, accepting the praise.

'Her schoolwork's the real thing, of course,' Becky hears her mum say. 'But it's nice to have a hobby.'

Becky rolls her eyes inwardly. Her mother has clearly been worrying that the great medical or teaching career will be in jeopardy if Becky gets the acting bug. She knows what dreams her parents have in mind for her. Her dad says something about

'Living in the moment for once.' Her mother makes a sharp remark. Becky allows herself to be parted from them in the surge of people.

Gradually, all the parents begin to fold away, as is the arrangement. The after-show party is not intended for them.

Becky changes into her comfy jeans and a sparkly top – no more body-con dresses, thanks – and helps the other students strike the set, taking down the minimal scenery. Finally, the stage is cleared, the (soft) drinks are served, and an old honky-tonk piano is wheeled out – for those who aren't already hoarse, there are plenty more show tunes to be sung.

Becky is looking round for Andy when Caitlin taps her on the elbow.

'Hey,' Caitlin says.

'Hey,' Becky replies.

'Listen, I'm sorry I've been off with you,' Caitlin continues. She seems nervous. 'I guess I was just jealous of how well things were going with you and Andy. He's really into you, you know.'

'Thanks.' Becky does know. She feels radiant with it.

'But, you know, I think what would really make him go that um, further distance,' Caitlin continues, 'is if he had a little competition.'

'What do you mean?' Becky asks. This sounds like one of Caitlin's bad ideas. Although, to be fair, the body-con dress hadn't been such a bad idea, nor had the whole drama course attendance.

'There's nothing that gets a boy lusting after you like a bit of jealousy,' Caitlin says.

Becky knows this is nonsense, but Caitlin's a friend, so she humours her.

'What are you suggesting?' Becky asks her.

'Why don't you snog someone else?' Caitlin replies, grinning wickedly.

Becky shakes her head. 'I'm not going to do that, Caitlin.

Anyway, who would you have me snog? You? That would turn him on no end!'

Caitlin backs away a little.

'Joking,' Becky says. 'Come on, lighten up.'

'OK, whatever. But I reckon you could totally aim over there.' And Caitlin nods to stage right.

Becky can't see any boys over there, just the drama teacher. 'Who?' she asks.

'Him.' Caitlin nods again, emphatically.

She *does* mean the teacher.

Becky laughs. Now she knows Caitlin must be joking.

'You're crazy,' she says. 'I'm going to find Andy.'

'I'm not crazy,' Caitlin tells her. 'Honestly, I've seen the way he looks at you. Can't resist touching you.' She mimics him. '"Oh, Becky, you're doing so well. Oh, Becky, let me just warm you up again."'

Despite herself, Becky feels herself blushing. Caitlin immediately begins crowing.

'See, I've touched a nerve! You know it's true. But I bet you couldn't pull it off. You're a one-hit wonder with Andy! Or maybe you're scared of going all the way with him.'

Becky begins backing away. She needs to find Andy. Caitlin has seriously lost the plot.

But then, almost as suddenly, Caitlin changes tack. 'Oh, look at your face! Come on, I'm just messing with you. Here, I got you your boring Diet Coke.' Caitlin hands her the drink in a plastic cup, which Becky accepts. 'Go on, off to Andy. See you later.'

Glad to be released, Becky does as she is told, and goes to find Andy. Out of the corner of her eye, she sees Caitlin opening conversation with the drama teacher. She's slightly worried about what Caitlin might be saying but pushes it out of her mind. It's Andy she cares about.

* * *

An hour later, she can't seem to find Andy. Rather, she can see him – he is there, sitting in the auditorium, with Caitlin. But for some reason, she doesn't seem to be able to call out to him, and her legs feel like they're made of jelly. She's sitting right at the back of the stage, talking to the drama teacher. She can't make out what he's saying. His words are indistinct, and fuzzy, like they've been drinking. But there's no alcohol here. Around them, raucous show tunes fill the air. As if they were in a gin palace. But it's dry here. The staff have made their views very clear.

It must be the adrenaline comedown. After her French oral at GCSE, she remembers she had such a shift that she couldn't get her words out at all – they were all blurry and strange for an hour or so. That's what this is. Yes, it must be, she thinks, as she finds herself sinking onto the drama teacher's shoulder. He'll understand. He's been here before.

Caitlin's words cross dimly through her mind. 'I bet you couldn't.'

She bets she could. It's just she doesn't want to. She wants Andy. But he's too far away.

Chapter 20

KIRSTEN, OCTOBER 2018

After Ian leaves for Croydon, Kirsten feels a slight pang. Perhaps she should have told him the whole truth. She watches him from the window, just to check he's going the right way (don't let Yvette meddle again, please, Ian …). Harriet sits reading next to her, her feet up on Kirsten's knee. Kirsten idly strokes her daughter's hair. Her gorgeous girl. Yes, there Ian goes, the right way. Slings his jacket over his shoulder and walks off out of view. Into his ignorance.

Because she knows what might have provoked that letter to Psychiatrist Clare. It was Kirsten's reply to letters she herself had received. Ian had brought the letters to her from the doormat, given them to her, shocked. She'd noticed the address. First Coventry. Then Watford. Getting closer. They'd agreed not to reply. (Ian had made all sorts of suggestions but none of them she liked – too conciliatory, and in the end 'do nothing' was all they could agree on.)

She'd been in two minds whether to burn the letters she received, or to keep them in case she needed to go to the police. But then she realised: she could never go to the police about her, could she? Because she, Kirsten, would be the one under arrest. She doesn't know for what archaic crime, she's not a lawyer. But there'll be one.

So yes, she burnt them. Ian watched her do it. Perhaps that would have been the time to say that she'd sent a reply.

Because in that letter, Kirsten said No.

Not in a million years.

Leave me alone.

… or words to that effect.

But the point is, Kirsten has already been asked. And Kirsten has already said 'no.' So there's not much scope for the nice arrangement that Ian has gone to try and broker.

Her reply didn't seem to have helped. Because now, Croydon – she's zoning in. Too near. Makes Kirsten think she won't stick at letters. Or at least, letters to them. Should Kirsten even have sent Ian off there? She might be dangerous. Maybe they will have to go to the police in the end – maybe she shouldn't have burnt the evidence.

Suddenly Harriet jumps up and starts banging frantically on the window, jolting Kirsten out of her reverie. Her heart tightens with perceived threat. She looks out the window and sees it's that teacher, from Harriet's school. Ms Robertson. What's she doing, wandering past their house on a Sunday afternoon? Maybe she lives around here. Kirsten pulls up the window.

'What are you doing in this part of town on your weekend, Ms Robertson?' she asks.

It seems too officious, too nosy. Kirsten wants to bite it back.

But Ms Robertson smiles.

'Please, call me Miriam. I was just meeting a colleague. We were going over our thoughts for the week, and I was walking home when I heard and saw Harriet banging on the window.'

God, Kirsten suddenly feels lazy. People *do* work at weekends, she knew it – she should be working now, using Ian as childcare, not sending him on false errands.

Suddenly, Harriet is taking Kirsten's hand, of her own volition – and they're not crossing a road, which is usually the only time it happens now.

'Mummy, can Ms Robertson come in for tea?' Harriet asks, her voice loud enough to carry down to the steps to Ms Robertson – sorry, Miriam.

'I'm sure Ms Robertson has better things to do with her Sunday afternoon than have tea with us, Harriet.'

Harriet's hand drops away from Kirsten's again. She already understands, then, the grown-up speak for, 'I don't think that's such a good idea.'

Kirsten wants that hand back. Even if just for a moment. So she pushes the bounds of Sunday afternoon decorum.

'Miriam, if you're not rushing off somewhere, though, it would be lovely to have you in for tea, just briefly? We could catch up on how school is going. It's always such a rush at drop-off.'

Kirsten holds her breath. She can feel Harriet's fingers snaking into hers again. Hallelujah.

Miriam looks at Harriet, then at her phone, then at Harriet again. Then she smiles.

'Of course I can spare the time. I'd love to. I just need to text someone, then I'll be right in.'

She does some lightning-speed tapping on her phone that only a millennial could manage, then she's with them. Kirsten goes round to open the front door. As Miriam bounds up the steps into their home, Kirsten feels Harriet's hand slide out of hers. When Miriam reaches the front door, Harriet slides her hand into her teacher's instead. She leads her through into the living room, and Kirsten is left standing alone.

Kirsten takes a deep breath. It was she who invited the teacher in. She has to play the good host, the self-assured, non-jealous mummy.

'What can I get you?' she asks with forced joviality, putting her head into the living room. Harriet and Miriam are sitting next to each other on the sofa, flicking through *Matilda*. Kirsten has never read it. Maybe they should go and see the musical, if Harriet's enjoying it.

'Oh, just regular tea is fine – thank you, Mrs White.'

'Dr,' Kirsten says, before she can stop herself.

Miriam gives her a searching look, then smiles politely. 'Of course, Dr White.'

Kirsten shakes her head. 'Sorry, force of habit. Please, call me Kirsten. Harriet, what can I get for you? Some juice?'

Harriet tilts up her head and looks thoughtful. Kirsten sees a little mischievous grin she's never noticed before. She wonders if she can get her iPhone quickly enough to capture it – but no, that would be weird. She'll just have to use her memory, like in the olden days.

'Mm, I'd like some hot chocolate and whipped cream and a scone.'

Of course she would.

'Not sure about that, sweetie. I'll see what I can do.'

'Hot chocolate, whipped cream and a scone!' The mischief has gone now. There's an anger, and she's bouncing up and down on the sofa with her bottom. She goes on repeating herself, getting red in the face. Kirsten feels herself blushing.

'Harriet, none of that, or you won't get anything!' Kirsten's voice is too stern. Harriet starts to cry. Kirsten wants to cry a little bit too, forced by Miriam's presence actively to 'parent'. What would she usually do if Miriam wasn't here? Probably give Harriet a great big hug then come back with whatever she could find to make her daughter happy.

'Harriet, tears won't help,' Kirsten says.

Harriet flings herself, inconsolable, into Miriam's arms.

'Sorry about this,' Kirsten says to Miriam. 'I think she's just a bit overexcited.' She goes to detach the two of them, finding where Harriet's arms have taken root.

'It's all right, don't worry,' says Miriam, gently nudging Kirsten away. 'It's OK, isn't it, hey, Harriet? Shh …'

And Miriam buries her face in Harriet's hair, like Kirsten does. She rubs Harriet's back, and keeps shushing her until the crying stops. Standing there, Kirsten feels like an intruder.

'I'll go and get the tea things, then,' she says, and she leaves.

In the kitchen, there might be a bit more slamming of cupboards than is strictly necessary. Stupid teacher, coming to their house at the weekend. The kettle, roughly filled, gradually builds up steam. What was she thinking, accepting the invitation? The obvious thing for her to do was politely decline and carry on her merry way. But no, she comes into the house, makes Harriet cry, and spoils the rare alone time the two of them have together.

Kirsten opens the fridge and inspects the milk situation. Best before yesterday, the open carton. She does the sniff test. Definitely on the turn. She's half-tempted to give it to Miriam, serve her right. But no, if she's ill, there'll be no breakfast club tomorrow. And Kirsten can't bear to imagine that wrinkled upturned nose, the teacup put 'politely' to one side. Fresh milk it is then. Don't know if she takes sugar. Maybe. Or maybe she's saccharine enough without it.

Right. Now for Harriet. They do, as it happens, have hot chocolate. And some whipped cream. Plus, actually, some scones. An observant child, then. Unless Ian has spoilt her while Kirsten's back has been turned.

Kirsten sees her hand shake as she pours the milk into Harriet's hot chocolate. Spoilt. Such an ugly word. Kirsten can only think of one thing that would spoil Harriet for her. She suddenly needs to see Harriet urgently, so she bungs everything onto a tray, and carries it hastily through. A bit of spillage, maybe, but nothing she can't correct.

'Tea's up,' Kirsten says, brightly, plonking the tray down on the coffee table. There she is, there's her Harriet. Sitting snugly side by side with Miriam. 'And yes,' Kirsten says, as if Harriet is paying any attention to her, 'there's also hot chocolate and whipped cream and a scone for you, Harriet.'

Kirsten cuts Harriet's scone up and hands it to her. Harriet accepts it, but goes on reading her book with Miriam.

Kirsten will not be an observer in her own living room.

'So this is nice,' she says. 'Something a bit different. Miriam, is your tea OK for you?'

'Yes, it's lovely, thanks, Kirsten.' She gives Kirsten a smile. Kirsten sees her look around, eyes sweeping over the high ceilings, the Farrow & Ball wallpaper edging up neatly to the plaster cornice. 'You've got a gorgeous home here,' Miriam tells her. Kirsten starts to relax a little. Maybe it's not so bad, having her here.

'Thank you,' she says. 'We try our best. Hence all those breakfast clubs!'

Miriam gives a kind smile and looks into her tea.

'So, tell me – how is it going at St Anthony's?' Kirsten asks her.

She nods happily. 'Really well, thank you. I've got brilliant pupils—' she breaks off to ruffle Harriet's hair '—and it's so nice to be doing the breakfast club. I know how much it means to the mums, and dads. Plus it puts me in kind of a pastoral care role, you know? Checking the kids are OK.'

'Are some of them not?' Kirsten asks, surprised. St Anthony's is hardly that kind of school, after all.

'There are some I have my doubts about,' Miriam says. God, she can't mean them, can she? Kirsten picks up some crumbs of scone from the floor. 'Some I want to keep my eye on, more than others,' Miriam adds.

'Well, we don't need to worry about Harriet!' Kirsten says, her tone bluff. It's the voice she uses for patients when the little growth they are worrying about is plainly benign, or they are merrily taking their folic acid and right on track for a happy birth.

Miriam doesn't answer directly. Instead, she ruffles Harriet's hair again (does she suspect lice?). After a pause, she says, 'Is Harriet happy at home?'

Kirsten hates it when people do this – speak like children can't hear. Like certain words are coated in inaudibility, and will waft harmlessly over kids' ears. Kirsten is guilty of this too, sometimes, she realises, but it still rankles. You'd think a teacher would know better.

'Of course she's happy,' Kirsten says. Then she adds: 'Aren't you, Harriet?' But it's not a question, it's a rhetorical demand for support.

Harriet nods happily and eats more scone. Good. Kirsten knows the way to her child's heart.

Miriam scrunches her face up a bit, then looks at Kirsten again, like she knows the secret of the food bribes. Well, it's not her secret, it's the secret of all mothers, isn't it? Surely Miriam's not suggesting Harriet's unhappy? Particularly when she's basically barged into their house one Sunday afternoon?

'I'm sorry, Dr White,' Miriam says, carrying on. She must see Kirsten's Unimpressed Face developing. 'I'll get out of teacher mode, back into weekend mode. We're trained always to look for the worst – I forget that at this school, I'm with the best.'

'Well, I'll take that as a compliment. Now, can I pour you some more tea, or do you have to get on?'

'Don't go! Have another cup. I'll pour it,' says Harriet.

Kirsten sighs, internally (she hopes). 'Let's pour it together, Harriet. I don't want a Sunday in A&E with you burning yourself!' Imagine – that perfect skin, blistered. Kirsten couldn't stand the guilt.

Kirsten holds the teapot, and Harriet holds her hand and 'together' they pour tea, very carefully and neatly, no accidents.

'Lovely, thank you,' says Miriam, smiling at them both. Suddenly, Kirsten feels every inch the proper mummy.

She drains her tea, ready to pour a new cup, and think of some new conversational topics. Ah! That's it.

'So, do you think you'll ever have your own children?' Kirsten asks Miriam.

Kirsten watches as Miriam smiles, stirring her new tea,

evidently concocting some clever answer. She feels like telling her not to worry, she won't report her to the headmistress!

Kirsten moves the conversation on, in case she's embarrassed her. 'I wish we could have another. I had a sister – well, I still have.' Kirsten laughs too loudly at her own joke. Wants to share the sadness of two sisters not speaking, but can't without admitting why. 'So I know how close siblings can be. But Harriet's our only one.' Kirsten ruffles Harriet's hair. The only one. After the baby that didn't … work out.

'Yes, me too,' ventures Miriam. 'About the sister, I mean. Amazing how close that blood bond can be, isn't it?'

There's something about the way Miriam says blood that makes Kirsten shiver. But she looks up at Miriam and sees only a smile. Maybe Kirsten just needs to put the heating on.

'Anyway, I'd better be going,' Miriam says. 'I'll see you at parents' evening.'

It sounds like a threat. Or maybe that's just Kirsten's interpretation of it. Because it's never just the children who are under scrutiny at those things, is it? It's the parents. What more could they be doing? How many more times a day should they be reading with their children? Why have they not got a maths tutor yet? Don't they know their child needs to have fun in the evenings, not just do the aforementioned reading and maths – a combination that can only be achieved in a time warp. Not in a busy working life.

Kirsten hovers as Ms Robertson gathers her things, hampered slightly by Harriet insisting on holding her teacher's hand in the process. Just as Ms Robertson is finally about to leave the room, a key turns in the lock.

Ian? What's he doing back already?

'She wasn't there!' he calls out. 'I got to the flat but—'

And then he puts his face into the room. His words freeze on his lips, as he sees they have company.

He looks like a new word is about to form on his lips, but he cuts himself short.

Chapter 21

MIRIAM, OCTOBER 2018

Look at his eyes bulging. It's too much for him. Miriam can see him want to cry out her name, her real name: 'Becky!'

But of course, he doesn't. He shows more self-control than that first time. When he fathered her child.

Because dear sweet Kirsten doesn't know who Miriam really is. Never got round to meeting her before she took her child. Harriet.

Miriam – or let's call her Becky, now – takes the lead.

'Hi, you must be Mr White. I'm Miriam Robertson, Harriet's teacher. I was just passing by. Harriet spotted me and invited me in.'

'Hi,' Ian says, sticking out a hand. 'Nice to meet you.' For a former drama teacher he's a pretty shitty actor.

'Daddy!' says Harriet, and jumps up off the sofa and gives him a hug.

'Hi sweetie,' Ian says. He pulls her up and sits down, gathering her onto his knee. Look at those hands tightly clasped around her. Now the protective daddy comes out.

'I'm having hot chocolate and whipped cream and scones!' says Harriet, bouncing up on his knee.

'I can see that,' Ian says. 'But what else has been going on here?'

Becky would perfectly happily explain that, what's going on, is that she's taken a rare and unexpected opportunity to see her daughter. But Kirsten butts in. Of course she does.

'We've just been chatting about how happy Harriet is,' Kirsten tells him. Smug bitch. Of course Harriet's happy this minute, she's been doped with sugar. But is she really happy? No. That's why Becky's there.

'Were you?' Ian asks.

Becky gives a small, sad smile. 'Yes, I was just saying – I keep forgetting, I'm amongst the best of mothers here.'

Becky sees that Ian has to look away. The truth is too much for him, always has been.

'Did you have a coat or anything, Miriam?' Ian asks.

'Oh, is it time to go?' Becky asks him, pointedly.

'No, sorry, I just meant – do you want me to help you look for it?'

'Oh, I see. That's kind,' Becky says. 'No, I'm unencumbered at the moment. I'll probably want to change that, in a few months though,' she adds, giving a pointed look to Harriet.

'But I wouldn't mind using the bathroom, if you could show me where that is?' she says. Becky can't leave without talking to him. Really talking to him.

'It's just at the top of the stairs,' says Kirsten.

'I think we might be out of paper,' Ian says. 'I'll need to get some out of the cupboard.'

And he leads Becky from the room.

'Just up here!' he says loudly.

Leading Becky to the stairs, he turns to her. 'What are you doing here?' he hisses. 'I went over to Croydon to find you!'

'I know,' she whispers. 'I texted you to say not to bother.'

'Let's see about that paper,' Ian says, loudly again. Oh, he has all the little tricks of the unfaithful! Then, whispered: 'But what are you doing here? With Kirsten? It's mad!'

'You're not giving me much choice,' she says. 'I just want to see my daughter.'

'Shh!' he hisses.

'Ian, have you found the paper yet? Do you need a hand?' Kirsten calls out from below. Becky looks round, and sees Harriet standing at the bottom of the stairs too.

'Yes, just got it!' Ian says. 'Harriet, run along, let people use the bathroom in privacy.'

And so Ian has to leave her too.

Becky grips the edge of the basin and stares into the sink. So much unsaid, as ever.

Like the morning after it all happened.

She'd woken up, a drugged blur. Seen him in bed next to her. Felt the pain in her insides. Imagined she'd been raped, feared she'd thrown herself at him.

Had merely said, 'Morning.'

He'd done the talking. Swore something must have been slipped into his drink. Wasn't the sort of thing he did. Would never breach a student's trust like that. Not Ian White. Not him. And particularly not with such a good girl, like her.

But he'd done it. And not by halves. Nine months later, Harriet.

Her Harriet.

Becky still remembers Caitlin, ashen-faced, turning up at home in the weeks before Harriet was born. The school could only hush things up so much. Couldn't stop your old friends seeing you in the street. 'I'm so sorry,' Caitlin had said. 'I never meant for this to happen. If there's ever anything I can do to help you, ever, please let me know.' Caitlin confessed she'd drugged both Ian and Becky's drinks, that neither of them were in control of their actions. Becky is still thinking of suitable repayment.

And that was from a seventeen-year-old girl, who'd done a prank gone (pretty seriously) wrong. Yet, that vile woman downstairs shows not a shred of guilt at knowingly taking someone else's daughter. How can she pretend in innocence that Harriet is her own daughter? How does she have the cheek, every day of her life, to do that? Becky should just go downstairs now, denounce their lies and pretence, and take Harriet back for her own.

But it doesn't work like that. Becky knows. Not after so long.

Instead, she splashes cold water on her face, flushes the toilet (for show), and opens the door.

There they are at the bottom of the stairs.

Her arms around Harriet's shoulders, and Ian's arms round them both. Becky wants to run back into the bathroom and be sick. But she's got to go down the stairs, towards them. She's got to stay cool. What is Ian doing, tormenting her like this? The tears start to prickle again and she blinks them back, processing as she moves down the stairs. She feels like that walk into the school cafeteria, the first day she was sure everyone knew she was pregnant. Everyone staring. The horribly long distance to sit in an empty chair, with her sandwiches. She knew, back then, halfway through the walk, that she shouldn't have come. She needed to get out. She needed to get out and then she could cry.

It's the same now.

'I need to be going,' she says, trying to keep her voice level.

Oh, but she doesn't want to say goodbye to her Harriet! How can he make her, standing there? How can he not give Harriet to her now, confess to his horror of a wife, make it right?

'Harriet, darling, I'll see you at school tomorrow, OK?' Becky ruffles Harriet's hair again. Does Harriet feel it too, that bond, that they are meant to be together?

She must do, because she untangles herself from 'Mummy' and throws herself against Becky's legs for a long hug.

Gently, heartbreakingly, Ian draws Harriet away.

Becky gives her a final pat on the head, but Ian has her in a tight hug now. There's no access. Becky nods at the two adults.

'Mr White, Dr White. Thanks for having me. I'll see you at the parents' evening in a couple of weeks, if not before.'

Because she wants to remind them, remind Ian – this isn't it. It's just the beginning. That he'd sure as hell better be in touch.

But now she has to go. She gives them a nod and tries to let herself out. She's fumbling with the latch though, so Kirsten helps her get out of the house more quickly. Of course she does. Bitch, bitch, bitch!

Becky hugs her arms around herself as she goes down the steps. She's sure Harriet will be waving behind her, but she can't look back. The tears are already coming down her cheeks and as she passes safely out of view, she lets them stream and stream and stream, and the sobs come.

To be in that room, in that house, with her daughter, her DAUGHTER, and that woman, that Kirsten, that horrible, horrible reason why she's not with her Harriet. Kirsten hadn't had the decency to meet Becky back then. She let Ian and that awful psychiatrist deal with her. And however awful, Becky trusted that psychiatrist, trusted the diagnosis – 'at risk of severe post-natal depression and post-traumatic stress disorder due to nature of conception and young age'. Unlikely to be able to care for child safely. Recommendation – child to be put into care unless suitable alternative arrangements found. And that diagnosis came *before birth*. Ian arranged for Becky to have the child at home, then took the baby to the waiting car and drove home with Kirsten. Then registered the birth as if it was their own child.

And of course, it was Ian's. But never, never has her Harriet been Kirsten's. Suitable alternative arrangements? No. They are not. Becky had promised herself, she really had, that if Harriet was happy with Ian and Kirsten, she would leave Harriet be. She could still be close to her, with this teaching job, but she wouldn't interfere.

But Harriet's not happy, is she? Harriet clearly knows at some deep level that she isn't right in that family, with its ridiculous pretentions of perfection – the long hours at work just to pay for some shitty wallpaper and all the trimmings rather than being at home with Becky's darling, darling girl.

Is that how Maya's parents convinced themselves it would be a good thing to send their little four-year-old daughter across the sea from Syria to England? On the basis that she would be happier here? That horrible choice, the desperate wrench of parting, to go on without your children? To decide whether it's better to keep them with you and risk their futures, or send them away to the unknown, potentially never seeing them again? Was it made intellectually bearable by the idea that she would have a better life?

True, Becky knows, their situations are so very different – they had to let their child escape the dire situation of bombs and air strikes and starvation. Becky was told she should want to let her child escape her. Becky didn't understand the choice she was making, back then. For both sets of parents, maybe it wasn't presented as a choice, even though every day they must both have questioned whether it was the right one.

But they will have one luxury, if they are living, Maya's parents: they will not be able to see their child's trauma. Will not be able to see little Maya, by all accounts wordless, baffled by her new foreign world, bereft at being away from her parents, traumatised by past conflict.

Becky hasn't met her yet, but she can see her. They'll be able to see her too, her parents, in their minds, but perhaps it's the absence of shrapnel in the background that is the main focus of their mental picture. That she must therefore be happy. They must worry and worry and worry – while they will afford themselves that comfort. But Becky can see her Harriet. Really see her. Becky knows she isn't happy. She knows she'd be better off with her.

And even if Harriet was happy – Becky is not happy. And Becky matters. She realises that now. She's not just some screwy seventeen-year-old, whose so-called friends got her into bed with a fit teacher (oh, yes, it's a longer story than that, but that's the highlight), so spiked that neither of them thought to use a condom. She's not an inconvenient backstory that can be thrown away, thrown out by her parents (her behaviour not fitting their religious ideals, given they apparently hadn't read the bits of the bible about Jesus's mercy and compassion), estranged from both her sisters – one angry that she could give Harriet away, one angry about what Becky had apparently done to her niece – misdiagnosed by a 'professional' for the benefit of her friend, then left, somehow, to rebuild some semblance of a life.

She'd gone to Ian for help, when she found out she was pregnant. Ian said he and his wife would take care of her and the baby. But really, she'd been duped, cast aside. Now she understands, and she understands this too: *she matters*. And her motherhood of Harriet *matters*.

The presumption of that woman, saying 'Do you plan to have kids?' They all look at Becky's flat stomach, her young age and assume she hasn't had a child. But they know nothing about her. The flat stomach is from making do, having to do real exercise – not just some stupid yummy mummy yoga class. She bets that Kirsten enrolled in one of those, to 'shed the baby pounds'. When Kirsten would just have been fat. Fat under her stupid pregnancy suits that they bought. Oh yes, Becky knows all this. Ian told her, when he thought she was too young and stupid to care or remember. Explained it was his wife's price for silence, that the baby had to be fundamentally hers. The miracle of IVF, to her friends and family. But it wasn't her child and she didn't deserve one. Or at least not Becky's child. Becky's Harriet.

It's no good. She can't keep walking away from her daughter. She sits on a low wall near Angel tube and hunches herself over. Let people stare. Or more likely, let them avert their gaze. Think she's some other dosser. Well, she would have been, if it weren't for Ian – and also if it weren't for Ian, she wouldn't have been in that position in the first place.

But guilt, it has deep pockets. It's paid for a flat, her teacher training, the clothes on her back. It's invited her to hushed rendez-vous, whispered reassurances of the future, clandestine meetings in cars. Up until now. Now, she has a job. She's independent. She's a fine, upstanding member of society. She doesn't need his money. And Ian knows that. That's why he's scared. You could see it in his face. He knows things have to change.

Part of his fear is because she's told him. As soon as she real-ised Harriet wasn't right, Becky said: I need her back. She sent him texts, criticising his parenting, saying he needed to do more. But she knew he knew that wouldn't be enough. He'd told Becky, you see, when he explained the plan, back five years ago. Let us look after her for now. Then, when you're ready, we can talk about you having her back.

I'll be able to see her, won't I? Becky asked, even though the medics had pretty much tried to convince her that she was a monster, not fit to be in the same room as a child – she'd known, she'd known she would need to see her.

Yes, of course. Of course you will.

So Becky reeled off into the world. In her tart's flat, staring at the wall. As she's said – her so-called landlord.

A levels written off. School only too keen to suppress the scandal. Exams picked up again later, thanks to Ian's influence.

But now, here she is. She came back, like Ian agreed she could. An assumed name, a new start. She's ready. She wants to talk about having Harriet back. Because every day she aches with the pain of being without her. Sure, weekdays she sees her, teaches her. Yet it isn't the same as being permitted to show her love as only a mother can. The cuddles, the kisses, the closeness. The proud introductions: this is my daughter.

Kirsten, though, she's said no. She's said no and she sits in that house with Becky's child, not giving her the love she deserves. To idly stand and watch while a little girl cries because she wants something to eat and drink! And then – scones to supplement her breakfast crisps!

What kind of mothering is that?

Becky wipes away her tears. Kirsten's turn is over. Becky has had enough. She's getting Harriet back.

Because, she said, didn't she? Harriet's her vocation. Her favourite. Her daughter.

Chapter 22

BECKY, SEPTEMBER 2012

Back home, five weeks later, the drama course is far from a distant memory. That last night has stayed with her, irreparably. The next morning, she'd left in a blur. She thought she was doing a walk of shame, but no one knew, so how could it be shameful?

Well, almost no one. Caitlin spotted her returning to the dorm at 6 a.m.

Caitlin had sat up in bed, raised an eyebrow. 'Well, what happened, then?' she asked, cattily. The drama on stage being over, she clearly wanted a new one backstage.

But even Becky didn't really know what had happened, how she'd got there. She knows she has had sex. That makes her a grown-up, right? Or does it make her a slut? Or, in this case, a victim? She knows what Ian says, that their drinks were spiked. Does that mean it didn't count? That because she hadn't surrendered her virginity willingly, knowingly even, she still had it? And did Ian's words mean she was ugly, a nothing, just some geeky kid, who he wouldn't even have looked at if he hadn't been set up? And if Caitlin was behind it, with those drinks she gave to Becky and Ian, could Becky honestly say that she wouldn't have slept with Ian undrugged, given the chance? She didn't know then, about the consequences.

So she hadn't answered Caitlin. She just got her bags together. She didn't even say anything when she spotted that there was another person in Caitlin's bed: Andy. It didn't matter anymore.

Her parents, oblivious, carried her bags away from the accommodation after she'd snuck back there, the two of them prattling happily about how proud they were of her (but, of course, it was only a hobby – not a career, like medicine or law, or teaching). They are probably happy, now, that she's reverted to her serious, quiet self. Perhaps even quieter, in the last week.

Now, she stares at her sister's New Baby in the cot, in her room. It's crying. So's she.

She hates it.

She loves it.

She wants to hold it.

She wants never to see it again.

She wants her own, one day. But not yet. Definitely, definitely not yet.

The baby seems to be doing something odd. Is it meant to do that? She continues to stare at it. Then she knows what she has to do. It's not a choice, it's a compulsion. Now or never. She acts on her resolve.

She goes downstairs. Her sister comes upstairs. Screams out her name from the bedroom. Screams things about how she isn't safe, not fit to look after a child. Meanwhile, her parents scream at her downstairs, after they understand everything. The Bible is mentioned a lot. For months, that's all she hears about. That, and her guilt – that even if they went to the police, physically she is guilty, so how can she claim she was wronged? Becky hasn't the strength to fight them, so she lets them preach. And then, she doesn't hear anything more from them again. When they cut her off entirely, with only a Bible for the road.

Part Two

2018

Chapter 23

KIRSTEN

Kirsten's hands still shake as she holds the latest missive from Becky, even though she's already read it five times.

It was there on the mantelpiece when she came home from a day at KidZania with Harriet. The trip was a half-term treat that had meant hectic appointment schedules for the rest of the week. She'd dispatched an exhausted but exhilarated Harriet into the living room to watch *Peppa Pig*, while she made them both an afternoon sweet treat.

She'd been picturing the scene all of the drive back – curled up on the sofa, her with a tea and Harriet with a hot chocolate and a purpose-bought cupcake, happily reminiscing about their day. Kirsten would show Harriet the videos from her phone of their exploits – Harriet strutting her stuff in the fashion show zone, pretending to be a medical courier carrying hearts around, and even chaotically concocting a smoothie. A brilliant day, with Harriet really coming out of her shell.

Ian must have already opened and read it – it had a Post-it Note on it saying, 'You should read this.' Intrigued, Kirsten had flicked open the envelope. The neatly typed letter had already drained all the exhilaration from her. Now, as she reads it (sitting next to Harriet on the sofa, Harriet watching cartoons, perhaps puzzled by the sudden lack of communication), the panic has kicked in.

Dear Dr White,

Five years ago, you took my daughter from me.

Now, I want her back.

I am her true mother, and we deserve to be together.

Please contact me to make the necessary arrangements. Otherwise, I will be contacting the press and the police to explain what really happened.

Becky

And it gives her contact details and the Croydon address.

'What really happened.' When Ian confessed, teary and imploring her forgiveness, that weekend after the drama course, she had put aside natural, weak, suspicions of intent and jealous anger, and was horrified that her poor husband had been drugged, and admired his integrity for confessing. She wanted him to involve the police, but he said it wouldn't be right.

When Becky came to him begging for help, saying she was pregnant, Kirsten's thoughts became less generous: my husband has bedded a young fertile woman and impregnated her while I am going through successive failed attempts at IVF. Yes, he says both their drinks were spiked. But I have a right to that baby. Her rage and self-righteous sense of betrayal overwhelmed her.

When she calmed down, she thought (at least, she thinks she thought): oh, that poor young woman – she's in no state to look after a baby, and she'll have to put the child up for adoption or into care if we don't offer to look after it. And no one must know why she was looking after it, because it wouldn't be fair on any of them – Kirsten must raise the girl as her own, for the time being.

And then, five years ago, with that beautiful newborn Harriet gazing up at her, this is what she thought: this is my daughter. Unequivocal. Permanent.

But those times in between, the times since – the fear that any parent (she assumes) has of their child being taken from her is magnified. Because she knows there is a real basis on which they could do so. Sure, there would be hurdles. They'd managed, through Becky having a home birth in a rented flat (with a private midwife procured and paid off by Kirsten) to have Kirsten's name on the birth certificate. And all (well, almost all) of Kirsten and Ian's friends and relations thought it was a genuine conception by Kirsten, which they'd probably attest to if needed.

And there had been a genuine medical assessment at the time saying that, as a seventeen-year-old who'd conceived under traumatic circumstances, she was in no fit mental state to look after a child. Kirsten had asked Clare to make that assessment open-minded, but they were old friends and Clare knew how much Kirsten wanted a child. No surprise, then, that Clare's report was enough to convince Becky she couldn't care for her own child, or to convince her parents if they ever chose to look into it. And the assessment would be kept confidential so it wouldn't alert anyone to Becky having given birth.

But Kirsten always feared this day would come.

She looks at Harriet, her darling Harriet, eyes still bright from the excitement of the day (and now, the cupcake). Harriet looks back at her, and snuggles over to Kirsten's side of the sofa. Kirsten folds the letter and puts her head into Harriet's hair.

'It was such a fun day, Mummy! I love you.'

Kirsten looks up to the ceiling to try to stop her tears from falling or from cracking her voice.

'I love you too, sweetheart.'

'Can we go again for my birthday, please?'

'Of course we can,' says Kirsten. Because it's easier than saying, 'I don't know if I'll still be your mummy by the time of your birthday.'

When Ian comes home, there is an emergency hissed conference of war in the kitchen.

'What do we do?' asks Kirsten, waving the letter.

Ian stands, eyes closed, hands in his pockets.

'She's not going to go away, Kirsten,' he says.

'But why now? What do you think she wants?' Kirsten asks.

'I think she wants her child.'

Kirsten slumps. Of course that's what Becky wants. But Harriet isn't Becky's child anymore. She was Becky's baby. She'll always be the biological mother. Yet it's Kirsten who has nurtured and maintained and loved her these last five years. That must count for something, surely?

'She can't have her. I won't give her up!' she says. 'We'll move, change our names, everything!'

'It won't work,' Ian tells her. 'Becky knows what I look like, and I bet she's got a pretty good idea of what you look like too.'

'Well, we'll just denounce her – report her before she can report us.'

'For what?'

'Being a mad fantasist.'

'They'll do DNA tests,' Ian reminds her.

'We won't let them! Harriet can't consent for herself and we won't consent for her.'

'There'll be a court order.'

'Only if she fights it! And where is she going to get the money from?'

Ian doesn't reply immediately. Then he says, 'So that's your world view, is it? Only the rich should be able to hang on to their children?'

Kirsten puts her hands on the kitchen counter and pushes against it with all her might to stop herself crying out.

'Ian, we've got to stop her. You've got to stop her. Otherwise, if she goes to the press, your career is ruined, you remember? And you might even do jail time.'

128

'And you think you'll come off all squeaky clean, business empire intact?'

Kirsten shakes her head. 'That isn't the point. The point is keeping our daughter.'

Ian leans in close to Kirsten. 'But honey, that's just the thing – she isn't your daughter. She's Becky's. And they need to see each other. You need to talk to Becky.'

'I won't do it!' Kirsten is sobbing now. 'I won't! I will never, ever survive this if we have to let Harriet go.'

'Then you'd better come up with a Plan B.'

Chapter 24

BECKY

At the first breakfast club after half-term, Kirsten is visibly jumpy. A kid drops a plate, and Kirsten starts, like it's a shot ringing out.

But Becky doesn't care about Kirsten this morning. She cares about Harriet. And she knows, now, that this is a child she's qualified to look after, never mind what has gone before. A week is a long time not to see her.

'How was half-term?' Becky asks both of them.

'Brilliant!' says Harriet, and starts recounting tales of some play place. The rest of the time, she spent drawing pictures of Mummy's office, no doubt. Although Ian will have been around a bit, presumably, with it being half-term. Subject to any holiday-time drama camps, of course.

'It was fine,' Kirsten says. Ungrateful witch. Although, to be fair, Becky does know where she's coming from. Then again, it's not so nice being apart from Harriet. Becky would love to tell Kirsten now, see her face. But she needs to keep more than one route to her darling. In case Kirsten is as obstinate as Becky worries she will be.

'By the way, I was wondering,' Kirsten says, looking around

the room, still holding on to Harriet's hand. 'What are the security arrangements for these breakfasts, and the after-school clubs?'

Becky pretends not to know why this would be a concern. She crumples her brow. 'Exactly the same as the rest of the school, Dr White. If someone's not a parent or on our system, they can't collect a child. Simple as that.'

'But if someone wasn't a parent, but said they were a parent – what then?'

'I think we all know who our pupils' parents are, by now, Dr White. And don't worry, I wouldn't dream of sending Harriet home with someone who wasn't her real mummy or daddy.'

Kirsten looks sick to the stomach. Good. But then she seems to remember her manners. She smiles at Becky, says: 'It's such a relief I have you to rely on.'

If only she knew. Well, she will soon.

'Now, Harriet,' Becky says, holding out her hand. How she wants to feel that skin-to-skin contact again! 'Let's get you some breakfast, shall we?' And then to Kirsten: 'Why don't you get yourself a coffee on the way to work. No offence, but you look like you need it.'

And when Kirsten has turned, lower lip slightly trembly (probably thinking Becky can't see it but, oh, how she relishes it), Becky gives Harriet a huge hug. If anyone asks, she'll say Harriet was missing her mummy and daddy after spending all half-term with them. Truth is, Harriet is missing her mummy. She just doesn't know it yet.

* * *

During morning lessons, Becky is just about to tear her eyes away from Harriet and look at some of the other students. And they have a lot to prepare for: in two days' time, little Syrian refugee Maya will be joining them for half an hour in the classroom.

'You have to be very nice to her,' Becky tells the children. 'She'll be very shy. She won't understand your questions yet. We'll have a grown-up here who speaks her language, but she still may not want to answer you.'

'She doesn't say much,' confirms Tiffany, the child whose parents are looking after Maya.

'Does she play games with you, though, Tiffany?' Becky asks her.

Tiffany shrugs. 'Sometimes. But she mostly just sits and hugs her toy dog.'

'Well, she must be very sad,' Becky says. 'Imagine, if you had to leave your mummy and daddy behind and didn't know if you'd ever see them again.'

Becky looks at Harriet, thinking of herself. But then she realises: to Harriet, Ian and Kirsten *are* her mummy and daddy. She would be sad not to see them again. Becky pushes the thought out of her mind as quickly as it appeared. Once Harriet knew the truth, she would be delighted to be with Becky as her *real* mummy. They'd spend much more time together than Kirsten ever did. It would be a proper relationship, lasting them a lifetime.

The children spend the rest of the day thinking of questions for Maya, or things they can tell her about school life in the UK (depending on what group they are in). Becky vets their work. 'What is the last thing your mummy said to you?' is allowed. 'How do you know your mummy and daddy are still alive?' is not. Over-emphasis on pick-up and drop-off time (and seeing parents or siblings again) is discouraged; talking about running around in the playground is fine.

At the end of the school day, with all this activity, Becky is suddenly seized by a fear that she is saying goodbye to Harriet for the last time. Kirsten might do something rash, something dramatic. Becky should just take Harriet away with her now.

But no. As 'Miriam', the reliable Ms Robertson, she can continue to see Harriet each weekday. She knows that. If Kirsten won't play ball, then it will be time for more drastic action. Right now, Becky needs not to panic. She must be strong, for Harriet's sake. She must hand Harriet over to Kirsten a few more times, at least, before she wins back what is rightfully hers.

Chapter 25

KIRSTEN

Kirsten breathes a sigh of relief as she leaves the school. At least Harriet is safe there. Ms Robertson gave her that assurance. And the breakfast club will keep Harriet happy – she seems to be getting a lot of care and attention there. Kirsten can continue her journey to work.

But on the way to work that morning, everyone is Becky. The young woman who Kirsten only just stops for at the zebra crossing. The female driver who cuts her up as she tries to turn into the surgery. The patient already waiting for her when she arrives at reception. They are all the right age profile. She can imagine Ian with all of them all those years ago. And she can imagine any of them making off with Harriet. As she unlocks the door into her consulting room she sees her hands are shaking.

Kirsten writes herself a prescription for Valium, then changes it to Seroxat, then prints out one for both of them.

What is she going to do? Other than take sedatives and anti-depressants, that is.

There's another woman who wants to mother her child. Who maybe has a greater claim. But no way is Kirsten buying into

Ian's surprisingly hippyish philosophy that they should all just sit and talk it through. She's not going to achieve anything by having some heart-to-heart chat with Becky.

Kirsten jumps as her phone rings. It's a number she doesn't recognise.

Is it …?

No, it couldn't possibly be Becky, could it? That's absurd. But what if it is? What if Ian gave out her number in some misconceived attempt to help?

Kirsten stares at the phone so long that it rings out.

It starts ringing again.

She can't answer it now. She's not in the right mindset. She flicks the phone to silent, like she always does for her consulting days. She throws it into the bottom of her bag.

No. That's not good enough. This is about Harriet. If the caller is Becky, she has to answer.

Voicemail phones her. Taking a deep breath, she answers.

A female voice, could be her, Kirsten thinks for an instant. But no. It's automated. A PPI-bot.

Kirsten places her head on her desk. This powerless anxiety can't go on. She needs a plan.

For possibly the ten thousandth time since she heard the name Becky, and for at least the five hundredth time that week, Kirsten goes back to the Google searches. There's a three-minute window before her next appointment. Maybe she can find out more about Becky then? Some clever new combination of search terms.

'Becky, Ian White, school girl, baby, Croydon.'

No. Nothing.

Back in 2012, Kirsten had been delighted that Becky's school had hushed it up. Had been horrified that she'd even had to know the first name of another woman, had baulked at the idea of a surname. So now, she can't even get a picture, a social media profile, for this woman who wants to take away her daughter.

135

Her life. If only she'd met her, back then. At least she'd know who to look out for.

The next patient is due. She considers not buzzing them in, pretending that she is busy with urgent paperwork for a previous consultation. But she already tried that earlier, and Jess sent the patient through anyway. Her practice manager won't let things slide, even if Kirsten will.

So she sits through some man ya-da-yahing about how meaningless life has become, and pops him on the same prescriptive doses she has just assigned herself. Good. Another few minutes won. She turns back to Google.

Maybe they can just run away with Harriet. Ian said they'd be found, but would they? Really? They could all live in a barn in the middle of Norfolk. Be recluses. Live off the land. Home-school Harriet. Change all their names. That would work, wouldn't it? Kirsten goes onto Rightmove. You can get some excellent places, big gardens. Shame they wouldn't be able to let Harriet play in them. Because they'd always, always be hiding. Better prescribe Harriet that Vitamin D now, if she's to be perpetually out of the light.

Oh, this is nonsense! That wouldn't be a life for Harriet. And they'd have no money, because Kirsten would be too frightened to go out to work in case a Becky-spy recognised her. She and Ian would be at each other's throats the entire time, and Harriet would have to have counselling for her whole adult life – if she even made it that far without being snatched away.

No, she needed something more permanent. Maybe Ian was right. Maybe they needed something crafted by lawyers in the interests of all parties. Something privately agreed, so that the courts, with their obsession with biological parenthood, didn't get their hands on it.

* * *

That evening, Kirsten waits until Harriet must definitely be asleep, and then opens a bottle of wine. She pours Ian a glass, unprompted.

'We should talk,' she says.

He looks up from what is presumably yet more Ofsted admin, his glasses on his nose.

'I need to review these for tomorrow, for an all-staff meeting. Sorry, sweetheart.' He looks down again.

Kirsten repeats herself, quietly but firmly. 'No, Ian. We should talk. About Becky.'

Ian looks up again, takes his glasses off. Accepts the wine.

'Sure,' he says.

There's a pause. It's her conversation; she knows she must speak.

'I've been thinking about what you said,' she tells him. 'And you're right. We need to work something out. For everyone's benefit.'

'Go on,' Ian says.

'So, I think, if we got together – you, me, Becky – had a talk, agreed some terms, we could work out a split-custody arrangement. Visitation, anyway. Maybe throw in a little bit of pocket money for supervised trips out. That kind of thing.'

Kirsten knows that she is lessening the terms of a deal for Becky with each sentence. But custody? She can't bear the idea of letting Harriet stay with someone else. And trips out for Becky and Harriet? Alone? How can she possibly countenance that?

Ignoring Ian's raised eyebrows, she asks him, 'What do you think?'

He takes a sip of wine before answering. 'It's great that you're thinking about this. We need to try everything. But let me do the talking to her.'

'Shouldn't I go and meet her?' Part of Kirsten wants to meet the woman, hunt her down, be able to recognise her in the street if she comes too close to her child. The other part never wants to set eyes on her, for fear she might actually just be a normal human being. That Kirsten herself might feel empathy, and cave.

Ian pauses again, as if picking his words carefully. 'I think it may not be the easiest meeting. I think there's a degree of … hostility there for you.'

'How do you know that?'

Ian shakes his head. 'I don't know for certain. I just get the impression from conversations back at the time. That she may have seen you as the driving force. May have stored up the most resentment for you.'

'But that's ridiculous! You're the one who got her into this, not me.'

'I get that, of course. But that's my gut instinct. And this is so sensitive. Plus it's my mess. I should sort it out, shouldn't I?'

Kirsten toys with her wine. She can't decide. Ian hasn't made a good job of sorting it out to date. So why should he manage it on his own now?

As if sensing her uncertainty, Ian speaks again.

'Tell you what,' he says. 'Why don't I speak to her first? Warm her up. Then depending on how it's going, see if I can broker a meeting for all three of us?'

Kirsten nods. 'Maybe. OK, yes. Let's do that.'

'Great.' Ian gets up from his seat, gives Kirsten a kiss, then puts down his wine glass and goes back to his marking.

Kirsten stares at him. He seems oblivious.

'Well?' she asks.

'Well what?' Ian says, looking up. Then he seems to get it. 'What, you want me to go over there now?'

'Why not?'

Ian looks theatrically at his watch. 'Because it's 8.30 now. It will be gone 9, maybe even 9.30, by the time I get there. That's not a time for a visit like this!'

'Phone her, then. Get her number from directory enquiries. Or didn't she put it on the letter?'

'You really think this conversation is best to be had by phone?'

'Make it a pre-conversation. Set a date for a proper meeting. Say you need to talk. I don't know – you used to be a drama teacher, write a script!'

Ian gives a sigh. 'Fine. You're right. Of course, I can tee something up.'

He gets up off his chair and leaves the room.

While she waits for feedback, Kirsten goes and stands outside Harriet's room. She can just about see her sleeping form from here. She is so sweet, so lovely, so … hers. But even as she thinks it, Kirsten knows the biological claim is a strong one. A just one. And she is conscious that there is something very real, very tangible, that she would be denying her gorgeous, innocent Harriet.

That doesn't mean she is willing to surrender, though.

She hears Ian talking in murmurs below. She tries to make out the words, but can't. She should go downstairs and eavesdrop, but she wants to drink in all she can of Harriet, while she has the chance.

When the murmuring stops, she tears her eyes away from Harriet, and goes downstairs.

'Well?' she asks Ian.

He nods. 'She'll see me. Tomorrow night.'

Chapter 26

BECKY

So, it turns out Kirsten isn't just a bad mother. She's a bad wife, as well. Makes her husband do the dirty work. Oh sure, on the phone, he dressed it up well. Said he 'understood it would be emotionally difficult for everyone if Kirsten were to come round.' Not for Becky. The only difficult thing would be to restrain herself. For Kirsten, yeah, Becky imagines it would be difficult. That she would feel some trauma, for the rest of her life, at the concept of giving up her child.

Join the club.

But Becky needs to get past her anger. Or at least, to look like she has. She knows that. The fire of righteous indignation, no matter how justly burning, has a tendency to look mad, erratic, frightening to those who don't feel that heat. She needs to be cool, if this meeting with Ian is to have any effect. It's maybe the highest-stakes discussion she's ever had.

And so, she boils a kettle, readies a corkscrew, makes ready for anything he might desire. Well, not quite anything. Then, just a little after 8 p.m., there's a ring at the intercom.

Ian rejects the wine and opts for whisky. He's brought his own. Hah. The pressure must be getting to him, then.

'So, what does she say?' Becky asks. Because she knows this is about Kirsten, not Ian. Why hide it? 'When do I get my daughter?'

'She thinks we can come to some kind of arrangement,' Ian tells her.

'And what kind of "arrangement" is that? I don't want to be bought off. I'm taking back my daughter.'

'You've got to see it from Kirsten's point of view—'

'Have I?' Come on, Becky. Cool the fire. 'I mean, sure, of course. This must be very difficult for her.' But Becky can't make her voice match the words. Ordinarily, she'd at least try to empathise. Here, she can't. She knows who is in the right.

'She's open to all sorts of options,' Ian says. 'But you need to take it slow. Supervised visitation at first, take it from there, see how we go.'

'"Supervised visitation?" You're kidding me, right?' This is Becky's own child. Harriet lived inside her for nine months, and has lived in her brain for the past five years. They should be able to live in the same house.

'Just as a start,' Ian tells her.

Becky shakes her head. 'Why shouldn't I just go to the police? Then I can have my daughter back. No terms, no nothing.'

'Really? You sure about that?'

Becky crosses her arms. 'What do you mean?'

'You really think it will be that straightforward? That Kirsten won't challenge it on grounds of Harriet's welfare? That social services will suddenly let a woman who surrendered her child, under no legal framework, five years ago, immediately take that child back?' He shakes his head. 'I doubt it.'

Becky stares at him. 'You're bluffing. She's shit-scared, I bet she is, of your names being dragged through the mud.'

'She's scared of losing her daughter,' Ian says.

Becky sucks on her teeth. 'Harriet is not *her daughter*.'

Ian swigs some more whisky. Refills his glass from the bottle. 'She wants to meet with you,' he says.

'That's not possible right now,' Becky says. She doesn't need to give her reasons. She knows them. The longer her identity is secret from Kirsten, the more options she has. Besides, if 'supervised visitation' is the only option on the table, she already has that – through school. It's just that Harriet doesn't know the nature of the visitation. Doesn't know she has the luxury of being taught by her mother.

'It's all or nothing, Ian,' Becky says. 'If Kirsten won't give me all, then she gets left with nothing.'

Ian shakes his head. 'She won't do it. You know that.'

Becky waits a moment. She's thought through her game play, of course she has, but she doesn't always want it to seem that way.

'Tell her she has two weeks. If she doesn't give up Harriet by then, I'm going to the police. And if that doesn't work, the press.'

Ian raises his palms in an open-handed shrug. 'I'll tell her that. But you know what her answer will be.'

Becky downs her glass of wine, blinking back tears. Why does Kirsten have to make it so difficult? Doesn't she get that she's basically inviting Becky to take matters into her own hands? Or rather, to take Harriet.

Chapter 27

KIRSTEN

'So she's just not interested in meeting me, and she won't compromise?' Kirsten demands, summarising what Ian has told her.

They're sitting on the sofa downstairs, Kirsten curled up with a mug of hot chocolate, Ian still holding his coat. It's late; Ian didn't get back from Croydon until gone 11 p.m. But Kirsten wasn't going to be able to sleep until she'd heard what happened.

Ian spreads out his hands apologetically. 'I'm afraid that's about the size of it,' he says. 'I tried as hard as I could, but she just won't listen to reason.'

Kirsten takes a sip of her drink and tries to hide her tears inside it. But it doesn't work. Ian reaches over and gives her a hug.

'Hey, we'll work through this, OK?' Ian says. 'We're in it together.'

Kirsten doesn't say anything, just sits there, brooding.

After a while, she draws herself off the sofa. 'We should head up to bed. Another day tomorrow,' she says.

Ian reaches out to take her hand, but she ignores him. How

can he give her something so precious, yet so tainted that it has to be taken away?

In bed, Kirsten undresses as usual, slips under the duvet, and gives Ian a customary peck on the lips before turning off the light. Turning over onto her right side, facing away from Ian, she keeps her eyes open in the dark.

How convenient it would be if Becky wasn't here.

She won't accept money.

She won't accept dialogue.

She just wants 'her' daughter.

How convenient it would be if something happened to Becky.

Could Kirsten make it happen?

Failed brakes (but does Becky even drive)?

An assigned target to a contract killer (but what does Becky even look like)?

An innocent party-girl cocktail swapped for a lethal cocktail of prescription drugs (but where does Becky even go to drink)?

Kirsten just doesn't know enough about her target. And she can hardly Google – the first thing the police now do, it seems, in a murder case (Christ, murder? Why is she even thinking about this?) is to search suspects' internet browsing history. Besides, she doubted that contract killers ran paid Google ads, or that there was a neat sign saying 'Dark net? Click here.'

But in an alternate world, where she could be forensically undetectable, and had the right murky underground contacts, it would be ideal, wouldn't it? To bump off Becky, by proxy. Throw some money at the problem, hope it landed where it needed to.

In this world, it is just something she will have to do herself.

* * *

The next morning, Kirsten is horrified at herself. Was she genuinely considering murdering her child's biological mother? Christ.

She slips on a black silk shift dress, its funereal darkness reminding her, intentionally, of the seriousness of life. Of the consequences of death. And of being caught. Imagine, robbing Harriet of two mothers. Because there was no way, in this age, to murder someone without being caught, was there?

Ian gives her a kiss before he leaves for work. Harriet is searching round for a book in her room. 'We have to read to Maya today!' she is saying. 'She's coming to breakfast club!'

Kirsten has no idea who Maya is, but assumes she is some kind of teaching assistant. Kirsten has bigger problems to deal with. If they weren't going to run away to live in a remote barn, and if she wasn't going to start murdering people, then she needed to work out how to secure a sensible future with Harriet.

Sleeping on it, the next best step was this: finding Becky and talking to her. Ian had tried his best. Of course he had. But this girl needed confronting. Whether or not she wanted to talk was irrelevant. They needed to. For Harriet's sake.

So, Kirsten resolves, as she drops Harriet with Ms Robertson at breakfast club, she needs to find Becky. And then they will have it out.

'Look after her well, won't you?' she calls over her shoulder to Ms Robertson, as she leaves the school hall.

'Like she was my own,' Ms Robertson calls in response.

Chapter 28

BECKY

Perhaps it wasn't a good idea to invite Maya to breakfast club. The slightly unstructured, chaotic atmosphere of parents dropping kids off whenever it suits them isn't perhaps best for getting a shy girl to speak.

Not that she speaks English, yet, anyway. There is an interpreter sitting on one side of her, and her foster mother sitting on the other side. But speaking at all would be good. Apparently that hasn't happened since her voyage across the sea either.

'Maya, we're so happy to welcome you to our school today,' Becky says to her, speaking slowly for the benefit of the interpreter. 'This is a special club where children who need to come early can have breakfast, and bring along their favourite books. I want to make a safe haven for everyone.' Becky smiles round the room, trying to catch Harriet's eye. 'Do you have a favourite book, back home, Maya?'

Becky smiles encouragingly when the interpreter has finished that sentence.

Maya stares back, wide-eyed.

Poor kid. That question must evoke so much. Who knows

what home looked like by the time she left, whether it was still standing, what it must have been like to have Mummy and Daddy read to her and now be so many worlds apart from them.

'It doesn't matter, Maya. Maybe you'll like some of the books here. They've all got lovely pictures in them!'

How is this going to work? The little girl is just going to have to sit there, listening to books not in her language. And the other kids won't have the patience to wait for a translator, will they? Becky bites her lip. She should have organised some special textual translations. Or just have saved Maya's slot for the classroom later.

'OK, who's brought a book in for today?' Becky asks the rest of the group.

A couple of kids stick up their hands. One is waving a *Peppa Pig* book, the other *The Very Hungry Caterpillar*. Becky chooses the second one. You can't go far wrong with that, can you?

As she reads it to the group, listing out the delicacies that the caterpillar eats, children get up from their seats and wander back to the breakfast table to collect more food. All except Maya, who continues to look round her, wide-eyed. She doesn't have any food on her plate.

Becky breaks off from her reading.

'Maya, please, help yourself to some more food if you'd like some.'

She nods to the interpreter, and then to Maya.

Maya's foster mother turns to Maya and gestures to the table as well.

Maya sort of shrugs into herself.

Becky holds out her hand encouragingly, as if to lead Maya to the table.

If Maya had any intention of going to the table, she seems to have withdrawn from it now. She shrinks back into her seat and curls her knees back up to her chest. Maybe Becky's offer of a hand was one thing too many. Each hand offered, each act of kindness must take her further away from her real father and mother. Becky blinks back a tear, feeling oddly put out that her overture was rejected. A stupid, self-centred way to react, she knows, but she can't help it. Is this how it would be with her and Harriet, when Becky finally had her to herself? A failed relationship with a little girl traumatised by separation from her 'mummy'?

Becky carries on reading about the caterpillar. It's gone into its chrysalis now, waiting to transform. Then, hey presto, it becomes a beautiful butterfly. Becky looks at Harriet, who is smiling benignly at the book while sucking on a piece of toast. A chrysalis into a butterfly, that's what it would be like, Becky decides; even if Harriet went into a little cocoon initially, at the shock of a transfer from her fake mummy to her real mummy, she'd soon emerge resplendent from the transition.

Unlike poor little Maya. Her foster mother is trying to persuade her to eat some toast, but she's shaking her head, tears rolling down her face. Perhaps it will just take Maya longer to emerge from her chrysalis. Maybe she thinks if she stays in there long enough, all this will go away. Mummy and Daddy will come back, and she can go home. The truth is tough at that age. At any age.

After breakfast club, Becky has a quick chat with the foster mother, Mrs Reynolds.

'It was too much for her, I'm afraid,' says Mrs Reynolds.

'I'm so sorry,' Becky replies. 'We should just have waited until the classroom session later.'

Mrs Reynolds shrugs. 'I don't think that would have gone much better. It's a shame. I was hoping her being here, seeing some other children, would sort of normalise things a bit?'

Becky nods. 'Will she still be able to come along to the classroom?'

Mrs Reynolds looks over to Maya, still sitting hunched in her chair. She shakes her head. 'Not today, at least. I'm sorry. I know the kids will be disappointed, but my first duty has to be to little Maya.'

Damn. Becky has really messed up. Upsetting Maya and depriving her class of their planned event, which would have broadened their horizons so much. 'Of course, I totally understand.' So much for a safe haven.

That's going to be a tricky conversation later, with the head. Becky explaining how she managed to make a young refugee girl cry away breakfast, and ruin a great educational opportunity for her class. Poor judgement on her part, Mrs McGee will most likely think. Well, she'll just have to play the compassion message, invite the head to think of the bigger picture.

And it will come up at parents' evening, too, she bets. 'Oh, little Angelica was so disappointed …' But it's not show and tell; it's a little girl's life. Becky's sure once they get on to Angelica's excellent progress in violin lessons, little Maya will be forgotten.

How good it would be for all the parents here if they could step away from all these 'privileges' and focus on the one main privilege: their child being with them at all.

Probably not a great line for parents' evening. But there's only one interview Becky is interested in on parents' evening, and it's with Kirsten and Ian. Because painful though it might be, if Ian hasn't managed to convince Kirsten that the way forward is with Becky, then 'Miriam' will do her best to persuade her.

Chapter 29

KIRSTEN

Kirsten sits in her car outside Becky's block of flats in Croydon. She'd got the address from the letter to Dr Clare. Now all she needs to do is wait for some kind of movement. A girl Becky's age, she'll have a social life, won't she? Won't just sit inside at 8 p.m. on a Thursday evening? Kirsten told Ian she was at an important networking meeting (which is kind of true) – and made him be primary carer for Harriet, for once.

Kirsten knows there's a flaw in her plan. She's never seen Becky, so how will she know what she looks like, even if she does leave or enter the building? And what will Kirsten do even if she does work out who she is?

But she feels that she will somehow *sense* Becky. The right demographic. The right type. Plus, although she doesn't want to think about it, Becky should look like Harriet, right? And Kirsten thinks she's managed to figure out which flat it is – there, on the third floor, with the lights on. She tries to imagine Becky wandering round in there. Maybe she's pacing like a caged animal, ready to pounce. Maybe she's thinking constantly about *their* daughter (because Kirsten is beginning to realise that neither woman has the full claim). Perhaps plotting how she can take her back. Or maybe she doesn't care at that deep level – maybe she just has a sense of entitlement, and wants back what's 'hers'.

First nine o' clock, then ten o' clock draws on. Figures have come and gone, but none of them look right. There was one person in a hoody, who excited Kirsten's interest for a few moments, but they turned out to be a man.

Finally, at 11 o'clock, very aware she has to drive back to Islington and be up for breakfast club tomorrow, Kirsten decides to ring the buzzer. She doesn't need Becky to let her in – doesn't quite know what would happen if she did – but Kirsten needs a sense that she's got something out of this evening, other than a numb backside.

So she gets out of the car and crosses the street. She puts her gloved hand to the buzzer. She tries to hear where in the building it's sounding, but she can't. No reply. She tries again. Nothing. Kirsten stands back into the road a bit, to see if her buzzing has elicited some kind of curtain-twitching response from any of the flats. But nothing. The curtains that are open stay open, and the ones that are shut stay shut.

Sighing, Kirsten goes back to her car. What a wasted evening. She could have been playing with Harriet or putting her feet up on the sofa. Or even attending an important networking function. Plus, she's starving. She knows surveillance workers are supposed to eat donuts or bacon sarnies or something in their cars, but she didn't have the foresight to bring any. What business has Becky got going out at night, when she's supposed to be pining after Harriet? A sudden thought makes Kirsten shiver: maybe Becky is even now standing outside their house, looking in on Harriet.

Back home, Ian has already retreated upstairs by the time she returns. The bedroom light's on, though, so she'll have to make up a whinge about the non-existent networking event (prime target didn't show up, too few canapés – bit of truth in that). For now, she needs something to eat. Famished, she polishes off the remains of some hummus and pitta bread, with a glass of milk for extra lining for her grumbling stomach.

She feels bad misleading Ian, not telling him what she was doing with her evening. But he wouldn't understand. And he'd think she doubts his ability to sort out the Becky situation. Which she sort of does. But maybe for good reason? Besides, the most important thing is to keep Harriet safe.

Chapter 30

BECKY

Maybe it's not normal, as a teacher on the morning of parents' evening, to find yourself evaluating your own daughter. How perfect she is. In class yesterday, she had been the brightest, most biddable child there. She sat so neatly on the carpet at story time. Becky bet she'd never had a tantrum in her life, unlike most of the children. Plus she'd answered all the questions about the story with the sweet little homeless cat correctly and was the only one who'd linked it to the Maya theme of her own accord. She was so clever, and so pretty. That hair ... she could just stroke it endlessly. They needed to spend more time together, as mother and daughter. Imagine the fun they would have on days out. Will have. Soon, now. Unlike with Kirsten, cooped up in that unhappy house in Islington.

That should be her life. Becky should be living in that house in Islington, making it a happy home. Ian knew it. Kirsten knew it too, even though she didn't yet know who 'Becky' was – it was why she wouldn't admit it. Instead, she spent what should be precious time with her family going off to that surgery. Sure, work in the daytime when your child's at school. But not in the early morning and evening. And if that means you need to down-size, so be it. Greed. That's all it is. Clear, selfish greed.

Becky tries to focus on her notes about the children, so she can give good feedback. But her brain is full of the idea that she is going to have to sit opposite Kirsten, giving that odious woman feedback on her own child. Is she going to be expected to say something negative about Harriet? Impossible, when the only negative in Becky's mind is that Harriet lives in the wrong house, with the wrong mother. Or rather, she lives in the right house, with the wrong mother. It could all be so easily fixed.

'Hey, Miriam!'

A tap on her shoulder reminds Becky that she is still meant to be Miriam. She looks up. It's Ted. Becky winces internally. She realises she's hardly said anything to him since she ran away from their so-called date to see Ian. Time to make amends. You never know when you might need an ally.

'Hey, Ted, how are you doing?' She gives him her best smile.

'I'm good, thanks. Feels like it's been ages. You, ah, avoiding me?' He's trying to sound jocular, Becky can tell, but she knows he means it.

'No, of course not. I've just been swamped. Trying to sort out my project work seeing as we couldn't have little Maya in the class, you know?'

Ted nods. 'Sure. I was sorry to hear about that. It would have been great for the kids.'

'But maybe not so great for Maya, it turns out. We had to put her first.' Becky is practising her patter for the parents' evening. She puts her head to one side, in what she imagines is an empa-thetic manner.

Ted nods along. Good. Maybe she can get away with her error of judgement after all, the mistake of overwhelming Maya with breakfast club.

'And you never know,' she says. 'Maya might be able to come along later in the term.'

'Of course she might. That'd be great. Good luck sorting it out. Anyway, how are things generally? Can I …?' He gestures to the seat next to her.

'Of course, sit down!' Becky pushes her paperwork to one side. 'I'm taking up far too much space.'

There's some shuffling of papers, some apologising, and finally Ted is settled.

'How's it going, then?' he asks again.

Becky puffs out her cheeks. 'Oh, you know. Surviving. I'll be glad when this parents' evening is over!'

Ted nods in agreement. 'Tell me about it! There's only so many ways I can think of to tell the proud mums and dads that their little treasure is in fact perfectly normal. The worst moments are when they start playing you videos of their "bright little buttons" reading aloud!'

Becky laughs. 'No! Really? They do that?'

'Oh yeah, you'd better believe it!' Ted grins. 'Reading videos, counting to a thousand videos. "But my child is so bright!"' he mimics. '"Why can't they be streamed into the upper set?"'

Becky groans and rolls her eyes. 'They know there's like, three children across the whole reception class who get special tuition, right?'

'Right.'

'Ah, well, you can't blame them for trying. If it were my child, I'd want only the best for them, I guess.' She doesn't need to guess. Harriet would get the best. But it wouldn't be achieved through pushing her into advanced mathematics at the age of five. Becky doubts Kirsten even cares enough to give that kind of chat this evening, but maybe they all do it, these Islington types – the pushy parent trap they can't help but fall into.

'We all usually get a couple of bottles in the staffroom afterwards,' Ted says. 'When the parents are safely gone. Share war stories. Or horror stories.'

'If there's wine and bitching involved, I'm there!' Becky laughs.

'Great, I'll see you later then. Good luck!' Ted says.

'Thanks, I'll need it,' Becky groans.

As Ted walks away, her smile fades. The idea of a communal bitching session over some wine sounds like hell. Not that she doesn't want to bitch about Kirsten. Of course she does. But the one thing on her mind, she won't be able to say: I wish she would just give me back my child.

Or explain the lengths she's willing to go to if Kirsten won't oblige.

Chapter 31

KIRSTEN

Kirsten stumbles over her shoes as they walk to the school entrance. She reaches out for Ian's arm for support, but whatever instinctive reactions they used to have to each other have gone. He doesn't catch her, and the stumble becomes a fall.

A great start to parents' evening.

Back on her feet, cursing her choice to wear the too-high shiny beige heels, Kirsten fumbles with her handbag. There's too much in it, and the clasp won't shut. She should just have used her big purple workaday handbag, the one that looks like a Mulberry from a distance, but isn't. (Those cost a month of school fees.) For some reason, though, she felt like she had to put on a show tonight. So she's gripping the mother of pearl clutch that she had for her wedding. She's always thought of it as her ultimate occasion bag, but it's starting to look a little sad. One of the threads is threatening to fray, she notices. She tries one last time to close the clasp, and the bag revolts, throwing lipsticks, tissues, and banknotes up on the path. Ian is striding up ahead, oblivious.

'Ian!' she shouts out. 'Wait up!'

But no. He doesn't seem to hear her. Kirsten tries to lean down elegantly to pick up her belongings, twisting her legs to one side, but her knee-grazing skirt is too tight for that. The only way is to kneel on the tarmac. She's just weighing up whether she has to succumb, or whether it will be less embarrassing just to walk away leaving the items on the path, when someone calls out 'Let me help with that!'

She turns. It's another mum, she assumes, in a sensible but elegant trouser suit, jewelled flats, and a big bulky handbag.

'Makes us all clumsy, that fear of going back to school, right?'

The other mum bends down with no effort and quickly gathers together Kirsten's things.

'Thank you so much,' Kirsten says. 'I'm so sorry. It's a stupid bag, and my husband's gone on ahead.'

'It's not stupid; it's very nice. I just came straight from work so flung everything into this old sack.' The woman gestures at the worn-looking black bag. Kirsten can't help noticing the Mulberry insignia. 'I'm Ellie, by the way. My son Thomas is in transition. Nice to meet you.'

Kirsten holds out her hand to shake, but the clutch threatens to spew out all its belongings again.

Ellie smiles at her wryly, and starts to root around in her bag. 'I think I have … yep, here we go.'

She holds out a carrier bag to Kirsten. 'Only Boots, I'm afraid, and you might find the odd bit of prawn mayo in there from my lunch, but better than dropping everything again.'

'Thank you,' Kirsten says. 'Serves me right for using such a ridiculous bag. I've had one like yours sitting under my desk all day!'

'Oh, I just assumed you didn't work – you look so well put together.'

Kirsten doesn't tell her she carved out the final appointment of the day, and went home to change and make sure Ian was (a) there and (b) had a clue what they were supposed to be asking about. For a man who was a teacher, he'd been pretty vague about the whole parents' evening thing. Also, she'd wanted to make sure that she had enough time to monitor Yvette, who was babysitting Harriet. Make sure she wasn't meddling in her style of parenting, suggesting different routines, the ones she would have used if she had her own child. Maybe that's what this is about. Maybe Yvette is just making up for her sadness at not having her own child. Kirsten feels a sudden pang of compassion. She's the lucky one, after all, with (her) wonderful daughter. She should be kinder.

Feeling a sudden warmth at being a mother, she walks up the drive of the school with her new friend Ellie, chatting about their respective work, and how they think their kids are doing. It's so easy, so nice – and so *normal* talking to another working mum. Or rather, a woman who happened both to work and have kids. By the time they arrive at school, Kirsten feels a mixture of relaxation at talking to someone in the same boat as herself, and envy that Ellie seems to be so much more at ease with the role than she is.

That relaxation leaves her when she gets inside and sees Ian. He's found the wine. He is rocking on his heels, knocking the red stuff back as if he'd just walked through a desert. Kirsten bids goodbye to Ellie and watches wistfully as she goes and kisses a handsome 'too rich or intellectual to wear a suit' type, who sports a chunky red sweater and just the right amount of stubble.

'I was wondering where you'd got to,' Ian says in greeting. 'I got you a glass of wine.'

He hands her the half-empty glass of wine she saw him drinking from a moment a go.

'Don't worry about it,' she tells him.

'What time's our slot again?' he asks.

'It's 7.55,' she reminds him. Again. 'So, you remember, the teacher's name is Ms Robertson; she takes Harriet for breakfast club and all her lessons, except P.E., and we need to focus in particular on how her reading is going.'

'It'll be fine, sweetie,' Ian tells her, and puts his free hand round her shoulder. 'Hey? Relax.'

She wants to do as he says. She wants to sink back into the comfort of that arm. Share a drink, have a laugh. Not take all this too seriously. But she can't. There's too much going on. It could be her first and last parents' evening. She wriggles herself out of Ian's grasp and goes to the refreshments table. She opts for orange juice. She notices one of the staff doing a quick look at her tummy, unable to believe that a woman would opt for a soft drink unless they were pregnant. As if. 'I'm driving,' she says. Which she probably is, given Ian's approach to the red.

At 7.56, Kirsten and Ian take their seats opposite Ms Robertson.

'So,' Kirsten says.

'So,' says Ms Robertson.

'How's it all going?' Kirsten asks.

'Good, good,' Ms Robertson says, nodding her head. 'Harriet's a lovely child. I wish I could see more of her!'

Come on, Kirsten thinks. Get to the detail. We only have a ten-minute slot.

'We think she's doing well at her reading,' Kirsten offers.

'Oh, do you have a video to share?' Ms Robertson asks.

'What?' Kirsten looks to Ian, who shrugs. 'A video? Why?'

'Never mind, sorry, it was a joke but … anyway.' Ms Robertson clears her throat and continues. 'Harriet's reading.' Ms Robertson's eyes mist over. 'I think she was reading *Matilda*, wasn't she?'

Kirsten nods. 'Exactly. Which seems a bit old for her. And I just wanted to check. Should we be encouraging her with that? Or do you think she's just looking at the pictures and we should give her something more on the right level?'

'Let her read what she likes!' Ms Robertson snaps.

Kirsten jerks her head back, surprised. 'Um, I'm sorry, I'm not sure that kind of comment—'

Ian wades in. 'I'm sure what Ms Robertson meant was, Harriet's doing brilliantly for her age, and we should just let her read the books that make her happy. Right?'

Kirsten sees Ms Robertson shoot Ian a glance. 'Right,' the teacher says, taking his line. 'That's what I meant. I'm sorry, it's been a long evening.'

But it's your job, Kirsten thinks. You're paid to look after my child. And you seem … emotional? Drunk? Oh my God, is she *drunk*, this woman? Kirsten leans forward slightly, seeing if she can catch a whiff of anything on her breath. But she doesn't smell anything, just sees beads of perspiration on her brow. Wow. So maybe she is finding it tough.

'How is Harriet's numeracy going?' Kirsten asks.

'She's doing very well. Look, she's doing very well at everything. I don't know what more I can really say. Your daughter is talented, pretty, popular, she … excuse me a minute.'

Kirsten watches in amazement as the teacher gets up from her chair, goes to the refreshment table and gets a glass of white wine, her back to them. Instead of returning immediately, she raises her arm twice for swigs.

'What's with her?' Kirsten asks.

'I don't know.' Ian shrugs, but he is perplexed too, Kirsten can tell. His eyebrows have become a monobrow, knotted together in concern.

When the teacher comes back, her eyes are red.

'I think I must be coming down with something,' Ms Robertson says, by way of explanation.

'You should come and see me at my clinic!' Kirsten jokes.

'I don't think I could afford you,' Ms Robertson counters.

Kirsten's taken aback. It's a catty comment, but that's not all. How does the teacher call so readily to mind what it is Kirsten does, that she offers a paid for rather than NHS service? Kirsten shifts in her seat a little, unnerved.

'Do you have any other questions?' Ms Robertson asks.

'Oh, um, I don't know,' Kirsten says, thrown. She thought the teachers were meant to provide information unilaterally. 'Harriet seems perfectly happy at school. Is she?'

Ms Robertson nods slowly. 'At school she is, yes.'

The nuance isn't lost on Kirsten. 'What do you mean, at school?'

Ian butts in again. 'I think she means—'

Kirsten holds up a hand. 'No, Ian. Let Ms Robertson tell us what she means.'

Ms Robertson takes a couple of breaths. Kirsten sees her lower lip trembling. 'What I mean is—' And then there's a tear, plain as day, running down her face. Ms Robertson clears her throat. 'Dr White. Kirsten, what you need to know is—'

'Becky!' Kirsten hears Ian shout. 'That's enou—'

And as the name sinks in, Kirsten sees both of their faces freeze in turn, Ian's and the woman's. Their faces asking the question: did you hear that? And did you understand?

Yes. Yes, she did.

Chapter 32

BECKY

Ian. You idiot. You absolute idiot.

Becky sits fixed where she is, staring at Kirsten's face. She follows as emotions paint themselves there. White with shock. Head tilting back, mouth opening, as realisation mounts as to what this really means. Eyes widening with fear. Hatred, as the eyes flick to Ian. Anger, as she looks between both of them. Or maybe fury would be more accurate.

And then, what is perhaps most alarming to Becky is – nothing. There's a mask. Or rather, a veil comes down. Like Kirsten's somehow taken on some of Ian's old drama teaching. Or been playing too much poker. Because now her face is blank, cold, emotionless. Which means Becky has no idea what Kirsten is going to do.

What she does in fact do is, very slowly, get up from her chair, and walk away.

'Kirsten!' Ian calls after her.

She doesn't turn back.

'We need to follow her,' Ian says. 'I've never seen her like this.'

They catch her up. Ian takes Kirsten's arm. Kirsten shakes him off.

'Why don't you stay here with Ms Robertson? Seeing as you have clearly been getting on so intimately.' She spits out the last word. Her voice is low, controlled. 'I'm going home to see my daughter.'

Your daughter? Becky wants to shout. But there's something about Kirsten's tone that suggests it isn't wise to answer. If Ian hears it, he ignores it, because he speaks again.

'Kirsten, listen, I'm sorry, I didn't mean for you to find out like this, I wanted—'

'I always have to find out somehow, don't I, Ian?' Kirsten says. Beneath the bitterness, there's a tiredness in her voice. Becky feels almost sorry for her. Almost, but not quite.

'I'll come round to see you both tomorrow,' Becky says, finding her voice again. 'Now you know, well, there's a lot to discuss. About Harriet.' She tries a laugh. It comes out wrong, manic. Her throat is too dry and her eyes too wet. 'Funny, for a parents' evening.'

Kirsten leans in very close to her. So close that Becky has to force herself not to step back. Very quietly, she says, 'You will stay away from my house. And you will stay away from my child.'

Before Becky has a chance to respond, Kirsten is walking away. This time, Ian doesn't try to follow her. Becky begins sobbing. Loudly. She can't help it. She notices people staring. It's becoming a scene.

'Come on,' says Ian, quietly, taking her by the elbow.

'But I've got to see more parents,' she tells him.

'We need to resolve this,' he says. His face is white.

'I can't just leave. I can't. I'll—'

She knows she can't stay either, though. There are three more appointments. There's no way she can coherently talk her way through them. She spots Ted, getting himself a glass of water.

'Ted,' she says.

Before she's had a chance to say anything, he looks at her and exclaims. 'Becky! What's wrong?'

'Some mother's given me a bad time. And I think I'm coming down with something. Vomiting bug. I just nearly threw up over someone. Can you explain to the parents I'm meant to see? I'm sorry. I've just got to go.'

'Of course, you poor thing – I will do, but don't you think you should tell Mrs McGee?' he says. He nods over to the far wall. 'She's just over there.'

The thought of the confrontation, of walking past all the parents, is too much. 'I can't, Ted. I've just got to go.'

And she walks as quickly as she can out of the school hall, to where Ian is waiting. She feels her shame all over again, five years on. Like when her peers first knew. A dishevelled girl, too young for her world, too confused to do anything other than follow Ian White.

Outside, it is no better. Groups of parents mill round. She keeps her face down, her eyes covered, like there's something in them. Ian tries to steer her to a nearby pub, to calm himself as much as her, presumably. But she can't, she needs to get home. He hails them a cab, makes to get in it with her. She closes the door in his face. She needs to be home, and she needs to be alone, and she needs to work out how to solve this situation. For good.

Chapter 33

KIRSTEN

Once Kirsten has shown Yvette out from her babysitting duties and put the chain on, she does not move from Harriet's bedside. Not when Ian is pushing and pulling the front door to protest about the chain, not when he is in the garden shouting up at the house, not even to check where he's gone when all is silent. Perhaps he's still there. Perhaps he's left. It doesn't matter.

Harriet's room is the only place she can think. If she is elsewhere, she just starts to panic: what if Miriam-Becky breaks in and takes her? And life choices become too academic, too theoretical, taken in isolation. If she is sitting there, in front of Harriet, the truth is clear – that nothing else matters.

And so, Kirsten is free to think, to take it all in. Becky is Ms Robertson. And Ian knew, from the time that Becky 'call me Miriam' came over for afternoon tea, when she happened to be passing (hah) that Sunday afternoon, if not before. He knew that all those drop-offs at breakfast club were to the woman that Kirsten most feared. That Kirsten was unwittingly letting Harriet get closer to the woman who had both created and almost destroyed their family.

When Kirsten was out of the house, that night, looking for Becky, was she here, snuggling up with Ian and Harriet? And what about all the other times, over the last weeks – Christ, over the years! The clandestine texts, the possessiveness over his phone. Has it all been Becky? Has he been seeing her illicitly all that time?

And if so, what's his game? To gradually get Kirsten out of the picture? Or to have his cake and eat it – see his daughter, have a comfortable lifestyle, also his young bit on the side? Does he like the sex? She assumes they are sleeping together; it makes sense. Or is he just desperate to keep his name out of the press? Perhaps he's being blackmailed, maybe that's where all their money evaporates to, all of the time?

She doesn't know. It's like a nightmare version of one of the climbs she and Ian used to do. All the time she was going up, she thought Ian had neatly belayed all the ropes she would need for her ascent. But they were loose, illusory, and she's been left hanging, feet dangling in mid-air.

One thing is clear: Ian cannot be trusted to answer a single one of her questions. Why would he give her a straight answer now, after deceiving her for so long? Whatever plan he's working to, he knows what he wants. And he's presumably going to stick to that. If it was Kirsten, Harriet, and Ian as a family unit, he wouldn't have given everything away this evening. His tongue wouldn't have slipped, out of concern for his young lover. He would have absented himself. Anything, but that.

And as for Becky – well, there's no way she can be trusted with anything. Let alone Harriet. It's all too obvious now what Becky's plan had been: get close to Harriet, then lure her away, never let Kirsten see her again. Unless it was also money? Was that where Ian came in, or the letters to psychiatrist Clare? Was Becky going to blackmail her first, with their threats of ruining what she had built up, and give her no option but to hand over her child? And how did Ian think that would play out for him

– Becky wasn't a pupil at his school when he slept with her, and she was over sixteen, but a good prosecution lawyer would still tear him to shreds over his breach of responsibility. And he'd never work as a headteacher, or any kind of teacher, again. His precious school's reputation and his own would be ruined. He can't want all this in the public domain. So what, really, is the game?

Kirsten exhales, and Harriet rolls over in her sleep. Harriet opens her eyes and rubs them briefly.

'It's OK, sweetie. Go back to sleep,' Kirsten tells her, kissing the tip of that wonderful nose. And then a kiss on the cheek as well – so beautiful, so smooth. So innocent.

Harriet wriggles a little, then rolls over away from Kirsten, and goes back to sleep.

Kirsten lays her head on the edge of Harriet's bed. Maybe she needs to stop working through what's in Ian's mind, or Becky's mind, and sort out what's in her own.

She stands and walks to the window of Harriet's room. Ian is still outside. Slipping on her dressing gown, she goes down to the kitchen and opens the French windows onto the garden, but stays inside. She's not going to risk leaving Harriet alone in the house.

Ian runs towards her and makes to come in but she holds up a hand to stop him.

'You knew?' she says.

'Kirsten, I'm so sorry, I should have told you. I just thought—'

'I can't believe you knew! You let me send our daughter to her every day – not just to class but to breakfast club, after-school sessions, and you knew who she was! How could you?'

'She kept going on about telling the press, telling the police. I just thought, if I helped her, played her game, she'd keep quiet, and we could buy some time, until maybe …'

'Until what?' Realising something, she snorts. 'Oh, come on – this isn't about your Ofsted report again, is it? If you've jeopardised our lives for your worry that you're going to be exposed just when your grand project is coming off that's absurd! This is our life, Ian!'

'If you'd let me finish—'

'I don't have to let you do anything!' Kirsten hugs her arms round herself. 'Do you get how much of a betrayal this is? How could you let that woman move ever closer to us, to see our daughter every day? Christ, to think you care more about the kids in that washed-up school than you care—'

'I wanted to wait until you were being more reasonable!' Ian shouts. Kirsten stares at him. He lowers his voice slightly, but the message is the same. 'I've been shielding you from her, but I thought if I bought time you'd come round to letting them have some time together. For everyone's sakes. I figured if we could just avoid a confrontation, keep her happy, we might make it out OK.'

'I thought we were in this together, Ian,' Kirsten whispers. 'I thought we always had each other's backs. Literally. Climbing partners for life, we vowed. Remember?'

'I can't lose everything, Kirsten. I just can't. I've worked too hard. Trust me, we'll find a way—'

'How can I possibly trust you if you keep something like this from me? Are you sleeping with her, is that it?'

'Of course I'm not sleeping with her!'

Kirsten wants to believe him, but why should she?

'Listen,' Ian says. 'I'll get her off our backs, OK? I'll go round now, talk to her.' And he explains what he might say, what he might do. She starts to filter out the individual words, the wheedling tone. She feels like she heard it all before, five years ago, when he swore he wouldn't see Becky again.

She can't know, for sure, that Ian is still on her team. If he ever really has been. That's it, for them, as far as she's concerned. What's their marriage worth if they can't trust each other to guide them through? Instead, Kirsten must focus on her own plan, lay her own guide ropes, secure her own summit: Harriet. And she must do it now, before dawn.

'I can't see you anymore, tonight, Ian,' she tells him. 'Please, go.'

'Go where?'

'Anywhere. To Becky. To a hotel. Just somewhere. Away from here. Away from us.'

And she watches him go. Her husband. The father of her child. The most disappointing man she has ever met.

Chapter 34

BECKY

At 8.30 the morning after parents' evening, Becky is waiting outside Mrs McGee's study. If she can just catch her before she walks to the weekly assembly, then Becky can put her plan into action. It's not the plan she and Ian sat up all night discussing, once he'd given up trying to break into his own home. But for Becky, it's the only real plan.

She's seen how Kirsten looks at Harriet. Kirsten won't be blackmailed out of her child. She won't put her career first, whatever Ian thinks of his basically estranged wife. Sure, Kirsten works too hard, when she should be looking after Harriet. But Becky understands the desperation for having a child. Once acquired, you don't want to lose it. Everything else – cars, nice houses, the best interior design, the best job – might be a status symbol. But the ultimate status symbol is the child. Becky knows Kirsten won't let herself be the person who gives that away.

And so Becky must use her ultimate status symbol: the truth.

Mrs McGee's door opens. But to Becky's surprise, the head-mistress doesn't rush out to assembly. Instead, she looks Becky up and down, and invites her in to the office.

'Now, Ms Robertson. You've obviously anticipated me calling you in like this.'

'I've got something I have to tell you, Mrs McGee. It's about Harriet White. You see—'

'Yes, I know it's about Harriet White. Or rather Kirsten White. Now, nothing is proven yet, and of course you'll get a full hearing by the disciplinary board but—'

'What? What do you mean, disciplinary board? Harriet is my—'

'Dr White has come to me this morning with some very serious allegations about your behaviour. You'll receive a written copy, so it wouldn't be appropriate for me to go into them now. For the meantime, I'm putting you on suspension until further notice.'

'But Harriet White is my daughter!'

Mrs McGee gives a shake of her head. 'That's exactly what Dr White said that you would say. I've heard of these cases of fixation before, but … anyway, I'll be referring you to an occupational health specialist as well, who can speak to you about these delusions.'

'They aren't delusions! I can prove it! Do a DNA test!'

'Ms Robertson, you must understand that I can't run about asking parents to consent to invasive testing for their children. Anything you want to say, you can say to the disciplinary board.'

Becky puts her hands on the edge of Ms McGee's desk, knuckles white. 'You don't understand what she's doing. She's evil! Her husband basically raped me, when I was seventeen! Kidded me into giving Harriet up!'

Mrs McGee whistles softly. 'Listen to yourself, Ms Robertson. First the drunkenness at parents' evening, then Dr White's visit this morning, now this behaviour – do you expect me to believe you? Try to calm it down before the board. Now, I must ask you to leave the premises.'

'I'm not going. I want to see Harriet! She's my daughter.'

'Harriet White no longer attends this school, as of this morning. And judging by your reaction, it seems Dr White is quite wise to have taken that step.'

'Where is she? I want to see Harriet!'

'Ms Robertson, I really hope I'm not going to have to involve the police at this stage, am I? You are to go home, and stay away from Dr White and her family. Is that understood?'

Becky laughs despite herself. 'Stay away from her family? I'm the mother of their child!'

Mrs McGee puts a hand to the phone. 'I'm calling our security desk, who'll escort you out, and then I'm calling the police. I'm concerned about what action you might take. Is that understood?'

Becky pushes back her chair. 'You don't need to. I'm leaving. I won't go anywhere near Dr White or her family.'

Mrs McGee keeps her hand on the phone.

'I don't fancy your future if you do,' Mrs McGee says.

Becky swallows a few times. 'I understand. I over-reacted. I need to calm myself. I've got some meds. Sorry. I'll go home now and wait for the letter about the hearing. OK?'

Mrs McGee nods, and slowly takes her hand away from the phone. 'OK.'

Becky pushes back her chair. 'It's been a pleasure to work at your school,' she says, as she leaves.

And then she runs. She runs through the corridors, out through the school doors, down the steps, into the car park. In the hope that maybe, just maybe, Kirsten has taken her time, is only just leaving. That she will be able to catch up with her, that maybe she'll have Harriet there. That she can confront the 'mother', see the child.

But no. The car park is devoid of mums. Drop-off is over. Harriet is nowhere to be seen.

Becky simply stands there for a long while. The truth should have worked. Why didn't it work? How had Kirsten somehow alluded to the truth but presented it all as lies? Becky didn't know what she had come up with. But she could imagine. Poor deranged Miriam, she would have said, with her fixations on my child. She obviously needs help, but my child's safety can't be compromised.

The gall of it. But it means nothing – Becky will get that test done. She'll prove her parenthood.

Becky closes her eyes. But how? Mrs McGee was right. Kirsten is the one recognised as the mother. She'd have to consent on Harriet's behalf, and of course, she won't. The only way is a court order. And what judge is going to give her that – without some long drawn-out, costly court battle? There's no adoption paper-work to fall back on – the birth and all visits were done at home, on a cash-in-hand basis, through a private network of midwives and doulas, and Kirsten had managed to get her name on the birth certificate. So that Becky wasn't 'shackled' by the child, had been the argument at the time. How naïve she had been.

Her family might vouch for her version of events. But would they support her having custody of Harriet? Her stupid sister, the boring one, Helen, will probably speak up against her, after that incident years ago, with her niece. But it was such a difficult time. She'd just found out she was pregnant. Her sister's baby was terrifying and wonderful to her in equal measures. So she hadn't been at her best in that moment, in that room. She's definitely safe to look after children now. Her child.

She has to see what the disciplinary letter says. She has to challenge every last allegation. And she has to find out where Kirsten is now schooling Harriet. Stay away from Dr White's family? Of course she will. But to Becky, that means Kirsten's mother, father, sister, whoever else there is. Harriet is not part of Kirsten's family. She is part of Becky's family. So Becky will get as close as she likes. As close as she can.

Chapter 35

KIRSTEN

'Are you sure you don't want to eat anything? Not even some cake?'

Harriet shakes her head fiercely.

Kirsten sighs, and brings her head back out from under the desk. Most children would be delighted at being able to miss school and sit with Mummy at work, being offered cake. Perhaps it lost its appeal on the first day. Now, by day three, Harriet must quite rightly be wondering what is going on, and she's demanding to see her friends. Also, apparently they'd been due to make and paint clay ships this week, for some project or other. When Kirsten had offered to send Jess out to buy some play dough for boat making, Harriet had told Kirsten dismissively that 'Play dough's for kids.' Right. Of course.

This probably wasn't exactly what Mrs McGee had in mind when Kirsten told her that Harriet would be home-schooled for the foreseeable future. It also probably wasn't what her patients had in mind when they had booked an appointment – a bored five-year-old staring out from under a desk as they went through the intimate details of their medical history. The theory had been that if the desk was angled correctly, patients couldn't see Harriet underneath it, and Harriet could sit there reading or doing maths puzzles. Harriet, however, had not bought into this scheme.

Kirsten knew she'd have to do something else. At some point, the local authorities were going to want to check out her arrangements for home-schooling Harriet. And at some point, patients would get onto comment boards that this was a doctor who couldn't even offer a private consultation, as there was a surprise child staring out from under the desk.

But what else was she meant to do? It wouldn't be for long. Kirsten's plans didn't stop here. In the interim, though, she couldn't face the idea of letting Harriet play in the surgery reception, under the half-watchful eye of Jess. All it took was for Jess to be distracted on the phone, or to pop to the loo, and Becky could appear and snatch Harriet away. You wouldn't leave your laptop unattended in a doctor's waiting room, so why your child?

Taking her out of school and bringing her to work had seemed the only option, though, that sleepless night after the parents' evening. Attack is the best form of defence, right? And so, she had turned up at Mrs McGee's office at 7.45 a.m., with a bleary-eyed Harriet, and explained that matters couldn't go on. She'd explained about the impromptu, invasive weekend visit Ms Robertson had made (true), about the giving of inappropriate gifts (true – Kirsten had finally understood the 'Miss Honey' reference Becky had written in the front of *Matilda*), about the breakfast club that seemed to be centred around Harriet's need (true), and, of course, the threats and allegations (less true, but Kirsten had needed something to make Ms Robertson seem mad rather than just keen). And of course, Kirsten had explained, only just keeping her sobs at bay, it had all made sense to her when she saw Ms Robertson's chaotic behaviour at the parents' evening.

'Chaotic?' Mrs McGee had asked her.

'Well, I hadn't liked to say – but *drunk*. She was *drunk* and couldn't sit down with us. I'm convinced she's got the hots for my husband, and has somehow got it into her head that Harriet should be her own child. If anything were to happen to Harriet at the school ...'

And of course, then Mrs McGee couldn't take the risk. Particularly when Kirsten had made it clear that she would feel compelled to tell the other mums about what was going on, unless the school took decisive action because, as Kirsten said, wide-eyed: 'She just couldn't let them believe their children would be safe at the school.'

Mrs McGee had confirmed that Ms Robertson would be suspended with immediate effect while they looked into the allegations.

Obviously, Kirsten had explained, she couldn't leave Harriet at the school after that. Ms Robertson would know where to find Harriet, and so Harriet wouldn't be safe. Home-schooling would be the only possible option for a while. Mrs McGee had recommended another school in the group. But surely Ms Robertson would look there? Or (and Kirsten didn't tell Mrs McGee that) even if she didn't, Ian would, if Becky put him up to it. He knew how these things worked, and before Kirsten knew it, he'd have turned up and whisked Harriet away.

After the meeting with the headmistress, Kirsten wanted to go back home and hide with Harriet under the bedclothes. Wouldn't it be lovely if they could just have a duvet day, the pair of them, lazy and safe together? But being a grown-up isn't about that. You have to fight on, go to work, show your child how to face the world. Plus Kirsten didn't want to risk an encounter with Ian or Becky. True, they could turn up at the surgery. But if Kirsten's own attempts at stalking were any guide, the home of the person you were watching was the most obvious first stop.

And so, when it came to the last patient of the day – a sad case, most likely early onset Alzheimer's, which left her ruffled about how much could so quickly be taken away from anyone – Kirsten was reluctant to leave. She wondered if they could stay in a hotel for the night. But no. There was preparation to be done. And she'd taken every step she could to make it safe, working round the clock these last few days. A locksmith to change the locks – it would stop Ian temporarily, particularly if he didn't have proof of address on him to get them changed again. New surveillance lights outside, so she'd be able to see the outside of the house properly as they approached. A taxi would take them right to the door; she'd left the car at home, as a decoy. If they could just get from the taxi to the house, safely inside, chain and bolt it, they'd be OK. Until the next morning.

And then in just two more days, everything would change.

Chapter 36

BECKY

Anger propelling her legs forward, Becky strides from Angel tube to Kirsten's house. Phrases from the letter inviting her to a disciplinary board play through her mind.

'Threats to the security of Dr White and her child.'

Did they include any written evidence of these so-called threats? Of course not. It was all Kirsten's word against hers. And what a good word it appeared to be – a nice wealthy parent, a doctor no less, without apparent reason for fabrication. Except the whole thing was a fabrication.

'Unprovoked drunken declamations at parents' evening.'

Unprovoked? Hardly. The things Kirsten had done. Becky wanted the disciplinary hearing to be able to see back to her as a vulnerable seventeen-year-old. How she'd been the morning after her 'friends' had drugged her into sleeping with the drama tutor. How horrified she'd been when she'd discovered she was pregnant. How she had tried to get her parents' help in making the right decision, but time had ticked on, and they hadn't helped her, had done quite the opposite, leaving her no choice but to go through with the birth. How Kirsten had callously misrepresented the picture to her psychiatrist friend, so that Becky felt she had no option but to give up her daughter.

But the reaction of Mrs McGee had shown Becky that she didn't have the tools right now to stand up to Kirsten. Not without Ian's testimony, anyway. The letter had invited character witnesses. Ian wouldn't admit it. Of course he wouldn't. Ted, maybe? She would call him later. But he'd known her, what, three months? Even if he did have the hots for her, he wasn't going to vouch for what sounded, even to her ears, like shades of crazy.

So she was going to talk to Kirsten. Kirsten wanted her out of Harriet's life, for ever. And Becky wanted the same for Kirsten.

Finally arriving outside Kirsten's house, Becky stops with amazement. There are lorries and packing crates everywhere. Kirsten must be running away! She's escaping with Harriet, and who knows where she's taking her!

If Kirsten takes Harriet away, Becky might never see her daughter again! That is not a possible outcome.

Becky jogs up to the house. The front door is shut. She'd ring the bell, but Kirsten won't let her in. Instead Becky scouts round, looking for a more subtle opening. Windows all shut. But what's that? Men with packing crates coming through the back gate. She runs up to it, then slows, trying to look relaxed.

'Let me hold that gate for you,' she says, like she has some proprietary right to do so.

'Oh, thanks, love,' says the removal man, barrelling through with a box.

Once he's gone, Becky slips through the gate, and quietly, quietly pads into the garden.

There's Harriet! At first, Becky thinks her daughter is alone. There, in the middle of the garden, playing with a watering can. Becky's about to rush up to her, when there's a little 'ahem' from the corner of the garden. Becky turns, expecting to see Kirsten. Instead, it's a woman she doesn't recognise.

'I'm Yvette,' says the woman. 'I live next door.'

'I'm—' begins Becky.

'I know who you are,' Yvette says, softly.

Shit. Perhaps Becky should just run now. Try a different tactic, later.

But then the woman says something else. 'I think Harriet has been getting bored, waiting for her mummy. It's not right. She's due a little walk.'

For a moment, Becky can't quite understand what this Yvette woman is getting at. Then Yvette nods ever so slightly in the direction of the gate. Becky gives her a questioning look. Yvette nods at her.

Becky takes a deep breath, then walks up to Harriet and takes her hand.

Chapter 37

KIRSTEN

Amidst all the chaos, Kirsten would look to any observer like an oasis of calm. Around her are half-filled packing crates, workmen topping them up with long-loved items, briskly wrapped in tissue paper.

But Kirsten is not calm. Kirsten is holding a letter. A letter that dropped oh-so-casually onto the doormat this morning. A stiff envelope, a formal crest. With a name so convoluted that it must be a law firm's. It wasn't a letter that Kirsten could ignore or put aside for later. So, hurriedly, she'd opened it. Skim-read it. Then she'd had to sit down.

Dear Dr White, the letter said.

> *We act for Dr Clare Sergeant in the matter of antenatal advice given at your request five years ago.*
> *Our client has received the enclosed threatening letter from the individual in respect of whom you procured the advice. She regards its contents as defamatory and, in conjunction*

with the other letter she received recently, as amounting to criminal harassment. She wishes to take steps to prevent further publication. In our client's view, the individual is under your control, and must be regarded as acting as your agent in these matters. If you are not able to provide the necessary assurance that the individual will not write more letters such as this, or otherwise spread the defamatory content, and cease harassing our client, then (without further recourse to you) our client reserves the right to set the matter straight in the public domain, including your involvement.

We trust that we will hear from you shortly.

Kirsten had hardly dared to flick over to the enclosure, but she knew she had to.

It was another letter from the Croydon address. From Becky. And it was much more stark than the previous one.

Dear Dr Sergeant,

Perhaps I didn't make myself clear in my last letter.

When you agreed with your friend Kirsten White to make up the prognosis that I had post-natal depression and would be a danger to my baby, and arranged to have my daughter taken away from me, you were in breach of so much more than trust. You betrayed your Hippocratic oath, you were criminally negligent, and I can't believe you are still allowed to call yourself a doctor. I am going to report what you did to the medical authorities and to the press, and I hope you are struck off and put in prison. I hope that Kirsten White will join you there. You both deserve to be ruined.

UNLESS, that is, you are able to persuade Kirsten that she must give me back my daughter. You have seventy-two hours,

or I am going public with this. Get my girl back to me, and
none of this has to come out – your career and your liberty
will be safe. The choice is yours.

Very sincerely,
Becky

Kirsten sits, still staring at the letter. It's all going to come out then, regardless of what she does. She thought she had it all figured out: stick the house on the market, rent it out before it sells, get all their stuff stashed in storage, and head up north with Harriet to a caravan site. Live some kind of eco-existence before settling somewhere more permanent. It's amazing how quickly you can clear out when you throw money at a problem.

But after seeing this letter, maybe she needs to go further. Whether it's Clare or Becky who first breaks the story, then Kirsten, Ian and Harriet's pictures are going to be all over the news. There'll be people looking for them. And Harriet is so pretty, and Kirsten knows she herself is not unattractive – people will notice them. England is too small. She needs to go abroad. They need to get tickets to France or, ideally, somewhere outside Europe that doesn't need a visa. Somewhere not hugely swamped with international newspapers. She gets out her phone, begins Googling destinations. That's stupid, though. She should just take Harriet to the airport, see what flights they can get. And go.

Resolved, she gets to her feet. Thank God for Yvette looking after Harriet while this fresh new crisis broke. She'd offered, this morning, when she saw all the removal men, to lend a hand.

Kirsten wonders, as she walks through the hall to the kitchen, whether she should pack sundresses for herself and Harriet, if they end up flying to somewhere with winter sun. There's a sweet blue cotton one with parrots on, with a matching straw boater, that Harriet looks so pretty in. She can just visualise Harriet's beautiful face in it now.

She steps out into the back garden, expecting to see that same beautiful face.

But there's no Harriet. She scans the garden again. No Harriet. Just Yvette, sitting snoozing in a chair.

Chapter 38

BECKY

'Isn't this an adventure?' Becky asks Harriet, for perhaps the third time.

Harriet nods gamely. But her pace is slowing. Becky holds her hand more tightly, and picks up her own pace, scanning the horizon for taxis. If they get the tube, CCTV footage will show them for all to see – when the kidnap investigations begin. Finally, here it is, the outing with Harriet that she'd imagined. And look how good Harriet is being! Just like Becky had imagined she would be. Now's probably not the moment to post on Facebook, much as she'd like to. She'd dreamt of putting mother and daughter posts up, all the time she was looking at the posts her sister had made of the niece Becky doesn't see.

'Help me try and spot a taxi, OK, Harriet?' she says.

'Where are we going?' Harriet asks.

'It's a surprise,' Becky says. By which she means she doesn't know. She has until she finds a taxi to come up with a plan. They can't go home – it's the first place Kirsten will have the police look. St Pancras, maybe. Lots of trains go from there. To France, even. Except Becky doesn't have her passport. Or Harriet's. Shit.

Or the money. They'd last two days, tops. Get some wired from Ian? More guilt money. Or a ransom, she supposes. But they'd be traced. Ian will be traced.

She could hire a car. If she could drive.

Shit.

'There's a taxi!' Harriet shouts.

'Great,' Becky says, reluctantly sticking out her hand.

The driver pulls up along the side of the road. 'Hop in,' she tells Becky.

'Are we going to school?' Harriet asks once they're in.

'Ha, she's keen, isn't she?' The taxi driver laughs. 'School on a Saturday! Where can I take you two lovelies?'

'Victoria station,' Becky blurts out.

'Coach or train?' the driver asks.

They were in the same place, surely? Why must she keep making all these decisions?

'Um, coach,' she said. Because that's what women do, in all the films, don't they, when they want to disappear? They get a coach. After having dyed or cropped their hair, and bought a baseball cap. Fine, she and Harriet can get hats too. Except in those movies, women are travelling across America. Which is big. And they have a wad of cash in their backpack, or down their bras. So even if you know, plot wise, that it's going to be stolen from them, at least they start out with it. Oh, and importantly – they don't have a child in tow. Usually.

'Are we going to find Daddy?' Harriet asks.

'Not just yet, sweetie.' Becky says. 'We're playing Miss Honey and Matilda today.'

Harriet seems to accept this, sitting back further on her seat. But then: 'Is Mummy going to come and play it with us?'

This isn't the moment to say: actually, Harriet, I'm your mummy. Becky doesn't know when that moment will come, but it's not in the back of a taxi, where the driver can hear their every word. Instead, Becky endures the silent heartbreak.

'No, sweetie. It's just me and you. That's how the game works.'

'We can see Mummy later,' Harriet says, nodding sagely.

Becky nods along. Because Harriet is right. It's just not the same 'Mummy' that she's thinking about.

Chapter 39

KIRSTEN

'Yvette! Yvette!'

Kirsten is shaking her but she doesn't seem to understand the emergency. Very slowly, her eyes open. Then she stretches and yawns.

'How's it going?' is the first thing she says, as if this is a lazy Sunday afternoon, and cat-napping in the garden was part of their plans.

'Where's Harriet?'

'Ah, Harriet.'

'Yes, Harriet, my daughter, who you're meant to be looking after!' Kirsten can hear her voice getting high, histrionic. But so what? She'd left Yvette in charge!

'She must still be on her walk.'

'What do you mean, on her walk? She's five; you've just let her go for a walk? Shit!' Kirsten runs to the gate. 'How long ago did she leave? Did she say where she was going?' Kirsten's already out the other side of the gate before Yvette can even answer. She runs down to the street, looks left and right, but there's no sign of Harriet.

'Shit!' she says again, and runs back into the garden.

Yvette has got up from her chair.

'You go one way, I'll go the other,' Kirsten yells at her. She should never have left Harriet alone, never have trusted Yvette with her child. All for that stupid letter! And the stupid master plan!

'Kirsten,' Yvette says, quietly.

There's something in her tone that makes Kirsten stop dead.

'Yes?' she says.

'Harriet wasn't alone.'

There's a beat. The outer world is silent. In Kirsten's head, there's a storm of noise, names flying around.

'What do you mean? Who was she with?'

'She was with her mother.'

Kirsten stands and stares at Yvette.

'I'm her mother,' Kirsten says.

'No,' Yvette says, calmly. 'Her real mother.'

Kirsten slaps Yvette in the face.

Yvette stands there impassively.

'How dare you?' Kirsten shouts. Her voice cracks. She finds herself holding Yvette's shoulders, shaking them. 'How dare you?'

Eventually she becomes aware of her grip slipping, of Yvette's arm on her shoulder, of Yvette guiding her to the garden chair on which she was recently 'dozing'.

'How did you know?' Kirsten asks Yvette, her voice flat.

'I told you, remember? I know lots of things.'

'Yes, but how? And what, what do you know?'

'I know that when my friend sold me the house next door, she told me that the walls between the houses are not so thick that they'll disguise the worst marital arguments. That sometimes, you hear things, think they can't be true, move on with your life. But then she told me that you'd gone from not pregnant to suddenly very pregnant. When you came out of the house, that is. Yet on occasion, when she came to the door, and glimpsed you in the living room before you answered, you didn't look so pregnant at all. She had a theory. When I saw Ian with that young woman, that cemented it. And, you know, you get certain vibes from men who aren't always faithful. So as I say: Harriet has gone for a walk with her mother.'

For a time, Kirsten has no words. They'd thought they were so clever, Ian and Kirsten. That no one knew. No one apart from Clare. Or Kirsten's sister, Nina. Kirsten had confessed one evening when she couldn't hold the secret in any longer, when she'd needed to bitch about Ian, to share her despair but the possible joy of having a child. Nina had told her in no uncertain terms that she was doing the wrong thing: that she should leave Ian, and let the young mother make her own decisions about the child. Yes, even if it meant the child temporarily being put into social care. Kirsten shouldn't make the bonds, she'd do herself too much damage.

They hadn't seen each other since – nor had Kirsten been allowed to visit her niece.

And yet, here was her next-door neighbour, who had apparently inherited knowledge from the previous neighbour. All along, she'd known. Those times she'd dropped Harriet at school. Had she just been waiting, then, for her chance to 'do good', to reunite mother and child?

The anger comes back to Kirsten. And the fear.

'But what were you possibly thinking, letting Becky take her?'

'They'll be back soon,' Yvette says.

'No, no they won't.' Kirsten is on her feet again.

'They should have whatever time they need, Kirsten. You have, after all. It's not right, Kirsten.'

'That doesn't give you the entitlement to muscle in and sort things out yourself! We don't know anything about Becky. She might be unstable; we might lose Harriet for good!'

'They will come back. It's only been, what ten, twenty minutes?' Yvette looks at her watch. 'OK, maybe thirty minutes.' Her poise falters slightly. 'But maybe they just went to get a milkshake, or something?'

Kirsten shakes her head. 'She's taken her. Christ! OK, we need to call police, social services, the news – shit, who else do you tell? Who looks for children?'

Yvette uses her low, quiet tone again. 'And tell them what, Kirsten?'

'That my child's been kidnapped!' Kirsten shouts.

But she knows exactly what Yvette means. She can't tell the police anything, without telling them everything.

The only person she can call right now is Ian. He must know something. He must.

Chapter 40

BECKY

'Come on, keep your hat on, Harriet. It's part of the adventure!' Becky whispers to Harriet. She doesn't want to draw the other coach passengers' attention to the hat – that's not the point. It's the *opposite* of the point.

'But I don't like it!' Harriet protests.

Becky can't blame her. It's a drab, black beanie hat, grabbed with haste from a food and wine store where Becky had kept her head down and the transaction short.

'Look, I've got one too!' Becky says. 'Matching hats! Awesome, right?'

Harriet goes back to staring out the window.

It's a long way to Bristol.

But it's the only place Becky can think of to go. It's where her sister lives. Julia. The cool one, without children. Even if they can't stay with her, she'll have an idea of where to put them, right?

Becky doesn't know if it's safe to phone her, or even text her. If Kirsten's gone to the police, surely they'll have some whizzy way to put a track on the phone. It's best just to turn up on the doorstep, plead asylum. Becky knows it's one of the first places the police will look. But she just needs to be there for a night, get some sanity from her sister, then move on. Maybe her sister is good with kids. Maybe that's why she was so enraged when Becky gave hers up.

'The wheels on the bus go round and round,' Becky sings quietly to Harriet.

'They don't,' Harriet retorts. 'It's a coach, not a bus. You said.'

True, true, she had said that.

'It's the same sort of thing though, isn't it? They're from the same family.' *And by the way, so are we*, Becky wants to add. How is she going to tell her? When? Maybe when they get to Julia's place.

Harriet shrugs.

Why isn't it this difficult at school? Harriet always seems golden there, like she can do no wrong. That's the child Becky has daydreamed about being with. Not this sulky and difficult person.

Still, that's a good thing, right – she's getting to know her child properly. With all her imperfections. No, imperfections is the wrong word. Harriet is perfect. Of course she is. All her *idiosyncrasies*. Being a proper mother, not just admiring Harriet from afar.

'I'm hungry,' announces Harriet.

Becky brightens. She'd thought of this, at least. Proudly, she pulls out of her bag the two tortilla wraps she'd bought at the food and wine store, along with the hats.

Harriet looks at them and her little lips curl slightly.

'Mummy said we could have turkey dinosaurs for lunch.'

She would, wouldn't she – just the kind of trashy food that a woman like Kirsten, too busy to cook, would foist upon her daughter. Not that the tortillas are much better. But they're on the run. Different rules apply.

'We don't have any turkey dinosaurs, I'm afraid, sweetie. You'll just have to get some later. Maybe Auntie Julia will have some.'

'I don't have an Auntie Julia. And I want some turkey dinosaurs!'

Harriet's lower lip is starting to quiver, and her voice is rising higher. Becky really wishes she'd forgotten the healthy eating thing and just bought some crisps. Children like crisps, right?

'When can we get some proper food?' Harriet demands.

Becky suspects that 'in about two hours, if the traffic is good' isn't the kind of answer that Harriet's after. While she's thinking of what to say, a man's head appears between the seats in front of them.

'I couldn't help overhearing the little lady,' he says in a heavy Scottish accent. 'Would cake count as "proper food", by any chance?'

He holds up a chocolate muffin.

It's on the tip of Becky's tongue to say that they can't possibly accept food from strangers, but Harriet is too quick for her.

'Cake!' she shouts in glee.

The man smiles widely and passes the muffin over the seat.

'Are you sure?' Becky asks.

But if he isn't, it's too late, as most of the cake seems to already be in Harriet's mouth or spread over her face.

'Aye, I'm sure. I could do wi' losing a little weight, anyways!'

'It's very kind of you,' Becky says. 'Thank you.' Even though, she is, of course worrying that (a) this man might be a paedophile who will later try and lure her child away and (b) this incident means that he will remember them if later quizzed about it.

But nothing now is worrying Harriet at all, it seems. Soon, the bus/coach dichotomy is forgotten, and Harriet is happily singing about wheels going round. She repays the kindness of the man in front by kicking the back of his seat repeatedly.

Maybe Becky has misjudged Kirsten ever so slightly. Maybe processed food and sugar do have their uses.

That's the only thing Becky is going to take any kind of guidance on from Kirsten, though. Becky knows she has it in her to be a better mother than Kirsten has even been. For a start, a biological entitlement to it. And so, if Becky has her way, Kirsten isn't going to see Harriet again.

Chapter 41

KIRSTEN

Kirsten slides into the car seat next to Ian. She takes in his appearance, and sees her own shock mirrored on his face. Yes, she probably looks like shit – his (ex?) lover has stolen her child. But he looks pretty awful too. Chin stubbly, eyes baggy, collar awry. She can't imagine that going down well with Ofsted. The car isn't in much better condition either. There's a sleeping bag on the back seat, covered with random bits of paper. Ofsted work, presumably. It doesn't cease just because Harriet has gone.

Kirsten sees him following her gaze.

'We're so nearly there,' he says, his voice rasping. Is that whisky on his breath? 'The final inspection is coming up. If I can just—'

'Our daughter, Ian,' Kirsten says gently.

'Yes, of course.' He nods, but Kirsten senses his brain isn't really there. It's like she's communicating with someone on the other side of a precipice. 'I don't know anything,' he says.

'You must do,' Kirsten says.

It's a reprise of the conversation on the phone. But Kirsten thought if she could put aside her sense of betrayal, for just a few minutes, look Ian in the eye, she'd be able to deduce whether Ian was telling the truth.

'We can go to her flat, if you like,' Ian volunteers. 'Kirsten, I want to help, but—'

'But how would we get into her flat?' Kirsten asks, voice sharp. Is he sleeping with her, after all?

'I'm sort of the landlord,' he says. 'I've got keys.'

What that probably means is that their money – her money – has been funding Becky's accommodation for years. Ian had said he wanted to avoid confrontation with her but what an expensive – and risky – way of doing it! Keep your enemies closer and closer, so that they move gradually nearer to you, in a flat you pay for yourself … this could so easily descend into a marital spat, but now is not the time. Kirsten's not even sure if there's a marriage left to spat about. 'If you've got the keys to her flat, why not go and live there?' she asks, looking round the car again.

Ian looks down at his hands. 'I thought about it. Tried it, even. But when I got there, it seemed too much of a transgression. After everything. I'm responsible, Kirsten. For all of it.'

And that is whisky on his breath. Because he takes another swig of it now.

Kirsten takes the bottle from him and puts it in the back seat. 'You're not responsible, Ian. Your drink was spiked.'

'I was physically responsible, and she was in my care. I just need to prove I can be better, that I'm not that man; if I can just buy a bit more time, stop it coming out before we get the school sorted, there's a chance people will see, understand, I'm not like that, I'm better, I'm …' He trails off, hand over his face. Sobbing.

Kirsten puts a hand on his shoulder.

'Give me the car keys,' she says gently. She doesn't want to see her husband like this. But she wants to find her daughter more.

When they get to the flat, Kirsten sees that, more likely than not, Becky didn't have a plan. In the bathroom, there's a tooth-brush in a holder by the sink, a dressing gown slung over the side of the bath. It's not the flat of someone who's taken everything and fled. But the main thing is – there's no sign of Harriet. No Frozen kiddy toothbrush or lurid toothpaste, no Minnie Mouse flannel, like at home.

Kirsten wipes away a tear. This can't be happening.

In the main living space – the cramped sitting room with adjoining kitchenette – there's nothing given away either. Some exercise books and other work-type papers slung in a corner. Unwashed coffee cups. More of them over in the kitchen. There probably isn't a dishwasher. The whole place has a stale, hopeless air. It's no place for her child.

'When did you last talk to Becky?' Kirsten asks, again.

'This morning, I told you,' Ian says. 'She phoned me. She said she got a letter from the school, then said she was going out. Over to our house.'

Kirsten ignores the 'our'. There's nothing for Ian there at the moment.

'What did she say she was going to do when she got there?'

Ian shrugs. 'I don't know. Talk to you. Try to see Harriet. Something.'

Kirsten stares at him. 'For Christ's sake, Ian – do you get how important this is? She's run off with our child!'

'She's run off with her child.'

'Why are you being so black and white, and biological about this? We've been bringing Harriet up for five years. And who knows what Becky is planning!'

'She won't try to harm her, if that's what you mean.'

'You can't know that! And what do you mean by "harm"? Imagine how Harriet must be feeling, swept away like this. She must be terrified!'

Ian puts his hands up in front of him, an old gesture of backing down. 'OK. OK, you're right,' he says.

'And I've had a letter from Clare's lawyers, in case you care, threatening to go public after Becky wrote to Clare again.

Apparently Becky's in our control – if we don't contain her, Clare's going public. With everything. And if she doesn't, then apparently Becky will. Unless we give up Harriet.'

Kirsten watches as Ian runs a hand through his hair. Does that mean he cares? She can't tell anymore.

'And you're still not willing to compromise?' he asks her.

She ignores the question.

'Where would she go?' Kirsten asks him. 'Come on, you must know something about her! Any friends, any family, that she'd run to.'

Ian wrinkles his nose. 'They're mostly estranged, I think.'

'Why, what's she done to them?'

Ian looks at his hands. 'I think it's mostly about what we've done to them.'

'I've done nothing to anyone,' Kirsten says.

'You still believe that?' Ian asks.

Kirsten looks out the window, draws in the desire to yell at Ian. She's about to start again when Ian pipes up with: 'Can't you just give them some time together? It might contain this whole business. Becky might calm down a bit, once she's spent some time with Harriet. She might stop this line about talking to the press and deal with it calmly.'

The man just finds it impossible to think about anything but himself, and that school, his name, his reputation, Kirsten realises. It's become his fixation, just like keeping Harriet safe has been hers.

Kirsten shakes her head. She can barely control the rage now. '"This whole business"?' she parrots back at him scornfully. 'Ian. This is about Harriet. A person. Not your career. A small girl's life. Harriet is not safe. She's with a woman who you've just admitted isn't calm, apparently has no plan, but has kidnapped Harriet. If we leave Becky to do that, and the press gets hold of it, we're in a worse position – apparently negligently not giving a shit about our child. And if something, God forbid, happens to Harriet, beyond whatever she's already going through, even if your little secret doesn't come out, we will have to live with that for ever. Do you see that? Do you get it on any level?'

Ian begins to nod to himself.

'Right,' Kirsten says. 'Can you think about where the family live, have a look round, try to figure out which of them she might realistically contact?'

Ian nods. 'Her sister Julia's the most likely bet; she's slightly less estranged from that one. She lives in Bristol, I think.'

'Finally – thank you! Find out where she lives. Get onto her. I'm going to talk to the school. For all they know, this is their fault. They'd be shitting themselves, if they knew – it will ruin them, one of their teachers, kidnapping a student.'

Ian nods, but he has a distant look in his eyes.

'We have a plan then, do we?' Kirsten asks him. She's itching to get to the school, but she wants to know first that he's actually going to do something.

'Just one last thing,' Ian says.

'What?' snaps Kirsten.

'If I find Becky, what do you want me to do with her?' he asks.

Kirsten pauses. As much as she is furious with Ian at the moment, knows so little of his secret life, she detects a depth to his question.

'What do you mean?' she asks.

'You know what I mean,' he says, quietly. 'What do you want me to do with her?'

Kirsten swallows. So. Ian has been thinking the same thing Kirsten thought not long ago. That their life would be much simpler without Becky in it.

But she's not going to say that out loud to Ian. For all she knows, he might be recording this. His own leverage, for once.

'I think …' she says. 'I think you should do whatever seems

201

best at the time to get Harriet back to me safely. And to keep her with me.'

Ian nods. 'Fine.' And then he goes to the kitchen, opens the drawer, and takes out a knife. 'I'll be sure to take this, then.'

Chapter 42

BECKY

'Becky! Jesus, what a surprise, what are you—'

Julia stands on her doorstep, staring at Becky and Harriet. She's wearing a tight blue sequined dress, eye liner pen in hand.

Harriet bursts into tears. 'I want my mummy!'

'Hi, Julia,' Becky says.

Julia shakes her head. 'Shit, Becky! I don't know what you're doing. But come in.'

The hallway to Julia's house is full. Running shoes, party shoes, bags, a bike. For some reason, a 'Men at Work' road works sign – as in a real one, from a road. And now, a crying child and a long-lost sister.

'What's happening, Becky? Why didn't you call to say you were coming?'

'I didn't know if it was safe,' Becky says. Her words feel stupid, melodramatic. She tries to hug Harriet to her, but she won't yield.

'Why wouldn't it be safe? Becky, who's the child?'

Julia bends down to Harriet. 'Hey, kiddo. What's your name?'

Harriet keeps crying.

'Can't you guess?' asks Becky.

Julia's jaw slackens. 'Becky, really? Shit. What's been going on? I'm so sorry, I had no idea you were living together, that you had her back. That's amazing! You should have told me!'

Becky would love for her sister to believe this alternate reality. That Becky somehow officially 'had Harriet back'.

But it's a fairy story. And it will only take thirty seconds for Julia's brain to catch up – that a girl wailing for her mummy isn't consistent with Becky being in maternal bliss. Or, indeed, in Bristol.

There, Julia's face is clouding over.

'I don't totally have her back,' Becky admits. 'But I'm working on it.'

Harriet cuts off whatever Julia was going to say in reaction by making a bid for freedom through the still-open door.

'Harriet!' Becky shouts. 'Come back, sweetie!' She grabs Harriet's cardigan, and pulls her back through the door, shutting it behind them. She puts on the chain. Harriet is in proper sob mode, more like a toddler than a child in reception year. Snot is streaming unchecked down her face, and her lashes are stuck together with tears. Becky loves her and hates her. She just wants her to stop crying. Like she had with her niece, all those years ago.

'OK, look, whatever's going on, we have to calm this child down, OK?' Julia says. 'Or we'll have all the neighbours calling the police, if they're not already following you.'

Becky sees the quick look Julia flashes at her, assessing whether the police might already be about to turn up. Becky looks away.

'Shit, Becky! Right, what can we do for you, young Harriet?'

Julia bends down to Harriet and talks to her with the practised ease of one used to talking to young children. She must be a good auntie to her other niece, daughter of the boring (conventional) sister Becky still isn't allowed to see.

'She likes cake,' Becky says. Maybe that will solve everything this time too.

'Um, the only brownies I have are ones I wouldn't recommend you share with a child,' Julia confesses. 'Some special ingredients.'

Becky rolls her eyes. Julia – still the party animal.

'Harriet, do you want to watch something?' Julia asks.

There's a slight break in the crying.

'Come on.' Julia holds out her hand. Harriet takes it, scuttling away from Becky.

Becky follows Julia into the living room. It smells musky, incensey, but it's not dingy – there are bold Warhol-style prints on the walls, bright pink throws on the sofas. The walls are lined with books, but also eclectic objects – a silver teapot, a waving Chinese 'lucky cat', and what looks like a bong. Julia lives life. Without her, Becky realises sadly. There's no evidence of another sister or niece-shaped gap here.

'Right, so, let's see what I've got,' Julia says. 'How about *Wizard of Oz*? Do you like that?' Julia looks up at Becky. 'Does she like that?'

Becky can't bring herself to admit that she doesn't have any idea what Harriet likes.

'That'll be great,' she says. 'Thanks, Julia.'

Julia bends down and puts the DVD into the player. She pats the sofa, and Harriet climbs up, wiping her nose on the throw. Julia doesn't seem to mind, and she ruffles Harriet's hair.

'There you go, kiddo. You enjoy that, while me and Becky chat, OK?'

While Dorothy whirls away from the home she loves ('Shit, I'd forgotten about that bit – do you want me to fast forward?' Julia asks), Becky and Julia sit close on the other sofa.

'So, what's going on?' Julia asks in a murmur.

'The woman who's been looking after her—' Becky starts.

'What, the teacher's wife? Christ, are they still together?'

'Yes and sort of yes – they're still married, anyway. She wouldn't let me see Harriet.'

'Bitch.'

'Exactly. She wouldn't let me see her so—'

'Wait, Becky, sorry – backtrack. How have you even been? You were ill, when we last spoke. I'm so sorry I haven't been in touch. I was just so angry. My lovely pretty geek of a sister, with so much promise, just thrown away.'

'I didn't do the throwing. My drink was spiked.'

'I guess I just didn't fully believe that,' Julia says. She looks embarrassed. 'And I was furious with you for giving the baby away. It seemed so wrong. It *was* so wrong.'

'I didn't have a choice there either,' Becky says.

'Sure you didn't,' says Julia, clearly still sceptical.

'I didn't,' Becky says. 'I was bullied into it, in a way that seemed legitimate. But now I have a choice, and I'm making it. I've made it.'

'I had a choice too,' Julia says. 'And I made the wrong one. I should have been there for you. I'm sorry.'

Becky looks at Julia, her gorgeous curly brown hair, her lively green eyes, the usually jovial slim face, now serious. She wants her back in her life.

'Apology accepted,' she says, even though the pain will probably linger for ever. They share a quick, tight hug.

'So, you were ill, I was a shit, you didn't get to see your child – does that bring us up to date?' Julia asks.

'Pretty much,' Becky says. 'I got a job teaching in Harriet's school.'

'Sneaky. And lucky,' Julia says.

'I know, it was a dream come true. Ian helped me with references.'

'Ian's the bastard, right?' Julia asks.

'Ian's the father,' Becky says.

'Like I said. The bastard. Carry on.'

'I didn't mean to do anything; I just wanted to be close to her. But I saw that she wasn't being looked after properly. I knew we had to be back together, so I tried to make Kirsten—'

'The wicked witch?'

On the TV, the bright green Wicked Witch of the West is bullying Dorothy.

'I'd go for something stronger, rhyming with it, but yes, that's right.'

'So you arrive like good witch Glinda in your bubble, try to ask for Harriet back …'

'And they say no. Pretty much. Kirsten got freaked out when she realised I was Harriet's teacher and also her, you know,' Becky doesn't want to say 'mother', in case Harriet is listening. It shouldn't be the way she finds out.

Julia nods.

'So she was trying to run away with Harriet. I freaked out, and thought I'd never see her again – and yeah, I kind of …'

'Kidnapped her?' Julia summarises.

'Yeah,' Becky says. 'But I should have a right.'

Julia shakes her head. 'Maybe. But it's not the way to go about it. Look at her, Bex.'

Julia gestures to Harriet. She's lying on the sofa, sucking her thumb. Her eyes are slowly closing, like Dorothy's in the poppy field.

'I know,' Becky admits. 'But also – look at her. She's gorgeous, isn't she? And she's mine.'

'The witch won't accept it, you know,' Julia says. 'You'll have the police on you. We should be checking the news now, see if there's anything about you.' Julia gets out her phone, does a few taps and swipes. 'I can't see anything – yet,' she says. 'But it can't be long.'

'Maybe they won't go to the police,' Becky says. 'They're both shit-scared of being found out – how Harriet was conceived, how they kept her from me. Ian in particular. It's game over for their careers, for their income. And the witch is such a career woman.'

'That's not a failing, Becky. You know that.'

Becky had forgotten Julia is all set to be something marvellous, career-wise. Last time they spoke, she was working in a lab, testing exciting things in petri dishes. She's probably halfway to a universal cure for all illness by now.

'But I want someone to be there to look after my child!'

'Remember how hard Mum and Dad worked? We hardly saw them.'

'I figured they thought God was our real dad, so why did we need them,' Becky jokes.

'And so we all had our rebellion against Him, like good teenagers.' Julia laughs.

'I didn't cause my rebellion, my friends did,' Becky says, serious again.

'Some friends.' Julia pauses. 'Some sister. Bex, I'm so sorry I wasn't there for you. I'll make it up to you, OK?'

'We can stay?'

'For tonight, yes. But then you need to sort yourself out. Do this properly. We can't have you in prison when you should be finding some way of having a relationship with …' She mouths 'your daughter.'

Becky shakes her head. 'I can't go back. Kirsten will run off with her again.'

'So get social services involved. Get DNA tests done, all that sort of thing. You haven't got anything to hide.' Julia narrows her eyes. 'Have you?'

Becky shakes her head. 'Of course I haven't. But you don't get it. Kirsten's poisoned everyone against me. The school's suspended me, thinks I'm a nut job. No one's going to believe me.'

'I'll be there to back you up.'

Becky shakes her head. 'I can't take her back there, Julia. Not yet, anyway.'

Becky and Julia both look over at Harriet. She's fast asleep, knees curled up to her chest.

Julia's face softens. 'I can't believe I'm an auntie to two such lovely little people.'

'You're very good at it,' Becky says, meaning it. 'Better than I am at being a mother. I couldn't even get her to stop crying!'

Julia rubs Becky's leg. 'Give yourself a break. You've had a shit time. I've practised on Helen's daughter. You'll get there, OK?'

Becky nods. 'Thanks, sis.'

Julia springs up from the sofa. 'Right, I'd better carry on getting ready!'

Becky looks at her, amazed. 'What, you're still going out?'

'Hot date, Becky!' She winces. 'Look, I know the timing's shitty. I know we should stay in and catch up over a bottle of wine. But I've been waiting since for ever to go out with this guy. Our diaries are both mad. And I really like him. He could be the one.'

'Like all the other ones?' Becky asks. She doesn't know, but she's guessing.

Julia's face hardens again. 'Bex, you can't just turn up here and insult me. I'll find you some bedding, you can kip down here, and we'll have a lazy breakfast tomorrow, OK? We'll figure out what you're going to do. You look knackered, anyway – I bet you'd have one sip of wine and you'd be snoring like your daughter!'

Becky shrugs. Logically, the argument works. But it's like being abandoned by her big sister all over again. 'Sure,' she says. 'Thanks.'

So Julia brings down the bedding, then (looking stunning, her face fully made up), heads off into the night for her date. 'Text me if the police come knocking!' she calls, as she leaves. Maybe that's it, then, Becky thinks. Maybe Julia doesn't want to be drawn in to whatever's happening.

Becky snuggles down on the sofa. She's taller than it is. The living room curtains let in the street lamps, and don't entirely shield her from view. She's not expecting a great night's sleep. Just as she's closing her eyes, her phone buzzes into life. Harriet stirs on the other sofa. Please don't wake up, little one!

Becky grabs her phone. It's an unknown number. Shit. Someone's onto her. She cancels the call. A few moments later, her phone rings again. This time, it says Ian. Well, she's not answering it. It will be the tenth missed call from him today. Surely he should have understood by now? She can't talk to him. Not just now.

She turns off her phone. It's just her and Harriet now. As it should be. But she's not sure the reality is quite what she'd hoped for.

Chapter 43

KIRSTEN

Sunday morning sees Kirsten and Harriet's headmistress having a coffee in a cold café on Islington's Upper Street. Kirsten would have invited Mrs McGee to the house – she knows she needs to stay close in case Harriet returns – but the abandoned packing crates and the 'for sale' sign would have raised too many questions. And Kirsten needs to be the one who's in charge of something – given she has no control over Becky.

It feels surreal to be outside at all. She's been awake all night (how could she possibly sleep?), sitting in Harriet's room, pointlessly Googling things like 'Bristol kidnap'. Inputting numbers for the missing persons hotline onto her phone, even 999, but never pressing dial. But she needs somehow to focus on this meeting.

'As I said on the phone, I'm expecting the school to be fully supportive,' Kirsten says.

'We'll do everything we can to help, of course we will,' Mrs McGee says. 'This must be horrible for you. But on behalf of the governors, I do need to make it clear that the school accepts no responsibility whatsoever for—'

'One of your teachers has kidnapped my daughter,' Kirsten

says. 'And I'd warned you she was harassing us. I think you're pretty firmly on the hook.'

'According to the school's lawyers—'

Kirsten cuts her off again. What is it with everyone and lawyers? First Clare, now the school. 'If you're consulting lawyers, you know you're in the shit, frankly, Mrs McGee. And unless your lawyers are going to magically find my daughter, I'd suggest the school's efforts are better placed elsewhere. Is there anyone on the staff she's particularly close to?'

Mrs McGee shakes her head. 'I don't understand why you aren't involving the police,' she says. 'That's the best way of finding them. The sheer resources the police have available to them. And you know what they say about the first twenty-four hours?'

'What, the time window when you were on the phone to your lawyers, you mean?' Kirsten sighs. 'Look, I understand – completely – what you say about the police. But my husband feels that if Ms Robertson knows the police are involved, she'll panic and do something stupid. The last thing we want is some great big media campaign.'

'But she's mentally unhinged!' Mrs McGee protests. 'She might do anything!'

Kirsten grips her coffee cup harder. The red bitten ends of her fingers (the fingernails themselves ran out at about 2 a.m. this morning) become white against the cup. 'While Ms Robertson is operating under the delusion that she's Harriet's mother, I don't think she'll harm her. And my husband is following up a lead. You just need to focus on doing what you can. Do you know anyone she would have contacted?'

Mrs McGee shrugs. 'I just don't keep tabs on who my staff are chummy with. I'll make some calls this afternoon – just saying we are concerned about Ms Robertson's wellbeing, and does anyone know where she might be. See if that winkles anything out.'

'OK. Good,' says Kirsten, with more hope than she feels. 'Keep me posted.'

She checks her phone again, while Mrs McGee gathers her belongings together. Nothing from Ian. Maybe he's busy calling the landline. She calls his mobile, waving a silent goodbye to Mrs McGee.

'Yes?' Ian says when he answers. 'I'm driving.'

'Where to?' Kirsten asks.

'The sister's. I've found her address in Becky's stuff.'

Kirsten nods in acknowledgement. For once, Ian has done something right.

'How long till you get there?' she asks.

'About an hour,' Ian says.

'Keep me posted,' Kirsten says.

'Are we still on the original plan?' he asks. He means the knife. Making her an accomplice, or accessory, whatever the word is. Maybe she should get lawyers, too.

'Just do what you need to do,' she says, her voice hushed. 'But for God's sake, don't let Harriet see anything!'

The line goes dead. Ian's rung off. Kirsten shivers, putting on her coat. It sounds like all she can do is go home and wait.

Chapter 44

BECKY

So much for catching up over a long breakfast, Becky thinks to herself bitterly, as she opens cupboards trying to find something suitable for Harriet. There's no noise from upstairs. Becky doesn't even know if Julia's up there. The date must have gone *really* well.

Harriet has refused to budge from the living room. She wet the sofa in the night, something Becky hadn't anticipated, and despite Becky opening the windows to let the cold fresh air in, Harriet didn't want to go into another room.

Finally, Becky finds some non-mouldy bread and some cornflakes. The milk fails the sniff test, so the cereal will just have to be extra crunchy.

'Here we go, sweetie,' Becky says, handing the breakfast things to Harriet in the living room.

'Are we going home today?' Harriet asks.

Becky takes a breath. Maybe this is the moment. It's not ideal, but then, when will be? She kneels down in front of Harriet, on the floor.

'Harriet, sweetie, there's something I have to tell you. It might be a bit of a shock – but your home's going to be with me from now on.'

Harriet's lip begins to wobble again. 'Home is with my mummy! In London!' she says, snatching her hand away like Becky's hit it.

'The thing is, Harriet, darling – the person you think is your mummy isn't your real mummy. It's actually me. I'm your mummy.'

Harriet looks at Becky for a moment, then gives a long, guttural wail. 'You're not my mummy!' she shouts.

'Harriet, sweetie, I know it's a big piece of news, but—'

'You're not my mummy, you're not my mummy, YOU'RE NOT MY MUMMY!'

Harriet gets down onto the floor and starts screaming. It's textbook 'Keeping Safe' behaviour, which Becky knows from lessons she's taught at school – it's exactly what they tell children to do if a stranger tries to take them away.

Becky tries to soothe Harriet, stroking her hair, holding her shoulders, but it just makes Harriet scream louder.

There's the sound of running feet on the stairs, and Julia appears, wrapping a slinky dressing gown around herself. 'What's going on?' she asks, looking from Becky to Harriet.

'I tried to explain who I am,' Becky tells her. 'It seemed like the right thing to do.'

Julia crouches down in front of Harriet. 'Shh, it's OK, it's OK, kiddo.'

'She's not my mummy!' Harriet whimpers.

'It sounds to me like you're the luckiest little girl alive, with two mummies!' says Julia.

'I want my other mummy!' Harriet cries, her voice getting louder again. 'I want my real mummy!'

'And that's fine,' says Julia. 'You'll see your other mummy again soon. Won't she, Becky?'

Becky sees her big sister's fierce gaze and feels like she herself is Harriet's age again. Maybe the time when Becky had drawn on a wall, or pulled the legs off a doll, and Julia would glare and her and say: 'You're going to tell Mum it was you, aren't you?' Back then, there was no arguing. Now it's different. It's Becky's child they're talking about. What Becky says, goes.

'She's just had a shock, that's all,' Becky says. 'She'll be fine soon. Once she understands properly.'

Harriet remains sitting on the floor, tear-covered face turning between Becky and Julia.

Julia shakes her head and tightens her lips. 'This is all wrong, Becky.' Then, to Harriet: 'What would you like for breakfast, kiddo?'

'I've already made her breakfast,' Becky snaps.

'Ah, but Becky didn't know about my secret stash of …' Julia vanishes for a few moments, then returns with a Tupperware box labelled 'Open only in emergency.'

'Cheerios!' she announces proudly. 'My guilty pleasure. I'm trying to limit myself. They go right to your hips at my age, kiddo – but sometimes I need them on ice cream if a boy's been mean to me. You can have them for breakfast though!'

Harriet's face brightens momentarily. 'Can I have them on ice cream?' she asks.

'Well, let's see – we might be able to achieve—'

'Julia, come on, don't be ridiculous, it's breakfast time,' Becky admonishes.

Julia gives her another look, as if to say: Seriously? You try to turn her world upside down and now you're sticking to breakfast rules?

Julia goes into the kitchen, and Harriet follows in pursuit of ice cream.

Julia inspects the freezer. 'Hmm, seems like we're fresh out of ice cream. But you know what, if you're really good, I'm going to throw on some clothes and run to the corner shop to buy you some, OK?'

Harriet nods. She doesn't smile, but she doesn't cry either.

'Great. Give me fifteen minutes, and we'll have you eating ice cream round this very table!'

Becky takes Julia's arm. 'Julia, this is nonsense!'

'What?' asks Julia. 'I stopped her crying, didn't I?'

'It's not always about that. Sometimes, as a parent, you've got to make your kids face difficult things.'

'What, in your vast experience?' Julia retorts. 'You've been in her life for about ten minutes.'

'Yeah? Which means you've been in it for about ten seconds. I gave birth to her, Julia. I have a right.'

'Helen was right,' Julia says. 'You haven't the judgement to look after a child.'

'Oh for God's sake, that was one time. I was a teenager, I'd just found out I was pregnant, I wasn't quite … connected that day.'

'It doesn't take much connection to see there's something wrong with a baby.'

Becky sighs. 'I didn't get that "watch the baby" meant actually intervene if it turned red.'

'What, if a baby turns red, then blue – you just ignore it?' Julia challenges. 'You knew she had problems with reflux, for God's sake – that's why Helen was staying with us.'

'Look, I told Helen I was sorry, OK?'

'Sorry means nothing in that situation. It was her *baby*. It's a good job she'd learnt CPR, and the hospital was close, otherwise …'

Maybe Julia had a point. Becky remembered how dulled her senses had been that day, a feeling that nothing really mattered because everything was lost. She'd sat in front of the cot watching Helen's baby. She knew, if she was honest with herself, that the baby didn't look right. But she felt so detached, so … *savage* almost. Not that she'd wanted the baby to die (and it didn't, thank God). At least, she didn't think she did. If she thought about it properly, afterwards. But in the moment, the moment where she should have been doing something, the baby was just an outward manifestation of her inner battle, her horrible discovery that she was growing one inside her. So she just left it, as it writhed in panic, not finding its breath, going blue.

Maybe the psychiatrist who said she wouldn't have been safe with her own baby was right. No. That can't be true. She'd never harm Harriet. They'd all been in the wrong – Helen, Kirsten, the psychiatrist, the lot of them. She was seventeen, knocked up by a teacher, terrified, and about to be kicked out by her parents. And ultimately, Helen's baby was fine.

'Jesus, Julia, you said at the time Helen over-reacted, all those pregnancy hormones still flying around. Don't start making a thing of it now!'

They glare at each other.

'How was your date?' Becky asks, pointedly. You didn't care enough to stick around last night, is what she means.

'A let-down. So I need some ice cream anyway,' Julia says. 'And Harriet can join in too, can't you, kiddo?'

Harriet nods.

Julia leaves the kitchen, and a few moments later, there's the sound of a shower going.

'Come on, Harriet, we're leaving.'

'But the ice cream!' Harriet protests. 'And the Cheerios!'

'Eat a handful of Cheerios now, but then we're going. Auntie Julia is being very naughty, and isn't making anything better. We're on an exciting adventure, you and me, and we're going to have a lovely time.'

Harriet sits on the kitchen floor and starts crying quietly.

It's not the sort of adventure picture you post on Facebook. Not the sort of picture Becky's other sister shares, that Becky likes to stare at. Still, her own time for smug mother-daughter selfies will come. Surely.

Becky turns her phone on and finds the local taxi app. 'Right, ten minutes, then we'll be off. Let's get your things together!'

Harriet shakes her head. 'I don't want to go,' she says. 'I like Auntie Julia.'

Becky takes a deep breath. 'The thing about Auntie Julia, sweetie, is she makes lots of promises, but when you need her most, she isn't there.'

Becky suddenly becomes aware of footsteps behind her.

'Am I not?' Julia says.

Becky turns to face her. 'You know you're not.'

'I'm here now, Bex. I'm trying to help.'

'We have to go. I've got a taxi coming.'

'This little one's going to tell the taxi driver you're not her mummy and cause a scene. You know that, right?'

Julia has a point.

'Have a cup of tea. Then I'll give you a lift somewhere, OK? It's too obvious for you to stay here.'

'You mean you'll support me?'

Julia looks at her and shakes her head. 'I don't agree with what you're doing. But you'll work it out for yourself soon enough.'

Becky had forgotten how annoyingly patronising she found her sister. Yet she wishes this had been Julia's response when Becky needed it most – when she was about to give birth to Harriet. When her parents had kicked her out (their strict religious teachings clearly not having covered God-like compassion and mercy) and she was living in sheltered accommodation, then a flat Ian rented. If Julia had been there for her then, she might never have listened to that doctor in the first place.

'We'll stay for one cup of tea, then you can drop us as a B&B or something, OK?'

In response, Julia puts the kettle on. Harriet sits at the kitchen table, listlessly picking at Cheerios.

So far, this is not the great bonding experience with her daughter that Becky had planned. But she knows she's right. Harriet is so much better off with her than with Kirsten. Of course she is.

Chapter 45

KIRSTEN

Still nothing from Ian. Kirsten paces up and down the living room, round the boxes. Occasionally she sits down to inspect her phone, then stands up again. This is absurd. She should have gone with him. What made her think she could trust him with something like this, given the number of times he's betrayed her in the past? The times he said that he was going round to talk to Becky, whose side had he been on? Whose case was he pleading? She should have gone with Mrs McGee, made her knock on the door of all the teachers at the school. Not just be left sitting here, waiting.

She calls Ian again, but it goes to voicemail, so she texts him:

Any news?

She knows she shouldn't be calling him, texting him, in case this ever becomes a police investigation. Ian and his knife. Why did he have to over-complicate things? Why did he have to care so much about his reputation?

And yet, Kirsten is grateful that he knows the world would be better without Becky. They'd have their child. And they'd have silence. Not just about their jobs. That's a niggle for Kirsten. But about the fact that someone else may have more right to Harriet than them. Or than Kirsten. Ian probably still has the same rights, given he's the biological father. What kind of a message is that? Be a shit dad, but because your drunken/drugged sperm happened to make her, you get a right to stay in her life.

Nothing from him. And a further ten minutes, still nothing.

Then, her phone comes to life. A text from Ian.

Just getting petrol. Be at target in 15 mins.

Is he mad? Unless the car's running on fumes, why would you stop at a petrol station so close to the scene of a crime you might be about to commit? And why would you not be driving like crazy to get there before your mad lover does something to your child?

Fifteen minutes come and go. Then twenty minutes, then half an hour. Kirsten longs to call Ian. But she knows she can't, not just now – he might be in the middle of … something. Kirsten covers her eyes as she has visions of a house full of blood, of Harriet witnessing a murder, of Becky getting the knife and stabbing all of them, Harriet included. 'Oh God, Oh God, Harriet, I'm sorry!' Kirsten whispers to herself, wiping tears from her eyes.

The phone rings. Kirsten nearly drops it. It's Ian calling. She swipes at the phone, but her wet fingers won't engage the answer button. 'Oh, shit, come on, come on!' she shouts, desperately wiping the face of the phone on the sofa, her hands on her top, then trying again.

'Hello!' she says as soon as she can, in case Ian is about to give up.

'I'm at the sister's house,' he says. 'Outside.'

Well go in, then! Kirsten wants to scream.

'There's no one there,' he says.

'Actually no one there, or they aren't answering the door?' Kirsten asks. Would someone answer the door if they were harbouring a kidnapped child?

'I've walked right round the house, and it looks like they've been there and gone. I peered in the living room window – there's a crack in the curtains – and there's breakfast stuff there. There's breakfast stuff round the back as well, lots of it – enough for three people. I tried to climb up a wall to see into the upstairs, but I couldn't. So it's possible they're hiding up there, I guess. But all the lights are off.'

Kirsten shivers and hugs herself, imagining Ian prowling round outside with a knife.

'Kirsten?' he asks.

'I'm still here,' she says. Although she's not sure she really is. This all seems very detached from anything like reality.

'What do you want me to do?' Ian asks.

Why does she always have to be the grown-up, making the right decisions? Ian seemed happy enough to make decisions in the past that would screw them over. Why not stick to it now? But he's not stupid, either, Ian – Kirsten knows he wants to be able to say that, whatever he did, she was part of it. Right up to the hilt.

What should he do, then? Should he wait? Break in? Should they call the police, now? There's no knowing that Becky actually went there at all.

'I'll wait, shall I, see if they come back – or come out if they're still there? Kirsten, what do you think?'

Kirsten takes a breath. 'Yes. Wait for them. Wait for them and get Harriet back. But please, please don't hurt her.'

Her voice cracks.

'Why would I hurt our child?' Ian says, and hangs up.

'I don't know,' Kirsten whispers to herself. 'I don't know, but I'm afraid.'

Chapter 46

BECKY

At the B&B, Becky puts on the TV. She bustles about, making tea, calls down to see if they have any Ribena for Harriet that she can heat up. She looks like the heat and the sweetness would do her good. Then she checks her phone, even though it's not on mute.

Harriet sits on the bed. That is all she has done since they got there. Sit on the bed, and stare into space. Occasionally a tear trickles down her face. Becky tries to engage her in conversation.

'Isn't this fun, Harriet?'

'I'm so lucky to be here with you, Harriet!'

'Hey, shall I see if I can find *Peppa Pig* on the TV, Harriet?'

All Becky's attempts have been met with no response. Becky thinks back to little Maya at the breakfast club. How even an interpreter wasn't enough to breach the sound barrier. How Maya was too traumatised, still, to speak. Had Becky done that now to her own child? Torn her away from her mother, taken her on an inexplicable journey, only to end up without her home comforts or what she thought of as her family?

Of course, an escape from somewhere like Syria, and the

torment that little Maya must have endured, wasn't comparable with a trip from Islington to Bristol. And nor was a stay with Julia, being offered ice cream and Cheerios, on a par with the staging posts and the squalor that Maya would have faced. But this listlessness, the refusal (inability?) to speak, a sort of shutting down – to Becky's guilty conscience, they seemed the same.

But she shouldn't feel guilty, should she? She was this girl's mother. They were meant to be together.

Becky tries again. She kneels down in front of Harriet, and gently strokes her hand. Harriet doesn't react at all – doesn't flinch, doesn't return the gesture, doesn't pull her hand away. Becky kisses Harriet's hair. Same story. Finally, she sits on the bed next to Harriet, so that their arms are touching. Becky would love for Harriet to rest her head on Becky's shoulder. To wriggle into her, to go for a hug. But no, still the impassive staring straight ahead. No doubt, if she had Dorothy's ruby slippers she'd be clicking her heels together to go home. She doesn't, so there's no movement at all.

Becky's phone bleeps. Sighing, she pulls herself off the bed and retrieves the mobile. It's from Ted. She opens it up.

Hey, we're all worried about you. Me especially. Where are you? Call me. x

So. The school is on her trail. And was apparently manipulating Ted into sending messages. They were probably all sitting there waiting for her to respond, as if that would give some great clue. She'd actually love to respond. She'd love to phone him, tell him everything, from Ian onwards. She'd love to cry down the phone about how horribly disappointing and overwhelming this was – that much as she loved being in a room with her beautiful Harriet, she hated it too because she despaired at what she was meant to do next, and could see only grudging tolerance down the line, at best, from her daughter.

Sod Kirsten. And sod Ian. How could it have come to this? It was their fault. Why couldn't they just have got over themselves, behaved like sensible people years ago – not have driven her to this?

Becky's phone rings. If it's Ted, she can't answer it. But no – it's Julia.

'Hello?' she answers.

'Are you guys all right?' she asks. She sounds breathless, urgent.

'Why, what's happened?' Becky asks.

'Someone followed me from the car. I think it was Ian. He was asking about you.'

'What? Where are you now?' Becky asks.

'Back home. I just managed to get in the door. But he might still be out there, Bex.'

'You didn't tell him where we are?'

'No, of course not. I said I hadn't seen you for years.'

'Did he buy it?'

'I don't know. He threatened me with the police, said that I was an accessory to kidnapping, that he'd find you. All that stuff. But it wasn't what he said, Bex. It was him; he gave me the creeps.'

'Why?' Ian could be a lot of things, but creepy wasn't how Becky would describe him. Charming, if he needed to be. Or just very ordinary, very reserved, when he didn't want to make a scene.

'Oh … just something about him. He was jumpy, nervy. Carrying something in a bag, I couldn't see what it was, but he was clutching it tight. You know when someone's not quite right? If I'd been on a bus with him, I'd have moved to sit closer to the driver. Or just have got off. That kind of thing.'

Becky shook her head. God knows what Kirsten had been saying to him – he was probably terrified the police were going to catch up with him, and all his sordid little lies would come to the surface. Or maybe he was genuinely worried about Harriet. Hah.

'Don't worry too much, Julia, OK? He's probably gone elsewhere now.'

There's a pause.

'I'm not sure, Bex. He'd have come into the house with me if I hadn't managed to shut the door on him.'

'He can't trace me and Harriet, though,' Becky tells her.

'Someone's going to find you two, you know – and if you're discovered, rather than handing yourselves in, you're not going to have any control over the consequences.'

Suddenly Becky realises where this is coming from. She'd forgotten how judgemental Julia could be.

'You've made this whole lot up, haven't you, Julia?' Becky storms.

'What?' Julia sounds shocked. Of course she does, she was always better at drama than Becky even after (especially after) the ill-fated drama course.

'"Oh, I think it was Ian, oh they're going to find you, oh you need to hand yourself in", Becky mimics. 'This is all because you don't think I'm doing the right thing. It's just a ploy to get me to take Harriet back to Kirsten! To make me call the police and confess!'

Becky sees Harriet look up at the mention of her 'mother's' name. Becky turns away from Harriet towards the room's small window, and starts banging her hand rhythmically against it. 'I'm doing the right thing, Julia!' she says. But she's not sure she believes it. Julia won't, and Harriet certainly doesn't.

'Yeah, you're right, I don't agree with you,' sounds Julia, her voice forceful down the phone. 'But I'm not making up some psycho stalking round outside my house, OK? You're paranoid! And you know what you're doing is wrong – don't project this back on me!'

'I'm not falling for this, Julia! I'm not calling the police!'

'Listen to yourself – you sound anxious, mad! Why would I make this up? I just wanted to check you were doing OK. Sounds like you're fine – it's just me who's stuck!'

'We're not fine!' shouts Becky. 'Harriet won't bloody say anything, I've no idea how to get from here to where I want to be, my employers are trying to trap me into saying where I am, and I can afford to stay here three nights tops. We are not fine!'

There's a silence on the other end of the line.

'Julia?' Becky prompts.

'Sorry, I was just checking out the window. I think he's still there.'

'Bullshit, Julia! If this is you trying to get me to go back to London, then it's not working!'

'I need to go,' Julia says.

Becky hangs up and throws the phone onto the bed, narrowly missing Harriet. 'Bitch!' she says.

This time, Harriet flinches.

'Not you, sweetheart! I didn't mean you.' Becky runs across the room, and tries to gather Harriet to her, but Harriet won't be gathered.

'What a mess, hey? What can we do? How do we sort this out?'

Becky sits back to look at Harriet. She gets nothing in return.

Chapter 47

KIRSTEN

She should call the police. It's been over forty-eight hours now. Never mind her and Ian's secrets. This is about Harriet. Harriet, whose absence means Kirsten hasn't eaten, hasn't slept, hasn't washed. Just stared out of the window, at her phone, at the internet. At Harriet's bedroom, at her photographs, at her Frozen toothbrush in the bathroom. Crying while she does it.

'Any news?' she asks when she phones Mrs McGee.

'Ms Robertson was apparently close with one of the male teachers. Went on a date, once. I don't encourage it, but it does happen. Of course, he's shocked to hear what's happening – couldn't believe it of her. Anyway, he's sent her a message.'

'And?' asks Kirsten.

'And she hasn't replied.'

'Is that all?' Kirsten asks. She knows she rang Mrs McGee; it's not like Mrs McGee phoned claiming to have an update. Although, frankly, she should have done – a link being established, a message being sent. That's something.

'Phone me if you have any more news,' Kirsten says, then hangs up.

Next she tries Ian again.

'Any update?' she asks.

'The sister's there,' Ian says. He's talking quietly, like he doesn't want to be overheard.

'Why didn't you phone me?' Kirsten asks. 'What's happening? Have you spoken to her?'

'She wasn't very forthcoming,' Ian says.

There's an edge to his voice. He sounds stressed, nervy.

'You didn't …' Kirsten asks, without really knowing what she is asking.

'What? Stab her?' Ian laughs.

Kirsten tenses. 'I don't know what's so funny.'

'Just because I'm out to "silence" one person, doesn't mean I'm suddenly a mass murderer, Kirsten.'

'No, I know, I just wondered if you'd, maybe, used the knife to – oh, I don't know, persuade her a bit.'

'She'd phone the police,' Ian says.

'What, and give away her sister's whereabouts?' Kirsten says. 'I'm assuming she hasn't told you anything.'

'Nothing,' Ian says. 'Swears blind she hasn't seen Becky for years. Didn't say anything about Harriet until I prompted her, so if she's lying, she's good.'

'I don't buy it. You'd go to family, at a time like this. Your sister would be there for you.'

'Would your sister?' Ian asks.

Kirsten ignores him. She doesn't want to get into the fact her sister hasn't spoken to her for five years. Wasn't there for her when, she supposed, she'd done a similar thing to what Becky has just done – taken Harriet away from her real mother.

'So where are you now?' Kirsten asks.

'Outside the sister's house still,' Ian says.

'What, in the car?' Kirsten asks.

'No,' Ian says. 'Outside. Like, outside her front door. In case she comes out. Or Becky comes out.'

Or Harriet, Kirsten thinks. She shivers at the thought of Ian lurking with the knife outside a house where their child might be living.

'What will you do if the sister does come out?' Kirsten asks.

'Try and make her talk again,' he says.

'But you said …' Kirsten trails off.

'I said I hadn't used the knife to try to persuade her. I didn't say I wouldn't.'

Chapter 48

BECKY

If Harriet's silence in the day was bad, her crying in the night is worse.

It starts at 1 a.m. Before that, Becky had been conscious of Harriet wriggling round in the bed next to her. After the wet sofa of the night before, Becky kept telling her to get up if she needed the toilet; once she even got up, turned the light on, and proffered a hand to lead her there.

But it wasn't that. It was the prelude to the tears. Harriet cries and cries and cries.

Like in those very first moments of her life. The first hour, to be precise, before her daughter was taken from her, given to Kirsten. Good strong lungs. They'd done skin-to-skin contact immediately after the birth, for the good of the baby, trying to keep her warm and content while Becky was sorted out. But it had nearly destroyed Becky. Crying herself now at the memory, at that brutal psychological wrench, Becky hugs and shushes Harriet, strokes her head, like she had done when she was so newly born. Finally, finally, she is here with her little daughter again.

But this time, looking at Harriet, she knows she is capable of taking care of her, however difficult it is. Last time, she couldn't understand how on the one hand she could feel such huge love for a little newborn creature but be told it would unleash some kind of monster in her. Kirsten and Ian must have paid Dr Clare well.

Becky shushes and cradles Harriet until she seems a little bit more peaceful. As they both seem to drift off to sleep, Becky feels a surge of pride that she has, at last, helped.

The tears, however, had apparently been a prelude to the nightmares.

'Mummy, mummy save me!' is the only intelligible scream that Harriet gives. The rest are murmurs, whimpers, cries. Along with them are shivers, trembles, sweats.

Becky turns on the side-light, and looks at the poor five-year-old girl in the sheets beside her. This isn't right. This isn't something that is going to 'sort itself out, given time.' This is creating trauma and terror in the little person that she loves above all else.

Julia is right. Becky knows what she needs to do. She must put her own hurt, her own trauma, to one side. She will get Harriet settled and the next day, Becky will speak to Kirsten. Arrange a meeting. Get something sorted out, so that they can work out a practical way of both being in Harriet's life. For Harriet's sake.

'It's OK, sweetie,' Becky whispers to Harriet. 'We'll call your mummy tomorrow, OK?'

And Harriet's body suddenly relaxes, the whimpering stops, and her child sleeps. Becky feels like finally she's done it, learnt the lesson – that motherhood is about putting your child first. That's enough for today.

Then the bedside phone rings. Becky had turned her mobile onto silent earlier, but she sees there are twenty missed calls from Julia. Shit. She picks up the landline.

'Hello?' she says.

'I'm putting through a call from your sister,' says a sleepy-sounding voice.

There's a click, then Julia comes on the line. 'You've got to get out,' she says, before Becky even says hello.

'What?' Becky asks, sitting upright.

'Ian knows where you are. He has a knife. You have to get out now!'

'Shit, what, you told him where we were?'

'Look, I'm not proud of it, but he had a knife, Bex – apparently fear makes me talk. But you have to go. Now.'

Shit. Becky jumps out of bed, still holding the handset. Why would Ian use a knife on her sister? Why was he so worked up to find out where they were? Had Kirsten been threatening to go public, or something? And should she really be worried? He was hardly going to harm the mother of his child, or his child. Was he?

'Becky, are you listening to me, you have to leave. He left five minutes ago; he'll be there in ten. Promise me you're going?'

There's panic in her voice. Becky can't argue.

'We're going. How about you, are you OK?'

'He didn't actually use the knife, just held it to my throat.'

'Shit, Julia!'

'I'm fine. Now go!'

Becky shakes Harriet awake. 'Harriet! Harriet! We have to get up!'

Harriet continues sleeping peacefully. Damn Becky's consoling words earlier – she hadn't thought that the idea of even just speaking to Kirsten would make such a difference.

Becky grabs their things, and tries shaking Harriet again. It doesn't work. Frantic, she takes the glass of water by Harriet's side of the bed and throws the water over her.

Harriet jolts, then wakes up.

'We have to go!' Becky says to her. 'Come on, get up, stick my jumper on over your clothes.' Harriet had left home in the middle of the day, wearing light clothes. It was the middle of the night, now; Harriet would be freezing.

'Are we going home to Mummy?' Harriet asks.

Her face is bright, and her eyes shine. Becky can see her yearning for the right answer. Amid the panic, she softens.

'Yes, Harriet, we're going home.'

After all, it was the last place Ian would look.

Chapter 49

KIRSTEN

Trust Ian to cock it up so massively. He'd managed to get the sister – Julia, apparently – to tell him where Becky and Harriet were, but he'd missed them. By the time he'd got to their B&B, hammered at the door to make the owners let him in, then up to Becky and Harriet's room, they had left. Some of their things were still in the room – Becky's coat, a hairbrush. Nothing of Harriet's. But she'd definitely been there – the receptionist had confirmed it with Ian.

'Well, they can't have gone far!' Kirsten had shouted to Ian. 'Drive around and look for them, for God's sake. Show people their pictures on your phone! Check the bus stations, the train stations. We need to find them.'

Christ, he should have killed the sister, stopped her tipping Becky off.

Kirsten puts her hand over her mouth in shock at the thought. But Ian ought to have done something, shouldn't he, to stop Julia calling Becky? Like taken her phone, locked her out of her house, something. But he'd screwed it up, and now Harriet was missing again.

That was four hours ago. Occasionally Ian phones her just to say he hasn't found them, but he hasn't phoned for an hour. He's probably fallen asleep in some lay-by somewhere. She should phone him, wake him up. But she's crashingly tired herself. She hasn't slept in about fifty hours now. She puts her head down on the arm of the sofa, just to doze.

She's awoken by a bell. She checks her phone, but it's not ringing. It tells her it's 7 a.m. It doesn't explain the bell. It sounds again.

Door.

She runs to open it. She's not expecting anyone, so it must be news of some kind. Through the glass of the front door, she sees two shadows. Oh God, it had better not be the police. Ian, Becky and Harriet – an incident, deaths. But hold on, one of the shadows is so small. It can't be …

She opens the door.

'Harriet! Oh my God, Harriet!'

Kirsten bends down, hugging Harriet to her, crying, laughing, stroking her little girl's head, kissing her, hugging her some more. Harriet clings to her, and won't be separated, even for Kirsten to look at her. Kirsten will never let her go, ever again.

Picking Harriet up, Kirsten looks now at the other figure.

Becky.

Kirsten wants to slam the door in the face. Or kick her down the stairs. She certainly doesn't want to invite her in. But she knows she has to.

'You'd better come through,' she says, her voice ice.

Together, they go into the living room. Kirsten puts Harriet onto her knee, where Harriet just clings on, thumb in her mouth, head on Kirsten's chest.

'Now, perhaps you'd like to tell me why you kidnapped my daughter.'

Kirsten expects her words to create an angry response. Expects to be told Harriet isn't her daughter. Expects to do battle.

236

'I'd rather explain why I brought her back,' is what Becky says.

'Be my guest,' Kirsten tells her, in probably the least hospitable tone she has.

'Harriet loves you,' Becky tells her.

Kirsten snorts. 'I think I knew that.'

Becky shakes her head. 'No, I mean really loves you. I had this fairy tale in my head whereby I would take her away, and make her happy – I thought she wasn't happy here, that all she needed was a day with me, her "real" mum—'

'Shh!' says Kirsten and covers Harriet's ears.

'She knows,' says Becky. 'That's why we're back. I explained to her that I was her mummy, but she wouldn't accept it. Wouldn't speak, wouldn't sleep – anything. She just pined for you. It wasn't right. So I brought her home.'

'Well, it's very good of you,' Kirsten says. What she wants to say is 'How dare you? How dare you do that to my child?' But Harriet has had a horrendous time. The last thing she needs is a fight in front of her. She needs security, safety, certainty. Always.

Kirsten has a plan forming in her mind.

'I mean it,' Kirsten says. 'It's good of you, to bring her back. You could have fled overseas, just ignored her views. Done worse. I thought I might never see her again.' Despite herself, Kirsten starts crying. Not little tears, that she could maybe rub away, pretend she had an itchy eye. Proper sobs escape her. Harriet wriggles closer in to her chest.

'It's all right, sweetie. You're home now. I'm just crying because I'm so happy to see you.'

'I'd like to be clear, though,' Becky says. 'We need to find a way for me to have a part in Harriet's life and for her to have a relationship with me. To understand who I am.'

Kirsten nods. 'Look, I get that now. I didn't before, and I'm in no way condoning what you did. It's been horrible for me and for Harriet.' Her voice gives way; she lets it. 'But it's made me understand how desperate you were to see her. Your little girl. I shouldn't have ignored that.'

Becky nods. 'Thank you.' She sheds a few tears of her own. Kirsten sees them roll down over the black shadows under Becky's eyes. Kirsten's plan might just work.

Kirsten continues. 'But look, you must be exhausted. I am, I haven't slept since Harriet … left. And by the looks of you and Harriet, you haven't either. I can't work out how we're going to do this until I've had some sleep.'

'I'm not leaving until we've worked something out,' Becky says.

Kirsten raises a reassuring hand. 'No, I get that; don't worry. I was going to offer if you wanted to kip in the spare room for a couple of hours, then we'll regroup. I'll get Harriet into bed with me.'

'How do I know you won't do a runner?' Becky asks.

Kirsten rolls her eyes. 'Look, you can barricade my door from the outside if you want to. What am I going to do – drive my dearly returned daughter in a car I'd almost certainly crash? Have you told the police on me? No – look, I understand we need to get this sorted out. For Harriet's sake.'

Becky nods. 'For Harriet's sake.'

Kirsten shows Becky to the spare room, Harriet holding Kirsten's hand the whole way. Kirsten is pleased now that she's always followed her mother's advice to keep the bed made up. Her mother used to say it made a house look civilised, and was less work if you wanted guests. To Kirsten, through her own tired eyes, she knows how inviting it must look. The soft bedding calling you in.

Becky turns to her. 'Thanks, Kirsten. This is so good of you. I didn't expect you to be so – decent.'

Kirsten shrugs. 'It's the only human thing to do,' she says.

Kirsten takes Harriet upstairs with her to the master bedroom. She wasn't lying; she needs to sleep too. And she is looking forward to curling up side by side with Harriet. But first she needs to call Ian.

'She's back,' Kirsten tells him. 'Becky's sleeping in the spare room now.'

Ian swears. 'I'm still roving round Bristol,' he resays.

'Well, come back. Fast. She'll be asleep for hours. She might not notice if someone stops her waking up.'

Ian doesn't say anything at first. Then he says, 'You still want me to …?'

'I'm not having Harriet taken away from me again. We're locking ourselves in the bedroom – I don't trust that woman not to take Harriet while I sleep, but give me a call when you get here. I'll come and let you in. Then it's between you and Becky.'

Ian is silent for a few moments. 'I do think it's best, you know.'

'I know,' Kirsten says, hugging Harriet to her.

Hanging up on Ian, she slides the bolt across the door of the bedroom.

Then she picks up Harriet, nuzzles her hair, and lifts her into bed. Hugging her daughter to her, she falls into a deep sleep.

Chapter 50

BECKY

Smoke.

That's the smell – or rather the taste – that wakes Becky. And not the kind of cosy smoke that comes from slightly overdone toast. Real smoke. And she can see it, billowing under the door. There's a high-pitched beeping sound as well, the feeble attempts of a smoke alarm to wake her. Who knows, maybe they did.

She jumps out of bed, but falls to the floor, weak. Shit. She must already have inhaled some. It's filling the room. Keeping low, she slides to the door and, praying she's not about to unleash an inferno, opens it.

Outside, the heat and the light are staggering. Has Kirsten torched her, then? Is this what the sleeping beauty routine was about? She'll be long gone, with Harriet, and a claim on the insurance.

But what if they're still here? What if Harriet's still here?

Becky had heard them go upstairs. She looks over the banisters. There's smoke billowing round the hallway, with flames licking at the staircase. It will be impassable in less than five minutes, maybe. Becky drags herself up the stairs. That's when she hears the banging.

'Help!' she hears Harriet calling. 'I can't open the door!'

Oh God. Harriet's in there, and she's trapped. Where's Kirsten, for God's sake? She wouldn't … no, of course she wouldn't.

'What's going on, Harriet? Is the door stuck?'

'It's locked, and I can't reach the bolt! And I can't wake Mummy!'

Ah. So Kirsten didn't trust her – that's what this was about. Fair enough in a way.

'We've got to get you out! The house is on fire! Is there something you can stand on?' Becky shouts through the door.

'No!'

'There must be!' Becky splutters. The smoke is getting worse, the fire getting louder. 'Is there a wardrobe? Look in there, for a shoebox or something.'

Failing that, Becky will have to find something to bash the door open. She can't see anything.

There's silence now from within. Becky looks down the stairwell and can see flames.

'Harriet!' she shouts. 'Come on, did you find anything?'

There's a faint scrabbling sound, and the door opens. Harriet is standing precariously on two shoe-boxes. When she sees Becky, she jumps off and quickly hugs her tight, then makes to run down the stairs.

Becky grabs her by the shoulder and propels her back into the room. 'There's no way out down there. Is there a flat roof or something up here we can climb onto?'

Becky sees Kirsten still sleeping on the bed. She is wearing an eye mask, and she is tightly curled up under the duvet. Little bits of drool are making a thread between her open mouth and the pillow. She'd probably die a quiet peaceful death, knocked out by the smoke fumes before she even woke up.

Becky shuts the door again, takes a blanket off the end of the bed and shoves it up against the gap between the bedroom door and the floor. Then she shakes Kirsten. And shakes her and shakes her.

241

'Gwwerr …' groans Kirsten.

'Kirsten you have to wake up; the house is on fire!'

'Five more minutes …' Kirsten says.

'There's a fire, Mummy – get up!' Harriet shouts. 'There's a fire! Please!' Harriet begins dragging Kirsten out of bed.

Becky sees Kirsten's eyes open fully, and her body go from the slump of sleep to fully taut.

'Becky, what?' Kirsten asks.

Becky nods. 'There's a fire. Downstairs. It's blocking the hallway. How do we get out from here?'

'OK, you call the fire brigade. We've got a fire ladder round here …' Kirsten's voice peters out as she clambers into the eaves of the room.

'We're trapped in the loft room of a house,' Becky tells the emergency operator. 'There's a massive fire spreading, and we've got a five-year-old girl here. You've got to get here!'

'Shit, it's heavy,' Kirsten says. 'Becky, will you help me?'

Together, they heave the ladder out of its casing. 'I always thought it would be Ian helping me with this,' she says.

'Now what do we do with it?' Becky asks.

'Open that window, as wide as it will go.'

'OK, I'm – Kirsten, it won't open, or at least not far, it's got an opening restraint on it!' Becky shouts, then coughs. Under the door, she can see smoke starting to in. 'Keep down low, Harriet,' she yells. 'Cover your mouth.'

Harriet whimpers, but she obeys.

'Shit, of course!' Kirsten says. 'I didn't want Harriet falling out. OK, there's a key round here somewhere. Um, um, it's meant to be on top of that bookcase.' Becky watches as Kirsten lifts photo frames, runs her hand over books. 'Shit, where is it?'

'Maybe it's fallen down the back?' Becky asks, moving to pull the bookcase away from the wall.

Kirsten shakes her head. 'If it has, we won't be able to get it

– the bookcase is still bracketed to the wall, from when Harriet was little. I didn't want it to fall on her.'

Becky puts her hands to her temple. All these things Kirsten has done to try to protect Harriet are going to kill their daughter! And the two of them.

Becky lies on the floor next to bookcase. 'I think I can see it,' she says. 'Get me a coat hanger or something. I'll see if I can ease it out.'

She reaches out her hand behind her, waiting to receive an implement. 'Quickly!' she says.

She feels a piece of wood in her hand. She turns to look at it. It's a posh, wood-mounted coat hanger. 'Not one of those!' she shouts to Kirsten. 'One of the wire ones!'

Kirsten shakes her head. 'We don't have any of those.'

No, right, of course – Princess Kirsten couldn't possibly sink to those depths.

Becky stands up. There must be something. The room is hazy now from the smoke. They can't have long. Harriet is curled up in a ball in a corner.

The curtain tracking! That will be narrow enough.

'Give me that coat hanger again!' Becky shouts at Kirsten. Becky snatches it from Kirsten, then puts the hanger behind the curtain track and pulls with all her strength. Nothing. No give at all.

'We need to smash the window, then!' Becky yells.

'With what? You can't smash it with a coat hanger. It's double-glazed, sound-proofed, all that stuff.'

'Have you got a boot, then? Something? Kirsten, come on! We're going to die up here otherwise. Harriet's going to die!'

Becky flicks a glance at Harriet. She is curled up in a corner, hand clamped over her face, eyes wide.

'It's no good,' Kirsten whispers. 'There's no way out. We're trapped.'

Becky looks wildly round the room. 'That's an en suite, right?' she says, pointing to another door.

Kirsten nods. 'Wet room.'

'Right, in there!' Becky shouts. 'Come on, Harriet!'

'Are you sure there's no way out downstairs?' Kirsten demands. 'Couldn't we fight through?'

Becky shakes her head. 'No. And if you open that door now, you risk getting a massive fireball.'

'I thought that was the other way round, if you opened a door from—'

'Just get in the wet room!' Becky yells.

Once inside, Becky shuts the door against the bedroom. She hoses down the door with shower water, grabs some towels from the rack and soaks them. She puts one under the door, and throws one each to Kirsten and Harriet. 'Put these over your mouths,' she says.

Then she starts to run the Jacuzzi bath in the corner, at the same time operating her mobile phone.

'What are you doing?' Kirsten screams.

'Just shut up and get Harriet in the bath. Hello, we called for a fire engine. Is it on its way?'

Becky turns the taps off momentarily so she can hear the response. The operator tells her it should be there by now. 'Well, it's not!' she shouts. 'Find out where it is. Tell them we're in the loft bathroom, round the back of the house. I've tried to make a water barrier but I think we're running out of—'

She stops speaking as there is a booming, whooshing noise from next door. The heat in the wet room suddenly increases, and there's a smell of singeing.

'The fire's made it through,' she says into the phone. 'I think they'll be too late.'

Chapter 51

KIRSTEN

Kirsten is covered in foil. In front of her, through an open door, she can see flames. So many flames. For one groggy moment, she thinks she's maybe in an oven. Or in hell. There are more foil people next to her. They don't seem to be doing much.

Then the vision takes on its real shape.

That's her house, burning down.

She's inside some kind of vehicle, with its doors open.

Beside her, Becky.

And that's her child.

Next to Becky, covered in foil. With an oxygen mask over her mouth.

'Harriet!' she shouts, but it comes out as a croak.

'It's OK.' Someone lays a restraining hand on her. 'The little one's all right. We're just giving her some oxygen as a precaution.'

'She's my daughter!' Kirsten declares.

She sees the woman – who must be a paramedic, she supposes – flash a quick, confused glance at Becky.

'We're both her mother,' Becky says.

Kirsten wants to protest, but she doesn't know on what grounds. She looks at the paramedic, and sees the cogs whirling in her brain, before she nods, accepting. Probably hit on some kind of surrogacy or lesbian relationship. OK, whatever. As long as it doesn't end in a social services visit.

'Well, you've all had a lucky escape,' the paramedic says. 'The fire crew said that whoever had the bright idea of creating a water barrier probably saved your lives. When they managed to get to the top of the house, the bedroom was on fire. The flames hadn't spread to the bathroom, and the smoke was limited by the towels under the door.'

Kirsten becomes aware of tears streaming down her face. The paramedic rubs Kirsten's shoulder again. 'You're OK, you've just had a real shock, and a bit of smoke inhalation. We'll get you sorted out, and the fire service will talk to you about next steps when you're ready,' she says.

Kirsten shoots a glance at Becky. She's looking at Harriet.

'Can you give us a minute?' Kirsten asks the paramedic. 'Only if it's safe.'

The paramedic nods. 'Of course.' She steps down out of the vehicle. 'I'll just be outside here.'

Kirsten turns to Becky. 'You saved our lives,' she says.

Becky shrugs. 'We had to get out.'

'No, but you could have left me there. Just concentrated on Harriet.'

Becky turns to face Kirsten fully. 'We're all in this together,' she says. 'That's what I was trying to explain this morning. Harriet needs us both. So we need each other.'

Kirsten nods. Thank God Ian hadn't come to kill Becky – if Becky had been stabbed, she and Harriet might have died in the fire. Although, she supposes she would have been awake, then, trying to get a dead body out of the house. She shivers, and pulls the foil blanket round her shoulders.

Standing up, she walks unsteadily over to Harriet. She strokes her shoulder, not wanting to hug her in case it dislodges the oxygen mask. 'Are you OK, sweetie?' she asks.

Harriet nods, and leans against Becky. Kirsten feels a surge of jealousy. She tries to push it down, but it's like bile. It keeps coming up again. She takes Harriet's hands, and rubs them. Harriet gets to her feet, and wraps her arms round Kirsten's middle.

Poor kid. What a horrendous few days she's had. And now she's probably lost her home, with all her things in it, too. Maybe Becky's right. Maybe she needs both of them.

She's about to say it, but the paramedic returns.

'Just need to check on our little lady here,' says the paramedic. She takes the oxygen mask off Harriet, and does some readings on a little machine.

'You're doing really well, sweetheart,' the paramedic says to Harriet. 'You've been so brave.'

'I don't want to be brave,' Harriet whispers, and clings to Kirsten's legs.

Kirsten bends down, and gives her a proper hug. 'I know, sweetie, I know. Don't worry, you're safe now.'

But she can't focus completely on Harriet.

The paramedic is satisfied with Harriet. One of the fire crew ducks his head into the ambulance.

'We've brought it under control,' he says, 'but there's a lot of damage.'

Kirsten nods, she hopes bravely, but her lower lip gives her away. 'I'm just glad we're all safe,' she says.

'Do you have any thoughts about how the fire started?' asks Becky.

The fireman looks at the ground. 'It's not my place to say at this stage, love.'

Becky nods. 'OK. Thanks.'

He nods back and takes his leave.

Kirsten looks at Becky. She dreads what Becky might say next because she knows it may be true. So instead, Kirsten voices it herself.

'He couldn't have, could he?'

Becky nods slowly. 'Yes, I think he probably could.'

Chapter 52

BECKY

'Think about it,' Becky whispers. 'It makes life so much easier for him, if none of us are around. Burn the evidence, you know?'

They're sitting in a neighbour's house – not Yvette's, her structure hasn't yet been declared safe – drinking yet another cup of tea. Harriet is sitting between them on the floor, drinking hot chocolate and playing with the neighbour's dog. Kirsten keeps being called away to talk to fire officials and insurers, but they're finally snatching five minutes together, unobserved.

'But *Harriet*?' Kirsten asks Becky. 'How could he even think about doing that to an innocent child?'

Becky looks at Kirsten. 'He's not the man you married, right?'

Kirsten shrugs. 'I don't know. Maybe he is. Maybe he's always been like this.'

'What – selfish, reckless, a liar?' Becky asks. She's glad Kirsten is putting the focus on Harriet. It stops Becky thinking about herself. After everything he's put her through, he would want to burn her to death too?

'You know he threatened my sister with a knife?' Becky asks Kirsten. It's a genuine question, and she wants the answer. Just how much did Kirsten know about Ian's trip up to Bristol? She watches as Kirsten's eyes widen.

'No,' says Kirsten.

'She narrowly avoided going to A&E. We'd been staying with her, me and Harriet. He could have got us then, too.'

Becky doesn't take her eyes off Kirsten. Is that a flash of recognition in her eyes?

Kirsten leans forward and strokes Harriet's hair. 'And then perhaps he would have come for me,' Kirsten says.

'What's to say he still won't?' Becky asks.

Kirsten turns to her. 'What do you mean?'

Becky gestures around her. 'It will be in the press, all this. Our lucky escape. He'll know he hasn't managed it. Probably try to make another attempt.'

Kirsten blows out her cheeks. 'You think we should go to the police?'

Becky scrunches her face up. 'Not necessarily.'

Now Becky feels herself being closely scrutinised.

'I thought you'd be only too pleased to tell them,' Kirsten says. 'After your threats to Dr Clare, and to us.'

Becky frowns. 'What threats?'

'Your letters! Telling her you'd go public with everything unless she persuaded me to give up my daughter. I mean, Harriet.'

Becky shakes her head. 'No, I'm sorry, I don't know what you're talking about.'

And she doesn't. It would have been quite a good idea, if she'd thought about it – putting pressure on that bitch of a doctor, make her put it on Kirsten.

Kirsten gives a dry laugh. 'I'm sorry, Becky, but I can't believe that. They came from your address in Croydon. Who else would …'

She trails off. In unison, they say: 'Ian.'

There's a pause. Becky watches the realisation hit home in Kirsten.

'Devious bastard,' Kirsten says softly. 'He wrote those letters, then made a fuss about them, brought them to my attention. Spoilt my trip with Harriet by leaving one out when he knew I'd be spending the day with her and be at my most vulnerable. Trying to jolt me into doing some kind of deal with you, I guess. Stop you going public.'

Becky speaks again. 'He's been shit-scared, all along, of losing his job—'

Kirsten interjects. 'His good name,' she says.

Becky nods. 'Right. And of going to prison even. Every last thing he's done has been in self-interest.'

She sees Kirsten look at her again. 'But what did you think when I replied to one of your letters, saying I wouldn't give Harriet back? If you didn't write them?'

Becky shrugs. 'I didn't receive any letters. Maybe Ian intercepted it.'

'In Watford?' Kirsten asks.

'Maybe when he told you he was travelling with work, he was elsewhere? He tried to show me a lot that he was helping, keep me sweet, I guess,' Becky suggests, her tone as kind as possible. She could so easily say 'You knew bugger all about your husband and he's a devious shit.' But there'd be no point in totally crushing Kirsten, satisfying as it would be. 'You can add manipulative bastard to his list of titles, if you like.'

'And here's me thinking you wanted to ride off into the sunset with him and Harriet.'

Becky shakes her head. 'No way. Everything I've done, it's been to get close to Harriet. I couldn't give a shit about Ian. Or rather, I could – a really big shit full of hate. He's messed up my life.'

Becky feels Kirsten's hand on hers momentarily. 'I think I'm probably partly to blame for that,' Kirsten says, softly.

Yes, of course you are, Becky thinks. And I hate you for it.

She shrugs. 'We'll move past that,' she says. 'Now that we have an agreement about Harriet.'

'We need to keep her safe – that's the priority,' Kirsten says. 'So what do we do about Ian? Why not go to the police?'

Becky stretches her hands above her head, then leans back to look fondly at Harriet. 'Think what the fallout would be. The police would want to know why we thought it was Ian, who we all are, in relation to Harriet. The full story will have to come out. And it will be all over the press. Harriet will get wind of it, eventually, whether it's now or in the future. How would you feel if you knew you were born out of a rape?'

'Ian didn't rape you, Becky – you were both drugged, by those hideous girls on the course!'

Becky shrugs. 'I sure as hell didn't consent. And do you know what – he shouldn't have put me in a position where people were able to think the two of us should be together. He'd overstepped a line. The girls weren't all as hideous as you think.' She thinks of Caitlin, her promise to help, when she found out that Becky was pregnant. A promise that neither of them had forgotten.

'But rape – it's different,' Kirsten says, apparently trying to salvage some good from her husband. 'With you, you were both victims. Ian, too.'

'That time, maybe,' Becky says.

She sees Kirsten flinch.

'What do you mean?' Kirsten asks her.

'I wasn't the only one,' Becky says. 'He seems to have enjoyed the summer school in another year too.'

'What, and he slept with another sixth former? After you?'

Becky leans forward, closer to Kirsten. It's the big news story, the one she's kept for when she's needed it.

'She wasn't a sixth former,' Becky says. 'She was fifteen. So there you have it – statutory rape. Which is why I don't think we need to go to the police to be safe from Ian. Not about us, anyway.'

Chapter 53

KIRSTEN

So now as well as attempted murderer and arsonist, her husband is a rapist? A sex offender, a paedophile? All that contrition after he'd got Becky pregnant, the late-night confession over what had happened. He slept with an underage girl? And then, even before that – she thinks back to the tenderness of their first years together. The holding her hand, physically and metaphorically, first through the miscarriage – the baby that hadn't worked out – then through all the IVF. She'd known him since they'd met at university – she was an undergrad, he was a postgrad, completing his teacher training. All that time, this monster was what was lurking beneath?

It's too much. She stands up, walks to the door of the neighbour's house, puts out her head for fresh air. But as she inhales, all she gets in her lungs is the ash of her former marital home.

She walks back in to Becky and Harriet.

Harriet looks up as she comes in. 'When is Daddy coming back?' she asks. 'Does he know about the fire?'

Kirsten wants to hug her dear sweet daughter to her, and tell her never to mind about Daddy again. To tell her that she must regard his sole contribution as having given her life – that maybe that is why he felt able to try to take it away.

Instead, she says: 'We're not seeing him right now, sweetie. And yes, I think he does know about the fire.'

Kirsten exchanges a look with Becky, then sits down beside her again.

'So what do we do?' she asks Becky.

Becky pulls her phone out of her pocket. 'This is her,' she says, loading up the screen. 'I knew her at school. She went to the drama school a year before me. She never told me about it at the time, but now I know everything. Ian confessed it to me when he found out I was pregnant. He felt so guilty that he'd interfered in two girls' lives.'

Kirsten peers over the screen. Caitlin. She's slim, pretty, fresh-faced. A spark in her eye. Whether or not the spark was there or not when she was fifteen, Ian should have known better. Perhaps it was this secret, then, that he'd really been so terrified about getting out there, not the Becky secret. The actual thing that would land him in prison, on a sex offenders list – more serious than sleeping with a seventeen-year-old student. And it had clearly been on his conscience, otherwise why would he have told Becky? For a moment, Kirsten feels sorry for Ian – so much plotting, but such a poor judge of character. Then she remembers what he tried to do to Harriet (and to her, and to Becky), and she hardens against him again.

'What's your plan?' she asks Becky.

'I'm already in touch with her,' Becky says. 'She's like a sleeper agent – I've been waiting to wake her when the time is right. Said I'd help her.'

'And is she ready to be woken? I mean, what's in it for her?'

Becky shrugs. 'If she gets some press money from telling her story, she can have a pretty excellent year off travelling the globe.'

Come on – what? Ian is going to be destroyed because a girl wants some air tickets?

Becky seems to sense Kirsten's reticence. 'We're not doing this just because of her. We're doing because of all of us – you, me, Harriet. Particularly Harriet.'

'You're right,' Kirsten says. And if Ian had been foolish enough to have underage sex with a student, then he deserved the punishment he would surely get.

Kirsten watches as Becky taps away on her phone. A few moments later, there's a buzzing. Becky holds up the phone and leaves the room.

Kirsten places her chin on Harriet's head, so Harriet's hair nestles up against her neck. 'You doing all right down there, sweetie? I know all this is a bit of a mess.'

'Can we get a dog when we get a new house, Mummy?' Harriet asks. She is busy stroking the ears of the neighbour's golden retriever. 'Bessie', her name tag says she's called.

'Why not?' Kirsten says. She doesn't say: I don't know if there'll be a new house, I don't know if the insurers will find out your dad set fire to it and won't pay out, I don't know if we'll have to live in rentals for ever, or if we're going to have to go and live in Becky's flat. I don't even know if you'll always call me Mummy, now that Becky's in your good books for saving our lives. So she says yes to the dog. Just to keep it simple for Harriet.

Kirsten sits back on the sofa and exhales. Christ, what a mess. All she wants to do is go back to sleep in the nice soft white sheets in her lovely house, the house that she'd put so much care into over the years, had added detail after detail to. The house she's shared with a man who would murder his own daughter. She shakes her head. Even if the house was repairable – which it wouldn't be – she couldn't go back. Life had moved on.

Becky comes back into the room. 'Done,' she says.

'What do you mean, "done"?' Kirsten asks.

'She's phoning the tabloids, and the police. Saying all the #metoo stuff has made her realise she can't stay quiet any longer.

It'll be all over the papers tomorrow, and the police will pick Ian up and charge him.'

'Really? They don't seem to have been too quick on charging all the other people who've been named as potential rapists in the media.'

'She was underage. In his care, as a student. He still teaches. It'll be a priority.'

Kirsten nods glumly. Of course. And she won't escape from being named in the press. She'll have to be 'unavailable for comment', won't she? She pretty much is – her landline, her mobile and her house are all in ashes. She feels prickles of sweat in her spine. The papers will love that story, won't they? They turn up to the house of the alleged rapist, and find that – coincidentally – it's been burned down. There'll be a profile of her, and what she knew about her husband. How could she live with a man like this? Had she burnt the house down when she found out? Maybe she'd better release a statement. Maybe it's all going to come out anyway.

She looks again at Harriet, playing innocently at her feet. They'll have to manage it. They key thing is to hold on to her. With Becky. Of course.

'Shall I say anything to the press?' she asks Becky.

Becky shrugs. 'Your choice. Either way, Ian is going to burn.'

Chapter 54

BECKY

Becky manages to find a quiet corner of the neighbour's house to phone her sister Julia. After Becky had texted her earlier to say what was going on, she'd had a barrage of calls, all of which she'd instinctively flipped to voicemail. But then she'd had a text: 'IF YOU DON'T CALL ME, I'M NEVER SPEAKING TO YOU AGAIN!' And she knows from past experience that Julia might just mean it.

'Do you believe me now that he's a bastard?' Becky starts the conversation.

'What do you mean?' Julia asks. Then there's a silence. Becky can't see her, but she can hear Julia gradually realising. 'Shit, what, Ian …?'

'That's not how we're bringing him down, though. So forget I said it. But I thought you needed to know. Policy of honesty going forward, and all that.'

'But why would you not tell the police? He'd be locked up for ever, attempted murder, arson, assault. He'd never bother you again!'

Becky shrugs. She doesn't need Julia to get it, just for her not to be a barrier. 'It's for Harriet,' she says. 'And Kirsten. And therefore for me. Everything would come out. It's better this way.'

'Which way?' Julia asks. Becky can hear the suspicion in her voice.

'Don't worry about it,' Becky says.

'What happened to your "policy of honesty going forward"?' Julia asks.

Becky considers. She's only just got Julia back onside. Which is going to be better – keeping secrets from her (and Julia knowing that), or telling the truth and risking her approbation?

She knows Julia. And Julia now knows what Ian is capable of, and how much Harriet means. Julia was the one who wouldn't speak to her for years simply because she thought Becky had given up on Harriet. This plan was now the opposite of giving up on Harriet.

So Becky takes a deep breath and explains everything to Julia. Everything she'll read about in the press in the coming days. And the inside story she'll never hear.

When she's done, Becky waits for Julia's reaction.

'What if it doesn't work?' Julia says. 'What if they decide not to prosecute, that it all happened too long ago?'

Trust Julia to voice the one thing that was worrying Becky. 'They will,' Becky says. 'Think of the political pressure. A teacher. An underage schoolgirl. The CPS will have to take the case – and if they don't, they'll have a whole load of ministers on their back. It will work.'

'And the jury? What about them? And what if Ian decides he's going to tell the whole sordid truth? That it will somehow help his defence?'

'What – hello, jury, not only do I commit statutory rape, I sleep with other students, steal their daughters, then burn down their homes?'

'He wouldn't be pleading it like that.'

Becky knows Julia's right. But she has a fragile agreement, with

Kirsten, even with Harriet. She doesn't want to admit the risk of it breaking down.

'Look, it's just Plan A, OK?' she tells Julia. 'We can do Plan B: the whole truth, at any time. Are you with me?'

'Does it matter?' Julia asks.

'Yes,' Becky says. 'It does.'

'In that case,' Julia says, 'I'm with you.'

They end the call, Julia agreeing to come to London as soon as Ian is in custody. 'The guy has a knife and a matchbox,' as she puts it. 'I'm not leaving Bristol until he's behind bars.'

'What about me and Harriet? What do we do?' Becky asks.

'Oh, I think you have that all figured out,' Julia says.

Which is true. She does.

Chapter 55

KIRSTEN

'Who were you speaking to?' Kirsten asks Becky, when she comes back into the room.

'No one,' says Becky.

Kirsten raises an eyebrow.

Becky shakes her head. 'Sorry. Force of habit. I've been trying to keep my background a secret. You get used to it. It was my sister.'

Kirsten nods. There it is – the usual stirring of nostalgia, of guilt, of longing, when someone mentions they have a sister. She wishes she could just call hers as easily as that.

'What does your sister make of all this?' Becky asks Kirsten.

Kirsten frowns. 'What do you mean?'

'You said you had a sister. That time, when I came round to tea. When I was "Miriam".'

Kirsten blushes. She hates thinking back to that tea. Her embarrassing assumption that Becky was just a young, childless teacher with a knack for spoiling Sunday afternoons. But that tea also now carries the fear of how it could all have ended, with 'Miriam' basically stalking them, getting creepily close to Harriet. How it could all still end.

She doesn't say all that to Becky, of course. 'I haven't told her. We don't really speak,' Kirsten explains.

'Anything to do with me?' Becky asks.

Kirsten smirks, despite the self-centred presumption of the question. 'A lot to do with you,' she says.

'Then I'm telling you to fix it,' Becky says. 'I fixed things with my sister, and it's so much better now. Having a confidante you can genuinely trust. Of course, me and you will end up becoming like sisters, the amount of time we'll spend together with Harriet. But it's not the same, is it?'

Kirsten closes herself down a little internally. She doesn't want to be like a sister to Becky. It's not the same, not at all. From what Kirsten can remember, with a real sister, you may hate each other at times but you know that, ultimately, they wouldn't do anything that would really screw you over. Maybe they'd hurt you. Maybe they'd put themselves first when they should have helped you. Maybe they'd just ignore you for years.

But they wouldn't steal your child.

'I'll try calling her,' Kirsten says.

She still knows Nina's number. Of course she does – they were sisters. Called each other every week, when they were younger, in the times when you learnt people's mobile numbers. Even with her mobile lost in the blaze, she's proud to think she can still get in touch.

Using Becky's mobile, she dials.

Invalid number.

Shit. Nina would be one of the few people to change her number. Kirsten wonders if it's because of her.

Kirsten calls her mum.

'Mum, hi,' she starts, forgetting for a moment that her house has been on the news in flames. There are endless questions: is she all right, is Harriet all right, is Ian keeping them safe?

Kirsten explains as much as she needs to, but nowhere near as much as she could. So far as her mum is concerned, Harriet is a true grandchild. She can't take that away from her. And how do you undo all those years of lying?

Once the onslaught is over, she asks the question. 'Do you have Nina's number? I've got the wrong one on my phone.'

There's a pause. 'Um, I'm not sure I should …'

'Come on, Mum,' Kirsten begs. 'I really want to speak to her, patch things up. The fire put everything into perspective. And she'll have seen it on the news; she must be wondering what's going on.'

'If she is, sweetheart, she hasn't said anything to me.'

So, Kirsten was already dead to her sister, was she? But she couldn't be. Not really. There must still be a flicker of something there. All those years together as children, as teenagers – the dressing up in sunglasses and pretending to be rock stars, doing botched dye jobs on each other's hair, testing each other on their homework, covering for each other if Mum and Dad thought they were revising but they were actually going out with a boy – that couldn't just be erased, could it? Beneath her *froideur*, Nina must be burning to talk to her. Mustn't she?

'Come on, Mum – can you please just give me her number?' Kirsten asks again.

Another pause, while her mother considers the competing demands of maternal diplomacy.

'No, I think I'd better not, sweetheart. I don't know what's gone on between you and your sister, but I don't want to be drawn into it. I gave Nina a promise when she changed her number. I'd love you to start talking again, darling, but I can't break a promise. I can't risk losing her like you've lost her.'

Kirsten feels herself close to tears. If only she could talk to her mother about the fear of losing her own child. That's why she needs to talk to Nina. She's the only one apart from Becky and Ian who know. And she can't be totally honest about her feelings with Becky. And she's certainly not talking to Ian.

Perhaps if Nina saw her, and Harriet, and Becky, all together, she would relent? Understand that Kirsten was doing 'the right thing'? And she'd yield?

'She still lives at the same address though, right?' Kirsten asks.

Her mother sighs, as if worn out by the conflict to come. 'Yes, yes she does.'

Then that's where Kirsten, Becky and Harriet would go. It was only Camden, so very close to them. Ian wouldn't think of looking for them there. And it would get them out of the neighbour's way – Kirsten wasn't stupid, she knew there were muttered conversations between husband and wife, wondering how long the fire refugees and their 'nanny' were going to stay.

'We're all going on a little trip,' Kirsten tells Harriet, having already explained to Becky. 'To see your auntie.'

'Auntie Julia?' Harriet asks excitedly.

Kirsten closes her eyes briefly. How confused their world had become. 'No, sweetheart, a different auntie.'

'Oh. Will Daddy be there too?'

'No, darling. At least, I hope he won't.'

* * *

Half an hour later, the three of them are standing outside a smart townhouse in Camden Square.

'Does well for herself, your sister,' Becky comments.

'Or rather, her husband does,' Kirsten says. When Nina had gone on maternity leave, she and her husband had agreed she didn't have to go back to work as a physiotherapist. At the time, his architecture firm was doing well and Nina not working saved on a nanny. Kirsten had no idea whether the arrangement remained the same – she hadn't asked her mother, and her mother hadn't volunteered the information. Perhaps another promise had been made. If the arrangement had changed, their chances of finding Nina at home were slim.

'Are we going inside?' Harriet asks, breaking into Kirsten's thoughts.

'We'd better try, I suppose,' Kirsten says.

Together, the three of them go through the gate to the house. Kirsten lines Becky and Harriet up next to each other, hopefully making it immediately obvious to Nina what is going on, so she doesn't slam the door in Kirsten's face. Or maybe that's too much to hope. Maybe Becky just looks like a nanny. Kirsten flicks a glance at her, then at Harriet.

No, she realises. She doesn't look like a nanny. She looks like the mother of the girl next to her. Kirsten has never really seen the resemblance before – or perhaps she's chosen to ignore it – but there it is. Like mother, like daughter. Harriet has Kirsten's mannerisms and gait, but the bone structure, the eyes, the shape of the forehead – they are all Becky's.

Kirsten rings the bell.

Nothing happens for a while, so Becky leans over and rings again.

Just as Kirsten is about to declare that nobody's in, there's a cry of 'Just a minute', and footsteps running to the door.

At first, it looks as though the door has opened by itself. But then Kirsten looks down. There's a little girl, a year (or rather, three hundred and forty days – Kirsten done the maths before) older than Harriet.

'Hello, Ruby,' Kirsten says. 'Is your mummy in?'

But Mummy soon comes to the door.

'Kirsten!' she exclaims. She's holding a tube of glitter glue in one hand, and there are blue smudges of it on her temple.

'And Harriet, and Becky,' Kirsten says. 'A lot has happened. Please, can we come in?'

Nina runs her hand through her hair. It becomes instantly covered in blue glitter.

'Um, you might want to wash your hand …' Kirsten says, indicating the glitter situation.

Nina either doesn't understand or ignores her. Finally, she speaks. 'Ruby, please take Harriet to play with your toys. These two ladies and I have a lot to discuss.'

* * *

While Harriet and Ruby play in the toy-strewn conservatory, Kirsten, Nina and Becky sit in the adjoining kitchen drinking tea. They could be three mum friends catching up on a play date. Except they're not that friendly. And it's a moot call who deserves the title 'mum.'

'It must have been so difficult for you,' Nina says, to Becky. There's a filthy look but no sympathy for Kirsten.

'It was Ian who was in the wrong, not Kirsten,' Becky says. Kirsten would like to believe that. But she knows it's not altogether true. And she doubts Becky believes it either. From the look on her face, Nina certainly doesn't.

'I thought I was saving a baby who would be put in care or adopted,' Kirsten says. Even though she already explained it to Nina, five years ago, and Nina wouldn't listen then.

'You should have done more,' Nina says. 'And certainly before now.'

'Finish playing your game, Harriet,' Kirsten calls out. 'I think we're going soon.' She shouldn't have bothered coming. It's the same argument as five years ago.

'No, wait,' Becky says. 'Come on – if I can forgive Kirsten, you can,' she says to Nina.

Nina looks at Becky. 'You can't have forgiven her,' she says. 'You're just tolerating her to be close to your daughter.'

Kirsten used to admire Nina for saying the things no one else would say, for calling them on their bullshit. Now she just wants to kick her. What right does she have to be so judgemental, so smug?

Kirsten looks over at Ruby and Harriet playing together. It's a lovely sight. They're both clever, beautiful girls. It reminds Kirsten of when she and Nina used to play together. Except as 'cousins' there is less conflict than there was between her and Nina as sisters. They know that when the play date ends, that's that. You can't send your sister packing after an hour. Or maybe you can.

Kirsten tries a different approach. 'When did you first fall in love with Ruby?' she asks Nina.

'The first moment I saw her,' Nina responds, automatically.

'Exactly,' says Kirsten. 'So what would you have done, in my place?' she asks.

She sees Nina look over to Ruby, her flesh-and-blood daughter. She knows Nina understands the question. She knows Nina would never have given Ruby away. That once you are mother to a child, however that comes about, you will do your utmost to hold on to it, if you can.

'It must have been so difficult for you, Becky,' Nina says again.

Quietly, Kirsten, Becky and Harriet take their leave. Kirsten tries not to cry as she opens the front door. She'd just hoped that biological bond, the nostalgic bind, would release some rush of love from Nina. But apparently not. Apparently she was on her own. Apart from a daughter who wasn't really hers. And the daughter's mother, who had saved their lives. Who knew what she planned to do with those lives now?

But at the door, just as they are about to leave, Kirsten feels a hand on her shoulder, a scribbled phone number thrust into her palm.

'Call me,' Nina whispers.

And there it is. Finally. The love.

Kirsten nods. She wants to hug Nina, seal the emotion. But maybe it's too much, too soon. So she just reaches out a hand to Nina, puts it on her elbow, holds her gaze, lets her eyes fill with tears.

When she turns, she sees Becky halfway down the path with Harriet.

She's stealing my child! is the immediate panic message from Kirsten's brain.

Except Becky and Harriet are hand in hand. No one is being stolen away; Harriet is going willingly.

Which is exactly what Kirsten can't allow. She cannot be distracted by whatever happens with Ian. She must keep herself in Harriet's life. Somehow.

Chapter 56

BECKY

Two days later, they're holed up in Becky's Croydon flat – Becky, Kirsten, Harriet. It's safe to be there again; the media reported yesterday that following Caitlin Parsons' shocking revelations about underage sex with a teacher, a man was being held in custody. Julia's joined them too, bringing sleeping bags. They're all sleeping like squashed sardines in the living room. No one can work out who would share with who without fracturing the fragile peace.

'Can we have Cheerios and ice cream?' Harriet had squealed when she saw Auntie Julia at the front door.

Julia ruffles Harriet's hair then flicks up the blind in the living room. She's warier than when Becky stayed with her in Bristol, her movements less fluid. That will be Ian's doing. 'How are those press vultures still out there? Haven't they got homes to go to?'

'Maybe Ian's burnt theirs down too,' Kirsten mutters. 'Come on, pull the blind down; we don't want to be papped!'

'All right, snappy,' Julia says. 'I know the insurers have pissed you off, but don't take it out on us!'

'I just don't know why they can't pay out pending an investigation. I didn't burn it down myself, that's for sure!'

'Um, because they know they'd never get the money back once they'd given it to you?' Julia suggests.

'Just be grateful they've offered you the temporary rental space,' Becky says.

She'd seen the pictures they'd sent through. It all looked fine. Kirsten would have one bedroom, Harriet another, and Becky could sleep on the sofa-bed in the living room. As long as they were all under one roof, it didn't matter. Except Becky suspects they'd somehow all end up sleeping in the same room, like they are now. Becky wants to see Harriet in the night, check she's still there. Kirsten had said that after the trauma of the fire, it was good to be together. But Becky suspects their reasons are the same. It's a question of trust.

Harriet had seen the photos of the insurer-properties they could move into too, and had expressed her opinion on which was the nicest. It was in Harrow, not Islington. Becky said they should go with that choice. She'd received a glare from Kirsten in return. Now, Harriet was sitting on the floor playing games on Becky's mobile. Occasionally Becky helped her get to the next level, but mostly she just sat watching. Her child. Finally, she was having a proper, meaningful relationship with her child.

Becky's landline phone goes again. She goes to answer it. 'Bound to be the insurers for you, though, Kirsten – more forms coming in the post, I'm sure.'

Kirsten groans and puts her head in her hands. 'I don't know where they think they're posting them to!' she exclaims. 'Idiots!'

Laughing, Becky picks up the receiver. It's not the insurer, though.

It's Ian.

'They said I was allowed a phone call,' he tells her.

'What do you want?' she asks.

'You know it's not true,' he says. 'Call her off. Make Caitlin tell the truth.'

Becky pauses. If only he'd called on her mobile. She could

have taken it into her room. Now, she's stuck in the middle of Julia, Kirsten and Harriet. With Ian saying what he's saying. She'll have to be smart – she doesn't want Kirsten finding out. Who knows what wifely feelings of empathy may still lurk in that treacherous breast?

'And are they going to add charges of attempted murder, arson and assault to that?' Becky says to Ian. She's going to have to play the part for her assembled audience, pretending he's said something else – hopefully he's not speaking loudly enough for the others to hear him. She'll put on a show, learn the lessons that he taught her, at drama camp. But keep Ian's name out of it. Harriet mustn't know it's her daddy. They must somehow preserve her innocence through all of this. And Ian needs to get the message. If he denies this, there's worse to come.

There's a silence in the room. The grown-ups know who it is now. Kirsten is staring.

'Becky, I'll be on the sex offenders list. I'll be in prison as a child rapist; I'll be slaughtered. Tell her to stop her accusations. I can't be that person. I can't.'

She thinks he might be crying.

'I think you know you have to plead guilty,' she says into the phone.

'I know I'm guilty, just not of that. Tell Kirsten, tell Harriet, I'm sorry, I'm so sorry, I don't know what I was thinking, I just, I wanted it all to go away.' Now he is definitely crying.

'No one wants to hear it, Ian.'

'I could ruin you, you know,' he says. His voice sounds wild, desperate. 'I could have you put in prison for perverting the court of justice, getting an old school friend to stitch me up. I bet you haven't been careful on your messages, on your calls. I'm not as stupid as you seem to think.'

'It's no good threatening me,' Becky says loudly.

She sees Julia frown. Kirsten mouths 'Can I speak to him?'

'I'd just like to point this out to you,' Becky continues. 'I'm sitting in a room with my sister, who you threatened with a knife. And there's a witness who saw you visiting the house. Oh, and here I am, another student you slept with. Good luck with your denial.'

The phone goes silent for a while. 'I'm not how you make me sound,' Ian says.

'I think you are,' Becky says. 'I think you have to accept your guilt.'

'I was only trying to do what was best,' he says. 'At least tell Kirsten I didn't do it – the underage stuff. Please.'

Becky covers the mouthpiece and addresses Kirsten. 'Ian says he loves you and he's sorry for what he's done.'

'Bastard!' Kirsten says. Becky sees her turn white, her hands shaking.

'Do you still want to speak to him?' Becky asks.

Kirsten shakes her head, and hugs Harriet to her. Becky will forgive that, this once.

Becky takes her hand away from the receiver again.

'It's over, Ian. You have to face up to your crimes.'

'After all I've done for you!' Ian shouts down the phone. 'Becky, please!'

'For you. It's always been you doing the best for you. Caitlin is going to do what's best for everyone.'

'Becky—'

'Don't phone again.'

Becky puts down the phone. She blows out her cheeks, like someone who's just been through a trial.

'That man is sick,' she finally says.

'Are you OK?' Kirsten says, coming over to her. 'What did he say?'

'Oh, that he'd come and get us, that he was going to deny everything, bring us all into it, that kind of thing.'

'Bring it on!' says Julia.

'Do you think he will?' asks Kirsten, biting her lip.

Becky shakes her head. 'He's got too much to lose,' she says. 'We've got too much on him.'

She walks over to Julia, Kirsten and Harriet in turn, puts one hand on their heads, as if blessing them. 'Don't worry,' she says. 'We'll be fine.'

'Is Daddy in prison?' Harriet asks.

Becky stares at her. This wonderful, intelligent creature that she and Kirsten have been pussy-footing around, trying to protect. And she knows everything. She really was Becky's own little Matilda.

'Don't worry about a thing,' Becky tells her.

And there's nothing to worry about. As long as Ian's sensible, and Caitlin plays her part. And Kirsten sticks to her word.

Becky's mobile flashes, and Harriet hands it to her. 'You've got a message,' she says.

Becky takes the phone from Harriet. It's a SnapChat message. Caitlin pouting in a selfie, giving her the thumbs-up. Becky smiles. Five years on, it's still the same Caitlin – long blonde hair, pink lip gloss. Presumably cut-off shorts too. Becky had called in the promised favour from Caitlin, given after Harriet's birth all those years ago. 'If there's anything I can ever do', Caitlin had said. And there was. Fit Ian up. It was the least Caitlin could do. Even though she'd done so much already – inadvertently giving Becky her Harriet.

'It's good to know people have got your back,' she says, out loud.

Kirsten nods. 'It is,' she says. 'We'll all look after each other,' she says. Becky hopes, for Kirsten's sake – for Harriet's sake – that she means it.

Chapter 57

KIRSTEN

It could be a normal school day. A mother fussing over her child's hair. Insisting that the little pink clips stay in, that the neat braids are not untied.

But it's not a normal day. Because the mother doing the fussing isn't her. It's the other mother. For herself, Kirsten thinks that the clips are too pink. That they should be gender-neutral, purple, if they're there at all. Becky disagrees. Kirsten's running late, so the pink clips stay in.

What a lucky girl Harriet is to have two mothers! What a lucky woman Kirsten is to be able to leave the house on time, knowing that her daughter's other mother will take their child to school, while Kirsten goes to her practice! Isn't this just the happiest, most idyllic scenario? Won't she just cry with anger and frustration as she drives the Lexus over from Alexandra Palace to Islington, while Harriet walks (presumably hand in hand) with Becky to the local primary school?

At least the house is just temporary – the rental accommodation that the insurers are providing. Kirsten told Becky that Harrow had fallen through, but really she just couldn't face the drive, even for a little while. She's pretty confident that now, three weeks after the fire, she'll be getting the payout after all.

'You should make it a life change,' Becky told her. 'Give up work, spend more time with Harriet.' This, from the woman who practically throws the keys at her to get her out of the door each morning.

Except at weekends. At weekends, they all have to sit eating croissants together at the breakfast table. Kirsten slathers her croissant with jam to stop herself choking on the crumbs. When Becky perkily announces that they should all go to the park together, Kirsten acquiesces. Except she usually insists on the red coat, not the pink one. And so Becky asks Harriet which one she'd prefer. Harriet doesn't want a coat at all. She just wants to run, by herself, in the park.

Just as Kirsten is about to leave this morning, looking forward to planting her customary kiss on gorgeous Harriet's head, Becky pulls Kirsten to one side.

'I think we're doing a marvellous job, you know,' Becky says. 'It's working so well. Thank you. Look how happy everyone is! I told you it would be just like having a nanny, but so much better!'

And Becky hugs Harriet to her. If Kirsten were to kiss Harriet's head now, she'd have to put her head into Becky's belly. She can't work out if Becky knows this, if Becky also has a plan. Either way, she has to leave without her kiss – she can't face the physical contact with Becky. She might snap, and headbutt her in the stomach by mistake. Destroy the illusion of perfection.

So instead she fakes a grin, and waves goodbye. Looking back at them, as they stand on the doorstep, she feels like she's been ejected from an Eden that Becky has created. There were three in the enchanted garden, which was too many; the serpent should have been the one that was ejected. Everyone knows it had to be two people, who if left to their own devices would have stayed in their gilded harmony for ever. And Becky makes sure that for a few minutes every day it is just her and Harriet.

But it was a false Eden, Becky must know that. Because a child cannot have two mothers, not like this. Two people trying to occupy exactly the same relationship space. Trying to fuss in different ways about the same things. Each having different models for their child's success. Both knowing they are right. Both trusting that, somehow, they will be supreme, and they will win.

And Kirsten fears so, so much that Becky will win. Because Becky can stay at home and help Harriet with her homework. She can be there at the school gates. She can stay up late making fun crafts and toys because she doesn't need to go to work the next day. She's a kept woman, the ideal stay-at-home mum. She is, of course, the real mother that Kirsten can never be. And so, Becky and Harriet drift ever closer.

But Kirsten goes out to work. Becky tells her she doesn't have to. But she does, doesn't she? Not because of a mortgage or school fees anymore – she can't use that excuse. 'Are we still on this topic, in the twenty-first century, questioning mothers going to work?' she says to Becky, playing the feminist, every time Becky makes the point. Yet that's not why. It's because of Harriet and Becky. Or not just because of them. She knows, though, that she can't be around them all the time; the jealousy would become too much. It's also because of herself. Because she has to keep something, out of the horror of knowing that her husband is sure at his forthcoming trial to be labelled a rapist, a sex offender; something of the life that came before these three weeks. Something to make her own existence feel real. And the medical practice does that.

Plus the time out gives her time to think. Time to think about how she can end this situation, the solution that doesn't solve anything. She thinks back to Ian and his knife. If only he'd got it right, if only he hadn't got greedy and tried to kill them all. Or if only she hadn't delegated it to him. Because this arrangement she and Becky have struck is unbearable. They can't just pretend they are both simply different sides of the same mothering coin – that this is an ideal situation, that Harriet has the luxury of a stay-at-home mum and a working mum, that they have somehow merged into one perfect woman who is doing it all. Life isn't like that. It's messier, more of a compromise. People have emotional agendas. Expectations. Resentments.

But this, this situation with Becky, it's too much of a compromise. It simply can't go on. Can it?

If it can't, Kirsten is going to have to take decisive action. Action that will no doubt harm her child, emotionally. Kirsten won't be popular. Motherhood isn't about popularity though, is it, or friendship? It's about doing what's best in the long run, not shying away from the difficult scenes.

Maybe. She doesn't know. Maybe you never know what motherhood is until you're right at the very end. Until your child is grown-up, and they have their own children, and you can see then whether they understand. All you did for them. All the choices you made. All the times you were torn.

She knows Becky won't be giving her own mother that recognition – there'd been messages, Becky had said, when all the press coverage about Caitlin Parsons came out. 'I didn't know he was such a monster,' one that Becky showed her had said. 'I'm sorry.' But Becky has said it's too late – that there's damage that can't be undone, reparations that can't be made. A mother's love should be unconditional, or at the very least a protective bubble against the world; thinking the best of your own child until someone else proves the worst. Becky's mother had failed that test.

Maybe that's what this was about for Becky – she needed to reclaim that notion of motherhood. She needed to be always there for her child, in a way her own mother wasn't. Kirsten knows she is lucky in that regard. She still meets her mother for lunch. They find things to talk about. Occasionally her sister comes too, their mother sensing a full reconciliation. So Kirsten doesn't have those issues.

But there are plenty to make up for them. Namely the mother-daughter-mother triangle to contend with, each facing the other, each with a tie to bind them to the other.

And so Kirsten drives on to work. It's all she can do, for now. But at the back of her mind, there's the constant refrain over the thrum of the engine: *there must be a way out. There must be a way out. I must be able to be the mother I want to be. And I must be able to do it alone.*

Chapter 58

BECKY

As soon as Kirsten leaves, Becky changes Harriet's hair-clips to purple. Becky doesn't want a pink-obsessed princess any more than Kirsten does. But you've got to play the game, haven't you? Becky can see, each time she wins a little point like that, Kirsten's heart breaking. Because Becky's heart breaks whenever Kirsten wins a point. All they each want is authority, the total autonomy to make decisions on Harriet's behalf. To be the absolute mother.

Kirsten will never have that. But Becky will. There'll come a time. Gradually, there'll be a flip over to when Harriet values Becky more than Kirsten. And when that day comes – be it in five months or five years – Kirsten will come home to emptiness.

The same emptiness Becky had for five years. Except Kirsten's will go on for ever. Kirsten will experience the same self-doubt, the same self-hatred that Becky had during that time. Imagine, seeing those perfect little blue eyes of baby Harriet for only an hour before she was taken away. Not being around long enough to witness the change to their present hazel. Not having a photo. No memento. Just a void. And she can't even get them back now, those memories, because all Kirsten's photos were lost in the fire.

Kirsten's mother has some, but they are sub-standard, cold, detached – not the ones a mother herself would take.

Becky thinks of this whenever some sympathy for Ian flares up. Ian, now locked up pending trial for a crime he didn't commit. She remembers, at the times when she pities him, how earnest and devoted to his craft he was at that summer school. How her skin had thrilled when he'd touched her for warm-up exercises. How sweet and tender the sex probably would have been if they hadn't both been drugged. But then he'd robbed her. In favouring his reputation and his marriage over her, by sliding from the horrified innocent guilt when he'd found out he'd unintentionally slept with and impregnated her, to shallow self-preservation, he'd connived to steal both her child and her future.

Becky could have been like Kirsten, going out to work, having someone else to look after her child – she had been all set, garnering the academic credentials to be a star. When Becky sees that expensive jeep going out of the drive, towards a rewarding career, she has a stab of jealousy. And that is all down to Ian. Ian and Kirsten. So the pair of them deserve all they get.

But they haven't managed to rob her utterly. Becky knows she has youth on her side. When Harriet is eighteen, able to make her own decisions, lead her own life, Becky will only be about as old as Kirsten is now. She can return to working, if that's what she wants to do. True, she might even have to do it before then, if she and Harriet are to be self-sufficient. And she can teach again; Kirsten had persuaded St Anthony's to drop the disciplinary charges, so Becky has a clean slate. Ian won't be able to teach again, ever; that's for sure.

So she'll carry on his legacy. He's taught her an awful lot. How to manipulate. How to lie. How to put the interests of yourself above all others. She'll be even better than him, though, because Harriet's interests will always be paramount. Like today, for example. Kirsten had announced she'd have no more appointments after 3 p.m., so she'd be home to come along on the school pick-up run. Sadly for Kirsten, she'll have someone make an appointment for 5 p.m. And then cancel. It's happened before. Kirsten never seems to realise Becky is behind the no-shows. But Harriet will get the benefit – because Harriet doesn't want both of them bothering her at home time. Having them both ask, with the same rapture, about her school day. Both of them wanting to straighten her socks, soothe the grazed knee, swing hands with her as they walk down the lane. Being three spoils it for each of them.

Becky takes Harriet's hand as they leave the house for school (wearing the red coat, not the pink one, because Kirsten will never know).

'What will you be doing at school, today, my little one?' she asks, as they walk along.

Harriet chatters about the project on bees that her form teacher, Ms Simmons, is doing with them. They are going to study hives, then all do a show about bees, buzzing around the stage.

'You'll be able to come and watch,' Harriet tells Becky. 'And Mummy too.'

Becky doubts that. There's not the space for them both on the front row among all the proud parents. Kirsten may have a surprise late appointment that day too.

Thank you, Ian, for all of this, Becky thinks. May you rot in jail, but you'll always be with me. And I know I'll always, always be in the thoughts of you and Kirsten. After all, no one forgets a good teacher. Right?

Acknowledgements

I am grateful to all those who have brought *The Classroom* to my readers, directly or indirectly.

My insightful agent Amanda Preston at LBA Books for helping me take the initial idea to a novel-worthy concept. My wonderful editor Clio Cornish at HQ Digital for pushing first draft to full manuscript. And the whole HQ Digital team for their work behind the scenes – I still love that cover design!

Of course, there's the whole domestic support team to acknowledge as well. My parents and my husband for being part of the childcare puzzle – and for everything else, over all the years. My sweet newborn son for putting up with sleeping on me while I type. And my lovely elder son for accepting that I can't always play all of the time. May you both be your safest and best selves always. Or just yourselves. That is enough.

Given the subject of the book, I'd also like to acknowledge two teachers: Susan Saunders and Joyce Robson, who taught me English and Philosophy respectively at Central Newcastle High School. They made the classroom a safe and emboldening place to explore the words and ideas that have so enriched my creative life.

Thank you, of course, to my readers, for wanting more – without you, these books would have no place in the world. In particular, thank you to those who have placed reviews of previous books online, which very much helps the writer's journey. I hope that is a large enough hint to those who would like to review *The Classroom!*

Reading Group Questions

1. To what extent did you sympathise with Kirsten? Did this change as the novel progressed?

2. What about Becky?

3. When a child is adopted fairly and legally, when do you think is the right time to explain their history to them? Is it ever right to keep a child's real parents a secret?

4. How much responsibility should Clare take for what happened?

5. Did Yvette do the right thing when Becky comes to the house? If not, what would have been the right thing to do?

6. Has there ever been a time when you have 'known too much' about a friend, neighbour or college and have chosen to intervene? To what extent do we have a social responsibility to do so?

7. Is it ever acceptable for a teacher to have a relationship with a student or former student, if the student is of age?

8. Did you have a teacher who changed your life, for good or for bad? How? Why do you think teachers make such an impression on us?

9. Do you think Becky's sister Julie reacted in the right way to the arrival of Becky and Harriet? What would you have done?

10. What do you think happens next?

Dear Reader,

Thank you so much for taking the time to read this book – we hope you enjoyed it! If you did, we'd be so appreciative if you left a review.

Here at HQ Digital we are dedicated to publishing fiction that will keep you turning the pages into the early hours. We publish a variety of genres, from heartwarming romance, to thrilling crime and sweeping historical fiction.

To find out more about our books, enter competitions and discover exclusive content, please join our community of readers by following us at:

🐦 @HQDigitalUK

📘 facebook.com/HQDigitalUK

Are you a budding writer? We're also looking for authors to join the HQ Digital family! Please submit your manuscript to:

HQDigital@harpercollins.co.uk.

Hope to hear from you soon!

Loved *The Classroom*? Keep reading for an extract from *The Good Mother*, another bestselling title from A.L. Bird – available now.

Prologue

The girl gets into the car that's waiting for her. She looks over her shoulder first, like he's told her to, to check Mummy isn't watching. Would Mummy really mind? She can't be sure. But he seems to think so. And he knows best, right? So she does the covert glance then slings her schoolbag into the back seat, like all the other times. He holds his cheek towards her for a kiss, which she dutifully bestows. Then he starts the engine with a vroom. Familiar buildings pass by. Buses on their way to places she recognises: Muswell Hill Broadway; Barnet (The Spires); North Finchley. There are a couple of kids from school. She raises her hand to wave but the man, seeing her, says, 'Best not.' So she lowers her hand and plays with the hem of her skirt, gazing absently out of the window.

Gradually, the territory becomes less familiar. The other man, the man they are going to meet, always insists on meeting outside of her home area. Says it's safer that way. She hopes he'll buy her a hot chocolate again. That was nice. Lots of whipped cream. Mummy always says whipped cream is bad: 'You'll end up big-boned. No one wants to be big-boned.' The girl commented that the women at Mummy's cupcake studio don't seem big-boned. And they have lots of cream. 'That's because they spend a lot of time in the bathroom after each session,' Mummy explained. That didn't make much sense. But still, after the last visit, she hung round in the bathroom for a good ten minutes, so that the cream didn't invade her bones and make them puff up.

And if there is hot chocolate, the girl thinks, it will be something to keep me busy. Because there's not a lot of talking on these trips, so far. The other man doesn't seem to know what to say. He looks at her a lot. Taking her in, from top to toe. She can feel his gaze travel down then up, up then down. Sometimes he gives a little smile. Other times a frown. She wants to please him, of course. She wants to please everyone. But when she tells him about the usual stuff – school, Mummy, music, boys even – he doesn't say much back. And the two men glare at each other whenever they're not looking at her. She can't figure out why they keep hanging around together. Or what they want her to do on these occasions. So perhaps better just to concentrate on pushing the little wooden stirrer stick up and down in the hot chocolate to make holes, revealing the hot chocolate below. You have to get it to just the right meltiness to drink it. Then it's delicious. She licks her lips in anticipation. Last time, the other man, the man they're going to visit, looked like he was anticipating hot chocolate the whole time. Kept licking his lips. If he wanted some of her drink, he should just have said.

This might be the last time at this place, though. Because the previous time the other man, the man they're going to see, had suggested they meet at his home. More relaxing. They could learn more about each other. He'd even given directions.

'I just want us to be close, Cara,' he'd said. 'You'll be quite safe. You'll have your chaperone there throughout.' He said 'chaperone' in a funny way. Like he was making a joke. Perhaps he only used that word because he didn't know what to call the man who brought her. She didn't, either, not really. Not once they'd had the little chat that evening in the car, his hand on her knee. Everything changed after that. She couldn't be herself around him, couldn't think of anything to say to him at all, never mind his name. She'd settled into the pattern after a while. But it was still odd. Of course it was odd. She would have asked Mummy. If Mummy were allowed to know.

Anyway, whatever he was called, the chaperon didn't seem to like the idea of going to the other man's home. So here they were, driving fast to the usual café. A bit faster than usual, maybe? Were they late? She looks at her watch, then realises she doesn't know what time they're meant to be there. And she doesn't really know where 'there' is.

So there is nothing to do but sink into the seat. It's out of her hands. But she's perfectly safe. Of course she is. It would be like all the other times. See the men. Then go home to Mummy. She looks across at the chaperone to smile, to show him she still trusts him after everything. But he doesn't smile back. He looks ahead and he frowns.

Chapter 1

My eyes flash open.

There's a bed, a room and a blankness.

I leap off the bed, a strange bed, a single bed, and collapse straight onto the floor.

Where am I? What's going on? Why am I so weak?

I put my hands over my eyes. Remove my hands again. But nothing becomes right. I've still no idea where I am. Why am I in this alien room? In pyjamas? Is it day, is it night, how long have I been here?

And, oh God.

Where's Cara? Where's my daughter?

Look round the room again. It looms and distorts weirdly before me. I don't trust my eyes.

I try to pull myself to my feet but black spots and nausea get in the way.

OK, Susan. Stop trembling. Try to remember.

A hallway. At home. The doorbell ringing. Delivery expected. Chain not on.

Going to answer the door.

Yes, that's it. A door. I see a door now, in this room. Maybe Cara is on the other side?

Crawl over the floor. One hand in front of the other. Grunt with the effort. Feel like I'm Cara when she was learning. Past a tray of partially eaten food. White fish. The smell makes me want to vomit.

Approach the door, in this room. Lean my hands against it, inch them higher and higher, climbing with my hands. Finally at the handle. Pull and pull. Handle up, handle down. Please! Open!

Nothing. It stays firmly shut.

In my mind, in my memories, the front door of my house opens. I've answered the door. Then blackness, blankness. Nothing but: Cara, my Cara, I must see Cara!

I'm shouting it now, out loud. Screaming it. Black dots back again before my eyes.

Come on. Comprehend. Don't panic.

Slide down from the door. Look around the room. It's clean, too clean, apart from the half-eaten fish. White walls. A pine chest of drawers. Potpourri on a dresser. Beige carpets. All normal. My hands ball in and out of fists. It is not normal to me.

And you are not here.

But why, Susan, why would she be here? Was she even at home when that doorbell rang? She's fifteen, why would she be there, at home, with Mum? She might be safe, somewhere else, happy, even now.

I shake my head. Wrong. It feels wrong. I need to know where you are. Something is telling me, the deep-rooted maternal instinct, that you're not safe. I need to see you.

Footsteps! From the other side of the door.

A key in the lock. I watch the handle turn. Slowly, the door pushes open.

Him.

How could I have forgotten about him?

We face each other, him standing, me on the floor. Bile rises in my throat.

So.

This is the now-known stranger who has locked me in here. Wherever 'here' is. It's been what – two . . . three days? He must have drugged the fish. That's why it took me a while, for any recollection to return.

He's holding a beaker of water.

'Thought you might like something to drink, Susan.'

He knows my name. A researched, not random, snatching then. Watching, from afar? For how long?

I stare at him.

'Where is she?' I manage. Not my usual voice. My throat is dry. The words are cracked, splitting each syllable in two.

'You mustn't hate me, Susan,' he says.

I wait for more. Some explanation. Nothing.

Could I jump him? Could I run past him, out of the door? I must try, mustn't I? Even if there is no 'past him'. He fills the whole doorway.

Stop thinking. Act! Forget the shaking legs. Go, go, go! Storm him, surprise him!

But he is too quick. He slips out. The door closes. The lock turns.

'They'll come looking!' I shout, slamming my hands against the door.

Because they will, won't they? Paul, even now, must be working with the police, following up trails, looking at traffic cameras, talking to witnesses. Find my wife, he'll be shouting to anyone who'll listen. Neighbours, dog-walkers, Mrs Smith from number thirty-nine with that blessed curtain twitching. My afternoon clients, they must have raised the alarm, when I wasn't there. Right? I must be a missing person by now. Please, whoever has lost me, come and find me.

And, please, let Cara be with you. Let my daughter be safe.

Images of Cara frightened, hunched, bound, dying.

No!

Just focus. Look at the room. How to get out of the room.

Look, a window! High up, narrow, darkness beyond it, but possible maybe?

There's a kind of ledge. I can pull myself up. Hands over the edge, like that, then come on – jump up, then hang on. Manage to stay there for a moment, before my weak arms fail me. Long enough to judge the window isn't glass. It's PCV. Unsmashable. And, of course, there is a window lock. And no key. Locked, I bet, but if I just stretch a hand – but no. I fall.

OK, so I need to put something under the window. That chair. Heavy. I push and pull it to under the window. Placing my hands on the back of the chair, I climb up onto the seat. With my new height, I stretch my arm to the window, then to the window latch.

Locked.

Still. A window is a window. People can see in, as well as out. When it's day again, I can wave, mouth a distress signal.

So do I sit and wait in the dark until morning? Until I can see the light again?

Or does this man, this man out there, have night-time plans for me? Because you don't just kidnap a woman and leave her in a room. You want to look at her, presumably, your toy, your little caged bird. Maybe he's looking at me even now. A camera, somewhere? I draw my legs up close to me and hug them. I stare at the ceiling, every corner. No. No. No. No. I can't see one.

Which means he must have another agenda.

I shudder.

Think of Cara. Be strong. What's your best memory of Cara? Proudest mummy moment?

Apart from every morning when I see that beautiful face. I will have that moment again. I will. Just as I've had that moment every day since I first held you.

Little baby girl wrapped in a blanket. So precious. Be safe, be warm, always.

But apart from that.

The concert!

Yes, the concert.

All the mums and dads and siblings and assorted hangers-on

filing into the school hall. The stage set up ready, music stands, empty chairs. Hustle, bustle, glasses of wine. Me chatting to Alice's mum – Paul working late – about nothing and everything. Then, the gradual hush of anticipation spreads round the room. The lights dim. On comes the orchestra! And there's Cara. Her beautiful blonde hair hanging loose, masking her face. She'll tuck it behind her ear in a minute, I think. And she does. Then the whole audience can see that lovely rose tint to her cheeks, the lips so perfectly cherub-bowed to play the flute that she holds. I want to stand up and say, 'that's my daughter!' Instead I just nudge Alice's mum and we have a grin. Then there's the customary fuss and flap as the kids take their seats. All trying to look professional, but someone drops their music, and someone else plucks a stray string of a violin. Not Cara, though. She is sitting straight, flicking stray glances out to the crowd, holding the flute tight on her lap. Come on, Cara, I say to her in my head. Just do it like you've practised. All those nights at home, performing to me sometimes so that you have an 'audience'. You'll be fine.

And she is fine. When the orchestra starts to play, it's like she has a solo. You can see the musicianship. All nervousness gone. Head bobbing and darting, fingers flying, like a true flautist. No pretention. Just perfection. Then her actual solo. The flute shining out, beautiful, clear. Wonderful phrasing, beautiful passion. Then she's frowning slightly – was that a wrong note? Just keep on, keep on, no one will notice. And she does, she keeps going, right to the end.

But what makes me proudest, happiest, is, when her solo is over, she has this magnificent pinky-red flush over the whole of her face, and she gives this quick smile of sheer joy at her accomplishment, a brief look into the audience, before she bows her head and gets back to playing with the rest of the orchestra. Oh, my beautiful bold-shy Cara. How I adore you!

And then.

The memory is spent.

I'm just here again.
In silence.
Waiting.
Alone.
Hoping, praying, that my daughter is safe.

Chapter 2

The headmistress of Cara's school is occupied with a small handful of girls she has brought together in her study. They're sitting on chairs in a semicircle surrounding her desk, sipping the tea that she's given them. Patterned china cups usually reserved for the governors are balanced precariously on saucers. The girls are too busy to worry if they are spilling their tea. Their attention is focused on the man next to the headmistress. He's a rarity in a school that only has two male teachers. And neither of them have beards. Or wear leather jackets and open-necked shirts. It's clean-shaven and smart suits or the door for Mrs Cavendish's staff.

'Who do you think he is?' whispers one girl, skinny, ginger, to her companion, slightly rounder, brunette.

Her companion shrugs. 'New teacher? A friend for Mr Adams and Mr Wilson?'

The skinny ginger girl shakes her head. 'I don't think so. I think it's about Cara.'

'Everything's about Cara,' whispers back the brunette, rolling her eyes.

And it is true. The police cordons. The letters home to parents. The visit from a special psychiatrist. The thoughts, the prayers they have been asked to give her and her family in her conspicuous absence. The anxiety they have shared.

The headmistress clears her throat.

'Girls, thank you for coming,' she says, as though there is a choice to disobey the headmistress's edict. 'As you will have guessed, this is about Cara.'

The brunette shoots a 'see what I mean?' glance at her ginger friend.

'I've asked you bunch here in particular because of your friendship with Cara. I know you must be very upset right now. You're doing really well. I'm proud of you.'

There's a sniff from a blonde girl at the outer reaches of the semicircle. The headmistress advances to her and puts a hand on her shoulder.

'I don't want to upset you by going through the details again. We've all heard what the police had to say, and of course it's been all over the news. But we've been asked to help a little more.'

The headmistress resumes her seat at the head of the semicircle.

'I'd like to introduce you to Mr Belvoir, a private investigator,' she tells the girls. 'He wants—well, Mr Belvoir, why don't you explain?'

'Thank you,' the man says. He stands up. Then, perhaps realising he towers over the girls, he sits down again.

'Sometimes, when the police are looking at these things, their approach can be . . . limited. Now, I'm not doing them down, it's a bit delicate, but . . . well, I explained to your headmistress that I've got a private instruction to look at what's happened. Cara's family, you know. Got to ask my own questions. Make discreet enquiries, with close friends. I hope that's OK with you?'

Five heads bob in the room. The ginger head doesn't bob.

'Alice?' prompts the headmistress.

After a moment, Alice, the ginger girl, nods her head.

But she excuses herself almost immediately. He must ask his questions later, she says. She has English homework to do, she says. But, as she runs from the room, ignoring the headmistress's calls that the homework can wait, it's not thoughts of poetry

298

composition that are spurring her on. It's the thought – or maybe the question – about secrets. Namely this: if your friend – your best friend, who's been your best friend since day one of reception – tells you something and makes you swear in confidence never ever to tell anyone, do you tell a man who is investigating something bad that's happened to that friend? When that man, after all, isn't even the police? And if it isn't even directly relevant? Or is it? Cara told her a secret and then—Oh Cara.

So Alice doesn't know what she should do. Cara would know what to do. She would just decide and have done with it. Impulsive and bold, that's Cara. Perhaps that's the problem. But Cara isn't here. Another problem. So, for once, Alice has to make up her own mind. The school hasn't prepared her for this sort of dilemma. Why don't they teach anything useful once in a while? Everyone knows it's friendships that count. Not books and sums and facts.

But she's stuck with those. And she'll just have to use them. And so she runs to the library, where she hides behind her textbooks. And until she has decided, she will avoid this Mr Belvoir. Even though she knows what she knows.

Chapter 3

Biting my nails. Putting my head in my hands. Walking about. Sitting down.

I can't do this.

I jump to my feet.

I shout. 'Let me out! Let me out! Let me out!'

Why am I here? Why aren't you at least in the room with me? He can't be scared of a woman and a girl uniting, can he? Not with all that muscle.

Do I just fuck him and hope for the best? That he'll let me out without killing me, and we can all be a happy family again?

Or am I meant to just stay in here and finish that piece of fish? Is he fattening me up? Does he have a fat fetish? Did he think that the proprietor of a cupcake store and studio would be all doughy? That she wouldn't be a salad-eating Pilates junky who would have to close the store if she put on a pound? Because the yummy mummies of leafy North London don't want to associate cupcakes with saturated fats and weight gain, do they? That's not the lifestyle. No. Perhaps they're bulimic. I don't care. That's not my lookout. It's important to watch what you eat. Of course. But not for their reasons. So, when I see them running round Alexandra Park, I nod and smile and remind them of the 'how to do deluxe frosting' session but I don't follow them when they go to the bathroom.

Which is a good point. Bathroom.

I bang the door of my room from the inside. I have a question. Or at least, a ruse to bring that bastard in here.

I keep banging until I hear footsteps along the corridor.

'Yes?' says the Captor from outside.

'What if I need to pee?' I ask.

There's a silence.

'Do you?' he says.

I don't, but I want to know what happens if I do. If it gives me a way out. Some hope of escape. Or at least seeing if Cara is out there.

'Really badly,' I say.

There's a pause, then a key in the lock. I expect to be handed a bucket when the door opens.

But no. He is empty-handed.

'Turn round,' he says.

I do as he asks.

Once I've turned, he takes hold of both of my arms from behind, clamps them together with one of his paw-like hands. I feel like my wrists will snap if I struggle.

He twists me round and pulls me out of the room.

We're in a short corridor. Look about, quickly. Nothing I recognise. It's as blank and beige as the room. Like it's been deliberately stripped. Or like he has no life at all, apart from ruining other people's. We pass one closed door next to mine. My stomach jumps closer to my heart. Cara? Is Cara in there?

Baby in one room, mummy in the other. Let me see her, I need to see her!

'Hello? Cara?'

He pulls me faster along the corridor. We stop in front of an open door. I see a toilet and bath and a shower enclosure in the corner. White tiling. Clean. Probably forensically bleached before and after each visit.

He pushes me into the room.

And follows me.

What have I done?

'There we go, then,' he says, nodding at the toilet. He releases me from the arm hold and nudges me towards the toilet. He stands at the door, arms folded, facing into the room. Like he has no intention of leaving.

'Are you going to give me some privacy?' I ask.

He shakes his head. Apologetically?

'The door doesn't have a lock,' he says.

'You're going to stand here watching me?'

He doesn't respond.

'You could at least turn your back,' I tell him. Then I could at least try to jump you, I think, even if it is with my trousers round my ankles.

He still doesn't say anything. Just keeps looking at me.

So. I'll have to carry on. But I'm not going to let him degrade me. I'm not going to let him see how vulnerable I feel as I pull down my pyjama shorts. I'm not going to let him know how my flesh creeps, how my insides clench and my legs tremble. I keep eye contact as I lower myself to the seat. I expect his gaze to drift downwards, to drink me in while I urinate. But he keeps his gaze level with my eyes. I make a show of squatting up fully to wipe myself. Still his gaze stays at my eyes. At first. And then he allows himself a quick flick down, towards my exposed parts. I pull up my shorts in a hurry.

I move to the sink to wash my hands. I struggle with the taps; my hands are shaking. The Captor helps me out.

'Careful,' he says. 'The water is very hot.'

As he leans in, I catch sight of the two of us in the mirror over the sink. I almost gasp. I'm not who I remember myself to be. My eyes have purple patches under them – tiredness beyond black circles. Or maybe he has punched me? My skin is so pale it is almost translucent. My lips are dry and cracked. My hair, unbrushed, but in a ponytail, sticks up wildly. And if I thought he was twice the size of me, I was wrong. He looks at least four times the size of me. And about four times as human – pink skin (neatly stubbled), hair combed, lips moist.

Steam covers the mirror and the comparison is lost.

I notice my hands are burning and I pull them out from under the tap.

Then I present my wrists meekly to the Captor. He takes hold of them and escorts me back to my room.

When he leaves I'm sick on the floor.

I try not to think what will happen when I need to shower.

When Cara needs to shower. If she's here.

All I want to do is hide in the bed in a foetal position. But I must be strong, for Cara. I must show him that it's not enough to leave me locked in here. Like I've had my bit of outside and now I'm stuck.

So I take a big breath and unleash the banshee. I cry and I scream and I shout. Maybe we are in the middle of a housing estate. Maybe I'll alert the neighbours.

The door opens before I even hear the key in the lock.

'What's wrong now?' he asks.

What's wrong? I want to shout back. *What's wrong? You've fucking kidnapped me, that's what's wrong. And done something, maybe, I don't know, to my daughter.* But I carry on with the wordless screaming. He moves towards me, closer and closer and closer, until—ow!

Stinging, on my cheek.

He's slapped me.

So I scream again. Louder.

He slaps me again, harder.

It brings tears to my eyes.

And there's a wet glittering in his.

'I didn't bring you here for this,' he says. There's a crack in his voice.

'Then why did you bring me here?' I hear my voice, high, wavering.

He shakes his head and moves back towards the door. I start screaming again.

He turns to me. This time his hand is in a fist. I flinch. He lowers his hand. But the warning is clear. No screaming. I lie down on the bed and face the wall. I can sense him standing there, watching me.

Eventually, I hear the door close. He's gone.

I fling myself over on the bed so that I'm facing the door that he's just exited.

Who is this man? I swear I hadn't seen him before I was abducted. What does he want? Can't he just tell me everything, like some kind of super villain confessing his evil plans? At least tell me he's got his cock out every night at the thought of me but he's just biding his time; tell me we had a chance encounter in a newsagent/ restaurant/ supermarket; tell me he has my daughter strapped inside a wheelie bin somewhere ready to be landfill unless I have sex with him. Just don't leave me here, not knowing.

I need to know what's happening. Why is no one telling me what's happening to my baby?

I need Cara. I need Paul. I need a hug, some tea, some air, some knowledge, some hope. I just need. Give me something. Please.

Chapter 4

The other side of the door

I could just have let her scream. Of course I could. I'm prepared.
Tough love, isn't it called? I've experience of that. I've hardened
myself for more. Had to. Grit your teeth, get on with it, think of
the greater purpose. The purpose she'll realise in due course.
Once that natural obsession with her daughter has abated. Of
course, she wants to know. And maybe I should tell her. But not
now. Not yet. Little by little we'll get there. Together. That's the
important bit. We'll always be together. I've succeeded in that
much. However difficult it might be, treating a woman like that
when all you want to do is hug her and kiss her and . . . all the
rest. The groundwork is done. We're together. Now I just need
to carry on. Day in, day out, as long as it takes.

Oh, she's resisting. Of course she is. Wants to be in and out
of that room like a jack-in-the-box. And it bothers me. Of course
it bothers me. In an ideal world, she'd take one look at me, one
morning, and she'd love me like I know she can. She'd thank me
for the delicious fish supper. Thank me for the warm bedding.
Thank me for taking care of her. But it's not an ideal world. Don't
we know it. All of us, under this roof.

So until that happens, she's got to stay there. Locked in that
room. And sometimes I may need to use force. Judge me, you

up there, if you want to. But just like you have your plans and work in mysterious ways, so do I. I didn't like slapping her. Of course I didn't. Yes, there was an element of me that liked the touch of her skin. So soft. English rose. Just like Cara. You want to caress skin like that, not hurt it. Needs must though. Even if she was more stunned than hurt. She'll forgive me in the end. She has to.

Slapping her, stopping her screaming, was the right thing to do. Selfish, partly. We need to communicate. We need to have a dialogue, even if for now it's full of hate from her. And I want to be able to hear her voice. Not just gaze at her from afar. If she's hoarse, we can't do that, can we? I've thought so much about her speaking to me nicely, silkily, calling me by name, that I don't want to ruin my chances by making her croak.

And there's the noise, of course. Screaming. I think we're safe. But I'm not big on attracting attention. Not now.

Of course, if she won't communicate as she should, however long she's in there, I'll need to come up with another plan. Perhaps I'll need to force her to understand. Something with more impact. Pierce that little bubble she thinks she can hide in, away from me, for ever. But for now I have to continue with what I've started. A new phase of life for us all.

If you enjoyed *The Classroom*, check out these other twisty thrillers from HQ Digital …

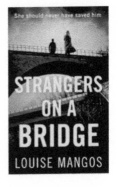